The Mirror Season

Also by Anna-Marie McLemore

Dark and Deepest Red

Blanca & Roja

Wild Beauty

When the Moon Was Ours

The Weight of Feathers

The MIRROR SEASON

ANNA-MARIE McLEMORE

Feiwel and Friends
New York

A Feiwel and Friends Book
An Imprint of Macmillan Publishing Group, LLC
120 Broadway, New York, NY 10271
fiercereads.com

Library of Congress Cataloging-in-Publication Data
Names: McLemore, Anna-Marie, author.
Title: The mirror season / Anna-Marie McLemore.
Description: First edition. | New York : Feiwel & Friends, 2021. |
  Audience: Ages 13–18. | Audience: Grades 10–12. | Summary: After Ciela
  and Lock are sexually assaulted at the same party, they develop a
  cautious friendship through her family's possibly magical pastelería
  and his secret forest of otherworldly trees.
Identifiers: LCCN 2020017596 | ISBN 9781250624123 (hardcover)
Subjects: CYAC: Rape—Fiction. | High schools—Fiction. | Schools—Fiction.|
  Dating (Social customs)—Fiction. | Hispanic Americans—Fiction. |
  Family life—California—San Juan Capistrano—Fiction. | San Juan
  Capistrano (Calif.)—Fiction.
Classification: LCC PZ7.1.M463 Mir 2021 | DDC [Fic]—dc23
  LC record available at https://lccn.loc.gov/2020017596

First edition, 2021
Book design by Liz Dresner
Printed in the United States of America
Feiwel and Friends logo designed by Filomena Tuosto
10 9 8 7 6 5 4 3 2 1

To the Jane Does who came before me,
the John Doe who came forward with me,
and everyone who helps us remember
we have names

This book contains discussions of sexual assault and PTSD. If you or someone you know has been sexually assaulted, please know that there's help, and there's hope.

If you don't know where to start, start with RAINN: rainn.org/resources or (800) 656-4673.

The Boy from the Surface
of the Moon

When my bisabuela first came to this country, the most valuable thing she carried with her was something only she could see. The rest was worth almost nothing. The varnished tin of her favorite necklace. The cloth full of the rose hips she seeded and then ate like hard candies. The shoes she wore nearly to dust getting to the house she would be paid to clean, and, eventually, cook in. Even her best dress—moths had eaten constellations of perfectly round holes that mirrored the desert stars they flew beneath.

Years later—when there had been a wedding ring, a new stove in a house of her own, a fine dress—the most valuable thing my great-grandmother ever owned was still her way of knowing what bread or sweet would leaven the heart of anyone she met. She could soothe lovesickness with polvorones de naranja, sweet as orange blossoms. She calmed frightened dreams with las nubes, sugared white as far-off stars.

It was a gift my great-grandmother had ever since she was a little girl. And when she died, she passed it to me, even though I was too small to remember her face.

I think of my bisabuela now, just for a second, because the first parking spot I find in the hospital lot is up against a rosebush, the hearty, scrub-like kind she ate rose hips off of.

Then I'm back to thinking about the boy slumped in my mother's car.

I don't know his name, or where he lives, or how to get him home, or why he was even at the party tonight. I heard he was visiting from Lancaster, but I also heard Bakersfield, and Ely, Nevada, so at this point he might as well be from the surface of the moon, because no one really knows.

I could check his pockets, but I'm counting on the hospital to do that for me.

Besides, nothing good ever came from a brown girl being seen taking a wallet off a white guy.

There was other talk about him at the party. Whispers not just about how he's from the middle of nowhere, but about how he's saving himself for marriage. *Too bad for him*, Victoria and her friends said. *He's cute, even with the acne.*

Victoria's compliments always come with qualifiers. *She looks good, even with the slutty eyeliner.* Or, *he's not as ugly as he was last year.* Or, the one I've gotten more than once, *she's kind of pretty, even though she's a little fat.*

Victoria and her friends declaring this boy cute may be the worst luck he's ever had.

I open the back passenger door. He's not tall, but he's taller than I am, which makes getting him out of my mother's car and into the doors of the ER even harder. His limbs are slack, like they're each trying to go a different direction. I have to hold on to him hard enough that my right boob is squished up against him. The curve of my hip shoves up against his leg, jeans fraying against jeans.

I wish I had help with him. I wish I had found Jess before I left the party.

But telling her would have meant having to explain.

The boy from Lancaster or the moon looks so bad that his face, washed-out as printer paper, and his lolling head pull two scrub-uniformed women out from behind the glass window. "They drugged him," I say, as though anyone here will know who *they* means. "We were at a party."

As they take him—he doesn't resist; he isn't conscious enough to resist—one of the nurses tells me, "The police are going to want to talk to you. Do you want to call your mom or dad?"

"What?" I ask.

I wince at the panic in my voice.

Classic brown-girl error.

My mother says I have to stop acting so jumpy. It makes me look guilty even if I didn't do anything, she says. It's the reason that, in sixth grade, when Jamie Kappe and two girls who were always following her around draped paper towel streamers all over the bathroom, and they pointed at me, the teacher believed them. I was nervous enough to look like I did it.

"They're just going to ask you some questions, okay?" the nurse says, apparently giving me and my panic the benefit of the doubt.

"I don't know who he is," I say, blurting it because some part of me thinks it'll get me out from under these fluorescents.

But it must sound like a confession, because the nurse gives me a bless-her-heart look.

"You're a good girl," she says. "For bringing him in."

This nurse, who looks like one of my cousins but with about half an ounce less eyebrow pencil, thinks I'm some kind of buen samaritano. A good-hearted stranger rescuing strange boys from the moral cesspool that is an Astin School party.

But I'm not the kind of girl she thinks I am. I'm the kind of girl who will make sure I'm gone before anyone can ask me anything.

If I'm not, I'll have to talk not just about what happened to this boy, but what happened to me. I will have to tell them everything I know about two awful things that happened at the same time, in two different rooms. Me in one, him in the other, the walls so thin I could hear him while I pressed my eyes shut and tried to pretend I was somewhere other than in my own body.

And if someone—especially this nurse who looks a little like my prima—asks me about it, I don't know if I'll be able to stay quiet. And I need to. Because nothing good will ever come from telling the truth about tonight. I already know that. Even under the buzz of the fluorescents and the bucking of my stomach, I know that.

In the morning, this boy and his parents will be informed that there was no sign of penetration, to him or by him. The fact of the lipstick on him will hover, unspoken, in the disinfectant-tinged air. He will know what it means. They will all know what it means.

He will elect not to have a rape kit done, partly out of shame, partly because he knows how difficult it will be to prove he didn't want it.

And because he has never heard of a girl forcing a boy.

His brain is not even sure it's possible, even as his body feels the violation tingeing his blood.

Right now, I don't know any of this. Later—much later—I will. And when I do, I will imagine this boy feeling like some specimen in a jar, a rare pinned moth, thinking it's his fault the pin went into him in the first place.

Maybe, if I knew all of that now, I wouldn't do what I'm about to do next. Maybe I wouldn't make the decision that will ensure this boy wakes up alone. Maybe if I knew that his mother is hours away, crying at the white lines of the highway because the voice on the phone tells her that her son is in a hospital in San Juan Capistrano, but will not tell her why, I would do it differently.

I want to think that. But I know I'm wrong. Because even in this moment, as I make this decision, I can guess that when he wakes up, the air will be thick with the vague but heavy sense that something bad has happened to him. But he will not know exactly what or who did it to him or why. A little like the feeling I am already dreading waking up with tomorrow morning, the reverse of that relief you get when you realize a nightmare isn't actually true, that you can let it go now.

I wrap my arms around myself, trying to hold my sobs in my throat until I get out to the parking lot. But they get so jammed in there I start choking on them.

The automatic doors slide shut behind me.

I do it without looking back. I leave this boy here, alone.

My abuela—my bisabuela's daughter—used to caution me that gifts like mine were delicate. She warned that if I did not guard my heart, all the sharp edges in the world could kill my gift, like salt deadening the soft rise of yeast.

As I walk across the parking lot, I decide I can do it, I can guard my heart against tonight. I can seal it off like it never happened.

Just as I'm about to open the car door, a wink of silver catches the moon. It draws my attention to the rosebush past the cement bumper.

One rose sits heavier than the rest of them. Its petals have lost their red, and now look as shiny and silver as liquid mercury.

I draw closer, watching how this silver rose gathers the light toward its glossed center. Its petals look like glass.

No. Not glass. Mirrors.

I reach out to it, to test its weight under my palm. But just as my fingers reach the hard edge of one petal, the whole thing shudders out of its cradle of leaves. It falls, hitting the asphalt and shattering into silver dust.

A shard catches my eye. It's small and coarse as sand, and I try to blink it out. But I feel it go deeper in. I don't know if I'm imagining the glint of it or if I can actually see it, but as I'm trying to blink it out, it turns the night to silver.

I don't know it yet. But that's how it happens.

Right there.

That fast.

One shard of mirrored glass changes my whole world.

This Is How You Lose It

When I get home, I try blinking it out, but I don't cry. I let my eye tear up as it tries to wash out that little speck of glass, but I don't cry. If I start crying, I'll start screaming.

The fleck of glass blurs my vision. It turns my bedspread and walls into a watercolor. It turns the two felted dolls my abuela made me into a wash of brown and pink. But I still can't find it. I catch it as a flash of silver against the brown of my iris or white of my eye, and then it disappears again.

The next morning, my vision settles. Everything is sharp and clear, the dresser my dad and I painted the yellow of a grapefruit's peel, the pictures of me and Jess in frames the color of candy buttons, the little felted dolls. The jeans and sweater I left on the floor last night. But I can still feel it, the scratch and prickle of glass crushed to sand.

I get to the pastelería a minute before my shift starts. On the way in the kitchen door, I cross my apron strings in the back and then loop them around to the front, using the extra to knot them. I steady myself with the things that have been here for years. The fluffy tissue paper flowers in sherbet orange and candy pink. The papel picado fluttering along the wall. The glass jars of rock candy decorating the back counter, in all the same colors as the pan dulce, that my tía put there because she liked how the light winked at them, and they winked back.

"Brace for the first rush." Jess throws me a hairnet.

Jessamyn Beverly. My ex-girlfriend and now best friend. Connoisseur of office supplies. Absolutely no talent for pan dulce dough, but meticulous with a piping bag and a cash register. And an actual, by-the-numbers genius. Which is unfortunate for me, because we were already a year apart at Astin, and she got admitted to nearby Laurel College a year early, which means she's graduating right after finals.

She'll still pinch-hit at the pastelería, where she used to help out so much my tía hired her. If she weren't my best friend, I might hate her a little for being the kind of person who can make change without thinking, and who can turn out a term paper in a night, provided she has a two-liter of Diet Coke and a Halloween-sized bag of gummy worms.

Jess pulls me toward the front counter.

I shudder at her grabbing hold of my elbow, but catch myself before she notices.

"Last crowd who came in was asking for the pastry witch of San Juan Capistrano," she says.

My bisabuela's gift has turned me into a reluctant and very obscure tourist attraction. La Bruja de los Pasteles, the girl who knows what kind of pan dulce you want before you do.

It's a little more complicated than that. If you asked me on the street, it'd be hit or miss. I only know for sure in our family's pastelería, surrounded by pan dulce made from recipes I know better than my cousins' middle names. I've memorized las especias in our swallow bread, how the orange yolks from my primas' grass-roaming chickens make our pan de yema seem like it has sun baked into it. I catch the invisible threads between our customers and the bakery case.

If I walk into another panadería, no guarantees; it's like trying to speak a language you know, but a dialect you don't. *Your bisabuela could*, my abuela used to tell me. *Anyone in the world, any pastelería in the world, she could do it. So will you, mija, if you're a good girl, if you care for tu don.*

I don't tell the gringos any of the details, no more than my tía would tell them her secrets for making concha sugar tops as smooth as dark velvet. Let them think whatever brings them in the front door.

"What happened to you last night?" Jess asks.

Jess gives me the look that reminds me why I avoided her before we started dating. It's an appraising look that speaks of her tabbed binders and the fact that she keeps a sweater shaver in her purse. And the fact that I only know what a sweater shaver is because of her.

We tried each other on as amantes, then realized, with no hard feelings, that we did not fit that way, that we were, instead, hermanas, and would be hermanas for our whole lives. And when I think about how differently she'd look at me if she knew about last night, if she knew how much of it was my fault, I feel as brittle as stale pan dulce.

"Nothing," I say, deciding as I say it, that it's going to be true. My body is still screaming with every secret written into it, but I'm going to make this true. "Nothing happened."

"So you just ditched me with the Kings and Queens of South Coast Plaza for no reason?" Jess sounds both annoyed and like she's trying it play it off. "That's cold, Cristales."

"Sorry," I say. "I felt sick and I went home."

Almost not a lie.

The first woman to come up to the counter looks expectantly at me. She's not ordering. She's waiting for La Bruja de los Pasteles to tell her what she wants.

Sometimes me knowing is just a feeling, like the charge in the air before a storm. It tells me someone would delight at pan dulce in a particular shape, like puerquitos or pajaritos. Sometimes it's like a flicker of light out of the corner of my vision, whispering something about cocoa powder or anís. Most of the time, it's more like a coil of wire lighting up in me, and I just know.

But right now, I don't.

Jess watches me, waits. I never take this long.

I wait for some flickering in my blood to tell me whether this woman will thrill at the flavor of a cream-filled cacahuate or the herb-laced dough of swallow bread.

My brain and blood and heart are quiet, all except for one syllable.

No.

My abuela warned me that such gifts were easy to lose, through pride or carelessness. She had heard about a young woman whose tears turned to perlas, but who had boasted so ruthlessly about it, had bragged how much better it made her than ordinary girls, that the saints took back her gift. In my bisabuela's own village, there had been a boy who inherited a sense for finding water from his grandfather, but had been so arrogant and so unwilling to listen to anything el viejo had to say, that he lost it forever.

No.

Once lost, my grandmother said, such gifts were gone for

good, like a wooden chest burning up, or a locket thrown into the sea.

No. My heart sings out the word *no.*

I try to catch some hint about this woman. Seed-flecked pan de cemita? The warmth of the coconut sugar in los ojos de buey?

Nothing.

Now I'm grasping for it, trying to read the air around her. The cinnamon-and-chile-spiced apple of empanadas de manzana? A sugared galleta?

There's no way to guess, no matter how many times I've done this before. My bisabuela was born speaking the language of flour and sugar, a language unlearnable, because it changed from one person to the next. A puerquito might delight one woman, but sadden another. A paloma that made one man brave might remind another that he would rather cower like a pigeon than face the world.

My blood is still. The humming sense that tells me what pan dulce will light up someone's heart is silent.

I go outside, not wanting to let the customers—or my tía—see my panic. I go to the back, not the front where the customers come in, but where everyone who works at the nail salon or the flower shop or the liquor store parks.

I wait for the brisk air to snap me into being La Bruja de los Pasteles.

The back kitchen door opens.

"Ciela?"

I hear my best friend's voice.

Jess stops alongside me. "What's wrong?"

"I can't do it." I breathe out one word at a time.

"What?" she asks.

"Guessing what people want. Guessing if they need a palmera or a peineta. I can't do it. I can always do it, but right now I can't."

"Maybe you're just having an off day."

"We don't have off days. Not with this, not in my family. My bisabuela never had an off day. She was in labor and she told the partera what pan dulce would make her stop fighting with her husband."

"Okay, that's just showing off."

Jess is trying to make me laugh. But there's no laugh in me right now.

"Just give it a day," Jess says. "It'll come back."

I make myself nod, even though I can feel how brittle and forced it must look.

"Breathe for a few minutes, okay?" Jess says. "I'll tell your tía you went to the drugstore."

"Why the drugstore?"

"I'll tell her you needed lipstick, because . . ."

I chime in with her so we end up quoting in unison: "Whatever the question, red lipstick is the answer."

We bob our heads, almost singsonging this phrase we've heard a dozen times from my mother and my tía, the shared motto of two sisters.

I still can't laugh, but my smile is almost real.

"Just don't stress yourself out," Jess says.

"This from the girl who used to bring antacids to standardized tests."

"Exactly." Jess stops at the door before going in. "I know of what I speak."

The kitchen door falls shut behind her, leaving me alone in the quiet back lot.

I didn't know it, how right my grandmother had been, how easily it could happen. How even a single shard of mirrored glass could get into me and kill the gift my bisabuela left me.

But standing there, feeling the sliver of glass burrowing deeper into me, that's the moment I know it's gone.

The most precious thing my bisabuela could ever have left me, a thread of magic passed down through our blood, and I lost it.

If I didn't know it from the feeling of that shard going in deeper, I would know it from the strange way the bushes are moving, a constellation of leaves hardening and turning to mirrored glass.

La Reina de las Nieves

I take them all. I carefully pick each silver leaf away from its branch, holding a hand under in case it falls. I wrap them in my apron, and I take them home.

That first mirrored rose appeared when I left that boy to wake up alone and wonder where he was, and now these leaves are appearing outside the pastelería, where I've grown up kneading dough and telling customers what they want before they even know. All this falls to me. I can't let another sliver of glass get into anyone else, not when I can still feel the pinch of one in my own heart.

I can't throw the pieces away or toss them into the ocean. I can't think of a way to get rid of them that won't risk them breaking and getting into someone else. So I hide them.

First, I tuck the leaves into the back of a drawer. But as the summer goes on, more mirrored glass finds me. A calla lily in my aunt's yard becomes a cup of flashing silver, and I pick it seconds before my uncle glances out the window. A delicate flag of papel picado turns, and I steal it off the bakery wall before anyone notices, tying together the two paper flags on either side.

Before an early shift, I find seven of my mother's gardenias have gone from cream-white to whirls of mirrored glass, and I have to rip them away before my mother wakes up. Later, I see her outside, wondering over the delicate branches, now bare of their vanilla-scented blooms, and I can feel my heart growing scar tissue around that sliver of glass.

It becomes too much for one drawer. So I clear out my closet, stuffing the clothes into my dresser and throwing the shoes under my bed. I move out anything I need, leaving only the stuffed animals, old textbooks—things I rarely touch anyway. I hide every piece of silver glass at the back.

I only sleep when I hold the tiny felted dolls my abuela made me, one in each hand. I gently close my fingers around their soft bodies, alternating hands until the rhythm makes me sleep. I dream of sugar as pale as snow, and of snow so cold it glitters like crushed diamonds.

My abuela used to tell me a story about snow like that, about a frozen queen called La Reina de las Nieves. She ruled the coldest land that ever existed, her palace glittering with sheared ice. I knew she was supposed to be la mala, la villana, the evil queen who steals a boy named Kai from a sweet, warm-hearted girl named Gerda.

To me, though, La Reina de las Nieves was magnificent. She not only survived the cold, she made beauty out of it. She crafted pillars of ice that caught the northern lights. She carved frozen rooms that glowed blue as gas stove flames.

But now, when I dream of cold, I do not dream of the Snow Queen's beautiful palace, glowing with aurora light. I dream of my body turning to icicles, snapping apart in careless hands. I dream of pale fingers pulling me apart like sugar dough. I dream of my skin turning to ice or glass, clear enough that everyone can see inside.

Mira, Se Fue

y, no," Pilar says when she finds me kneading dough for the elotes. "Don't kill it." She eases my hands away. "What did that dough ever do to you?"

I brush the flour off my hands and don't argue. There's a reason my aunt hired Pilar. She has as much feel for dough as I used to have for which pan dulce would speak to which heart.

"Go." Pilar takes over the kneading. "I won't have you pummeling this."

I slump against the sink and start on dishes.

It's been more than three months since I lost the gift that made me the Pastry Witch of San Juan Capistrano. It hasn't come back. When a customer doesn't know what they want, I have no ideas. They're better off throwing a dart at a menu board than letting me guess. La Bruja de los Pasteles now exists as no more than rumor. Soon las turistas will wonder if she was ever anything more than local lore.

I've lost the part of me that speaks the language of flour and sugar. I've lost the thread of magic handed down from my bisabuela, one that ran through my family for so long no one could remember when it started. One that helped her open her first pastelería in a storefront barely wider than its door.

So I try to make myself useful kneading dough. Except that I am, apparently, not even getting that right this morning. My aunt slips alongside me. "Don't take it so hard, mija." She leans against the edge of the sink. "It's a strange season right now. The wind's not even going. It'll all get better after it turns. El don, you'll get it back." She watches me spray hot water over a soaped-up cake pan. "When la llorona loses her voice, that's when you know it's the season, not you."

I give her a weak shrug, acknowledging her stories about how the howling of the Santa Ana winds is the voice of la llorona sweeping over the land. My tía assigns great importance to any year the Santa Anas come late, or not at all.

"Did you hear?" Pilar calls over to my tía. "Another tree. Gone. Into thin air."

I keep washing dishes, pretending I'm not straining to hear every word over the spray of water.

"¿De verdad?" my tía asks. "Which one?"

"The lilac," Pilar says. "On Los Rios. The owners"—she clucks her tongue—"you should have seen them, salían de sus casillas. I thought steam was going to come out of their ears."

I've lost count of how many that makes. For the past few weeks, whenever a yellow removal notice goes up, there's been a good chance the marked tree will vanish overnight, before it can be torn out. Last week it was a fringe tree in front of a mint-green house. Before that, a chaste tree, a redbud, some unloved fruit trees. All of them got tagged for removal and then just disappeared.

And a little corner of my brain, one that I can't make quiet, whispers that maybe it's my fault. Maybe each of these trees vanishes because they turn, in the middle of the night, to mirrored glass. Maybe they break into as many pieces as the mirrored rose did on the parking lot asphalt, so in the morning there's no trace of them except a wisp of silver in the air or deep in the grass.

"What do they care?" my tía asks. "They were going to rip it out anyway."

Pilar shakes her head over the dough. "People want to lose things on their own terms. Not when the night steals them. Plus their lawns are always a mess after. Always this California love affair with green lawns."

"¿Mi opinión?"—my aunt looks at both me and Pilar like she's asking permission to tell her *opinión*, but she's not— "Something's not right around here. Las golondrinas, they're restless. You can hear it in their wings."

"It's not las golondrinas." Pilar shoves the heels of her hands into the dough. "It's that silly TV program."

She means the renovation show that filmed a few blocks north of here earlier this year. The producers ordered the trees ripped out in favor of sod rolls and a clean-lined porch, and a dozen houses in the neighborhood have already tried to copy it. It's an aesthetic that demands everything be trimmed and manicured within an inch of its life, leaving no room for beautiful, gnarled roots or old, winding branches.

"TV's why people want to take the trees out," my aunt says. "It doesn't explain anything about the trees disappearing in the middle of the night." My tía checks her order book like the answer might be in there. "Something's not right."

"When did you become such a superstitious viejita?" Pilar asks.

"This from the woman who wouldn't let a broom near her daughters' feet until they were married."

"And every one is married now, so who was right?"

I want to keep washing dishes and hear what else Pilar might tell my tía about the trees, but then steps clatter across the front threshold.

My throat goes taut.

Brigid Marchand and Victoria Kinkopf come through the door first. PJ Delahooke and Chris Bernard stagger after them, their feet drowning out the sound of the bell.

I knew I'd have to see them at school. But seeing them here, in my family's pastelería, the one my bisabuela dreamed up all those years ago, is the next worst thing to having them in my house. Chris and PJ have come in before, picking up coffee for themselves and these two girls they're continually dating and breaking up with. But never the four of them at once.

"I've got it," I say. I don't want my tía dealing with them. Chris and PJ always talk to her in overly loud, exaggerated enunciation. I've given up trying to tell them she speaks better English than either of them.

Chris elbows PJ. "You got so fucked up last night."

"Me?" PJ shoves back. "You tried to drive your dad's car from the trunk."

They laugh, in the same crackling way they did in that room, and for a second I'm sure I'll be sick on the front counter.

My throat tightens thinking of either of them out on the road.

PJ and Chris tip their heads up in greeting.

They don't notice me flinch.

They either think nothing of that night or were too drunk to remember it.

"Four coffees, and four of whatever the greasiest thing you have is," Victoria says. "We have to sober up the brain trust over here."

She nods at PJ and Chris, the kind of long-suffering look that's meant to be shared, commiserated over, as though we're friends. As though I didn't have a wrecked boy in the back of my mother's car because of her.

I ring up four coffees and four buñuelos de viento.

Victoria gives me cash. When I go to make change, she lifts a hand to stop me.

"Keep it," she says, her voice bright. She points at my face, circling her finger. "For under-eye concealer."

"Yeah, you do look kind of tired," Brigid says, and then flits out after Victoria. PJ and Chris follow.

"Hey, Cristales." Chris turns back, nodding toward the parking lot. "You want a ride?"

"Not on you," PJ says, and laughs so hard at his own joke that he completely misses Victoria's withering eye roll. Chris shoves him hard enough that PJ has to stumble to keep his balance, but he's still laughing.

A column of heat goes through my throat, my heart, my stomach.

I don't watch them leave. I adjust the pasteles in the bakery case, to best show off the pink frosted roses, the sheen of apricot jam, the soft green of pistachio mazapán. I pretend I don't hear the laughing, a sound that reaches into my dreams, coarse and loud as a flame licking across dry paper.

The Welcoming Committee

Every time I shift my weight in bed, it sounds like I'm playing the xylophone.

I don't know exactly what went wrong when I was putting this bed together. It's the kind that has a skeleton of wooden slats in place of a box spring. You wouldn't think there was a wrong way to install it, but apparently I've achieved it.

My parents ask about the noise sometimes, as they're passing my room in the morning. But I've told them I like it, that I find it soothing, like built-in wind chimes, when in fact I find it irritating as hell.

I could ask my parents for help. It wouldn't be the first piece of IKEA furniture they'd put together. But I'm sure that if they take apart my bed looking for what's wrong, they'll find what's wrong with me. They will pull aside the mattress and they'll just see it.

So I've mostly learned to sleep through the xylophone. Except when I have the dreams I've been having all summer. Nightmares about cold water, about my body being made of icicles or pan dulce that grabbing hands break apart. I am as brittle as new ice, I am disintegrating into sugar and flour, I am nothing but something to freeze or consume.

I startle awake, gasping like I've come up from underwater.

The bed sings out again as I get up, get dressed for school. Uniform skirt. Shirts we're supposed to iron (it actually says that in the student handbook) but that I just throw in the dryer and then hang up. Sweater in the Astin purple that always looked good with the brown of Jess's skin but not against the brown of mine; you couldn't pick a shade that brings out the shadowing under my eyes any better.

My parents are downstairs, coffee maker on. I hear their steps on the uneven kitchen tile.

The hall window shows me the white crepe myrtle across the street, a distraction I need from the thought of walking into the locker hallway this morning. Its pale, tissue-papery blossoms look like stars against the autumn blue of the sky. Ever since I first saw its branches bloom, I've thought of that tree as the snow tree. The McKinleys, the family who lived in that house before its current owners, loved it as much as I did. Their grandchildren used to run under it, the blossoms falling like snowflakes.

As I take the first few stairs, I hear my mother's voice, half whisper.

"She's fine," my mother says.

"She's not fine," my father says.

I go still, as though they can see me through the walls.

"She's just stressed," my mother says.

"Is it that school? I've never liked how they push them. To them, she's not a student, she's a transcript."

My mother shushes his rising voice.

School. That's their running theory. I didn't correct them all summer, and I'm not going to now.

"We can't leave her alone," my father says, quieter now.

"And we can't stay home on our twentieth anniversary," my mother says. "She'll know we're worried about her."

"We *are* worried about her." I can hear my father trying not to raise his voice.

The knot that lives in my stomach contracts and tightens.

Their twentieth anniversary.

They can't actually be thinking of canceling their trip. They've been planning it since last Christmas, saving for it since I started high school. They've been talking for years about going to New Mexico, seeing the balloon festival, five hundred bright points of color against the impossible blue of the desert sky.

Now I imagine every one of those balloons deflating and sinking, because they think I'm too fragile to be left alone for ten days.

At the pastelería, I fill cup after cup of to-go coffee and slip pan dulce into wax-paper sleeves—fast, clean, efficient, a small apology for the fact that I am no longer La Bruja de los Pasteles—until my tía chases me out the back door.

"You're going to be late, mija," she says.

I fill in what she's not saying, what she would never say.

You're not half as useful as you used to be anyway.

I take the route to school that goes past the creek bed. Fluffy with poppies and sage grass, the creek bed is where I used to play with my primas before they grew up and moved to Los Feliz or San Bernardino. It's where Jess taught me the name of the mapacho plants and that the standing waters, muddy as agate, are called ephemeral pools.

The thought of walking back into school without Jess, without the bubble of goodwill I got to live in being her best friend, drones through the air around me. The dread of facing what everyone else thinks happened at that party—I know the rumors, I know they think I went into that room laughing, willing—is like the crash of distant clouds.

I fish in my bag for the slip of paper where I wrote my locker number, which lets me enter the building without making eye contact with anyone.

"Hey, Ciela." Andie Granville waves in greeting. But she passes as quickly and carefully as if I had a snarling dog walking alongside me. A minute later, so does her brother Anthony, a studio art prodigy who taught Jess and me to take pictures of each other with refraction rainbows.

I get those greetings along the whole length of the hall. *Hi, Ciela. Hey, Ciela.* Each one is an acknowledgment of how Jess and I always floated from table to table, bench to bleachers, hermanas who had given our allegiance to no particular group, and so who found ourselves welcome in all of them.

Except now, each greeting comes with a wary look.

I know what everyone thinks happened that night. I know the vague rumor that I blew PJ Delahooke, or fucked Chris Bernard, or the other way around, or both. And this has scared off any of the loose but friendly acquaintances who might have become my friends this year. Not so much because they think I'm a slut but because they think that I sided with boys who call them fat and ugly, and whose girlfriends call them stupid and poor.

It never occurred to me how much of a risk it was having a single best friend, one I ate with every lunch period and sat with during every assembly. I didn't realize how much I had counted on the fact that, after she was gone, I'd settle in somewhere else until graduation, another lunch table, another clustered group on the cement steps outside the library.

I never accounted for the fact that everyone I could have settled in with might suddenly back away.

I'm still braced to hear the words *slut* and *whore* covered by pointed coughs. When I open my locker, I expect to find disgusting artistic renderings of whatever acts I supposedly performed willingly. But everyone gives me that wide berth. Their eyes widen instead of glare. It's not respect. It's not that kind of eye-widening. More like fear. A look of *I-didn't-know-she-had-it-in-her*. The hesitating reverence given to a surprise slut.

I'll take it. The only thing worse than everyone thinking I went into a room with PJ and Chris willingly would be them knowing what actually happened.

I turn the corner near the history classrooms and stop short, enough that my low-tops skid against the linoleum.

For a second, I think I'm imagining him, the boy I last saw when I handed him over to the ER nurses. The boy who lives as a shadow deep in my nightmares. The boy I cannot stop imagining that next morning, waking up in a hospital bed, finding the stain of unfamiliar lipstick on him.

He's still not tall, but he's taller. His frame filled out a little over the summer. The acne has thinned out, but you can still see where it came on hardest. Scarring darkens his jawline like a five o'clock shadow. Instead of the flannel shirt and jeans that made Victoria almost fall over with laughter at the party—"Only lesbians and Mexicans wear plaid shirts like that," she said, in front of me and Jess, giving us both a look of *no offense*—he has on the Astin uniform. Khakis. Collared shirt. Dark purple sweater embroidered with the school emblem.

I look for what's still the same. The way he stands with his back and shoulders straight but dips his head a little. That pear-blond hair that falls in his face. Brown eyes that stare at his middle-third locker.

His middle-third locker that's covered in plastic squares.

It's papered over with them, so many different-color squares taped to the metal that he can't even loop his combination lock through. It looks like some awful imitation of how girls wrap each other's lockers in foiled paper and ribbons on their birthdays.

I shift my weight forward, about to take a step closer to him and say something—I have no idea what but I'm hoping I figure it out in the next few seconds—when PJ and Chris's laughter sounds from an empty classroom.

It freezes me still.

I just stand there, as the boy whose name I still don't know peels condom after condom off his locker.

Balloon Animals

What is he doing here? What is he doing here? The question rings in my brain. It bumps up against everything I've been working for months not to think about. That night. Those awful minutes of him getting hurt in one room, and me getting hurt in another.

"Cristales, Graciela," Mrs. Vanderlinden says, with an annoyance that tells me this is probably the second time she's said it. I raise my free hand to tell her I'm here, my other hand flipping the book open.

Brigid Marchand twists back in her seat. She's not looking at me. Not in a way I'm meant to notice. She's more glancing toward me and then back to her friends, whispering something I can't make out.

"I'm not the one who wanted to be friends with her last year," one of the other girls says. I don't look to see who. "You were."

"Wrong," Brigid objects. "That was all Vic."

"Then I guess she's just nicer than you," another girl says.

"I'm nice," Brigid says back. "Nice enough to tell you what a shitty job you did with your lashes."

"Language," Mrs. Vanderlinden says without looking up. She charges down the attendance list.

"Thomas, Lock," she says.

My attention sparks at the name. It's not one I know. In schools this small new names always stick out.

Mrs. Vanderlinden says the name again. This time, impatience thins her voice.

"Right here," says the boy who walks in just as she's about to mark him absent.

I turn my head to see him sliding into a back-row desk.

My pencil slips from my fingers.

Of course the desk next to mine is one of the few open ones.

He gives me a quick nod as he sits down, something that could be either generic greeting or recognition.

Does he remember me?

There's no way. Whatever they put in his drink knocked him out hard enough that I doubt he even remembers the nopal green of my mother's car.

Sure, we were talking early in the party, when it was mostly populated by bowls of chips, unopened two-liters, and those of us too stupid to learn you always show up to a party an hour after it supposedly starts.

The boy—Lock—unzips a pocket of his backpack.

About twenty wrapped condoms spill out.

Brigid's laugh bubbles up again. The girls around her echo it. They know that Brigid will inherit Victoria's place when Victoria graduates. These laughs are their way of showing respect, like reverence at the end of the ballet classes we took as little kids.

Rage rises up in me as Mrs. Vanderlinden finishes her notes about who's sitting where.

Even if Brigid wasn't the one to actually slip the condoms

into his backpack, she's in on the joke. It's a joke that doesn't even make sense. Brigid and Victoria didn't put a condom on Lock; the lipstick wouldn't have been where it was if they had. And PJ and Chris didn't even have any condoms with them. They kept trying to needle me with their insistence that *come on, you don't need one for this, this isn't even sex, it doesn't even count.*

Lock's face flushes as he tries to gather the condoms back into his backpack.

His jaw is tight. So are the muscles around his eyes.

No.

He cannot cry right now.

It's not like I blame him. Whatever reserve he had, he probably used it up taking condoms off his locker in front of half the junior class. But if he cries now, first day, it's blood in the water. They will know they can get to him. They will never leave him alone.

A shiver of heat goes through my hip, right where my one tattoo is. El escaramujo, the rose hip I got on my fifteenth birthday in honor of my bisabuela and how she ate them like sugared plums.

Right now it stings, a little like the needles inking in the black outline and filling in the coral and mauve. The prickling, vibrating feeling hums through me.

If there had been any condoms around anywhere that night, I don't know if I'd be able to do what I do next. But before I can second-guess it, I take one of the plastic squares he's missed. I unwrap it, and blow into it until it's inflated, just like Jess and I did with the free condoms we got at Pride.

It swells up, pale and translucent, like the white plastic globes Mr. Milner uses to show us the phases of the moon.

It works.

Lock Thomas sinks down into his seat, trying not to laugh.

I tie off the end of the balloon and let it bounce and settle on Lock's desk.

Then I look straight ahead, biting my lip.

I spent half this summer trying to get back the light, flirty laugh that used to come as easily as swiping polish over my nails. I went at it like a numbers game, one date after another. I went out on enough dates this summer that if each one were a bead I'd have a bracelet. The girl who showed me her illustrations of hedgehogs and foxes. The boy I ended up nudging toward calling the boy he really wanted to be out with. The nonbinary college freshman who knew a thousand facts about the history of language, and told me something about Finnish and Hungarian I wish I could remember. Each time one tried to hug me (the artist), or shake my hand (the linguist), or accidentally brushed my arm (the lovesick one), I shuddered back like they'd shocked me.

They were, mostly, people I would have loved to know, but who I couldn't laugh for and who I couldn't let touch me.

But now, I am somehow making someone else laugh.

The crinkle of plastic makes me look over. Now Lock is opening a condom. The soft whir of him inflating it follows. It spreads faster than mine did, bursting into a comically large sphere in the space of a second.

I sink down now, my shoulder blades almost to the base of the chair, my lips pressed together so tight I can feel my pulse. I am trembling with the effort not to laugh loud enough that Mrs. Vanderlinden will hear.

He lets the balloon stick to his desk.

I look over at him. There's no tightness in his face, no sheen on his eyes to warn me there's still a risk of him crying. He tilts his head toward me, almost a challenge.

I reach over and inflate another one, to get him back.

We have five condom balloons static-clinging to our desks and he's starting on a sixth by the time Mrs. Vanderlinden notices.

She sounds more weary than stern when she says, "Let's save the balloon animals for your physics lab, shall we?"

Lock takes out what looks like a shiny blue pencil and, still looking at Mrs. Vanderlinden, pops each balloon.

Mrs. Vanderlinden sighs and turns toward the board.

Brigid and the girls around her start chattering in whispers I can't hear. Every few seconds one glances back at Lock, their faces more interested than mocking.

Just as Mrs. Vanderlinden goes back to explaining our syllabus, the crunching of plastic starts up again.

Not condom balloons this time.

This time Lock has tossed a zip-top bag onto his desk, filled with something fluffy and round.

Yarn.

It's a ball of blue yarn.

Lock hooks the tail of it around the shiny pencil. I don't realize until he flicks it, making a few loops, that it's not a pencil but a crochet hook.

His fingers turn back and forth. Within one of Mrs. Vanderlinden's bullet points, the string of stitches is as long as his forearm.

Lock Thomas, a boy, is crocheting. In class. Where everyone can see.

But he's not checking to see if anyone's watching. His eyes move only between his hands and the board. He just keeps turning the yarn over while listening to Mrs. Vanderlinden.

When she starts with enough substantive material that he has to take out a pen, he sets down the crochet hook.

He moves his notebook as close to me as he can get it and still have it on his desk. In the upper right corner, he writes, by way of introduction I guess, the name I heard before. Lock. Neat, all caps, the first letter a little bigger than the others.

I reach over to his desk, and, just below his name, write mine.

It doesn't occur to me then that Brigid or one of her friends might notice this. It doesn't occur to me until later, when I open my locker and handfuls of condoms spill out.

Gallina

When I tell Jess, she gives a delighted gasp. "The guy you were talking to at that party?" It comes with a suggestive lift of one perfectly tweezed eyebrow.

I shush her. "No. No eyebrow. This is not an eyebrow situation."

"Hey, you were the one making eyes at him, not me."

My shoulder blades tense at the mention of the party, but I shrug it away. It's not her fault. She doesn't realize that I disappeared from the party around the same time PJ and Chris went upstairs, and that Lock went missing at the same time as Brigid and Victoria.

"You know I'm right," Jess says. "I haven't seen you look like that since Amber Lewis got married."

My face heats with the memory, my crush on the middle daughter of a family who lived down the street. The day my parents got the crisp white envelope inviting them to her wedding, Jess was the friend who came over with a bucket of rainbow sherbet and our favorite movies.

I wish I knew how to tell Jess that if there was ever a chance for there to be a Lock-and-me, it ended in those two rooms.

He turned from a boy I thought was cute to a reminder of the worst night of my life, and probably his.

Jess makes change for a customer as I restock the polvorones. We both give a farewell *thank you*.

"So what did our boy in plaid flannel do to lose your favor?" Jess sighs. "Men are so disappointing, aren't they?"

"He didn't do anything," I say. "I just didn't expect him to show up in first-period history. I didn't even know he was enrolled."

Jess sighs, like she's summoning her patience. "Is he wearing off-brand uniform pants?"

I didn't think of it because my mom makes my school skirts on my abuela's old machine, so they're always a shade or two off from everyone else's. Now that Jess mentions it, I realize so are Lock's pants, which means he's not buying anything he doesn't have to from the Astin School–approved uniform company—with its ridiculous markups—any more than I am.

"Yeah," I say.

"Secondhand books?" she asks.

"Yes," I realize as I say it. The corners of his books have the same slightly curled pages as mine.

"Scholarship," Jess says. "Just like you have, just like I had. Only my guess is he's on full, or why transfer all the way from wherever he came from?"

Everything slots together.

Like him visiting last spring from Lancaster or the moon. A written application and test scores probably convinced Astin that they wanted him, and a tour of the shining classrooms, the orderly chem labs, and the pristine athletics fields was probably meant to convince him that he wanted them.

Which means he was at the party because he was visiting, and he still decided to come here, to take the scholarship and the chance at everything he could get at Astin.

A blond girl—college or grad-school-aged, carrying a book-heavy canvas bag—comes into the pastelería.

I only look at her for a second, but there's that prickling feeling again along my hip.

This time, it brings something else with it. The thought of powdered sugar, vanilla, cinnamon, dough that's been baked enough to stand up to the cream slipped into the center.

She's a little in love. Vanilla and powdered sugar might give her the space in her heart to realize it, if she hasn't already. Cinnamon will give her enough nerve to do something about it.

One of the oven timers goes off in the back.

I lean into Jess. "Get her a gallina," I say. "It's what she wants even if she doesn't know it."

Jess looks at me. "What did you just say?" Her voice is thin, unadorned. There's no winking or eyebrow raising.

"Una gallina," I say, pointing at the bakery case. "You know. The round one with all the powdered sugar on top that looks like a chick."

Jess blinks at me.

Something in me hums and vibrates, like the coil in a light-bulb blazing to life.

My understanding snaps into place.

Did I just do what I haven't done in months?

Jess gives the girl her best smile as she recommends the gallinas, and the girl shyly answers, "Okay. Why not?"

As the girl leaves, she holds the wax sleeve close to her face, breathing in the smell of vanilla and cream. She lets out a reveling sigh, like something is settling for her, landing softly.

Jess waits until the girl is out of sight to stare at me again.

"Did you just . . ." She doesn't even finish the question. It's the same one I have.

Did I just look at someone, and know exactly what she wanted before she did?

Las Alverjillas

On my way into the house, I pretend I'm stopping to admire the delicate alverjillas overflowing my mother's flower beds. I pretend I'm smelling them, instead of snapping away the sweet peas that have turned to mirrored glass, and slipping them into the front pocket of my sweatshirt.

Inside, I startle just before the door to my room.

"Mom," I say, like the first time she caught me on the sofa with Jess.

I hold both my hands in my sweatshirt pocket, the mirrored petals cool against my fingers.

My eyes slip toward the closet. No sign that she's opened it. She doesn't usually go into my stuff without asking, but I really should put more of a mess in front of the closet door just to make sure.

"You need air in here." My mother opens the window. "It smells like Windex and that disgusting shower gel your father bought you."

"It's supposed to smell like the ocean," I say.

She jerks the window the rest of the way open. "It smells like a can of air freshener you put in a car." She taps at a hole in the window screen. "We've got to get this replaced."

"It's fine," I say. Anything to get her out of my room. "I'll put duct tape over it."

"Con clase," she says on her way out. "Come help me with dinner."

"In a minute," I say, pointedly setting down my book bag so she'll think I need to check something with my homework.

Once I hear her at the bottom of the stairs, I shut my bedroom door.

I ease the closet door open, to put the alverjillas inside with everything else. Squinting, I look for the familiar shapes of the edges, the leaves and papel picado that look like mercury glass. But I don't find them. Instead, the inside of the closet shimmers. It sparkles with silver dust.

Before I understand what I'm looking at—these pieces that have crumbled into shards—a draft from the window reaches into the closet. It draws out a glittering wisp of crushed pieces.

"No." I shut the closet door.

But it's already out.

I chase it toward the window, but it's too fast for me. The ribbon of air, sparkling like needles of frost, streams out through the hole in the window screen.

"No," I call after it.

I try to push the window screen out, but the shards of mirrored glass are already swirling away and into the world. It looks like the kind of snow that's so cold it glitters. It dances over the roofs, silver against the blue of the sky.

"Ciela?" my mother calls.

"Coming," I shout through my closed door, praying a sliver of glass doesn't get into anyone else the way it got into me.

It Goes with Us

I wake up to the hinges on my bedroom door creaking. A slice of gray morning cuts in from the hallway.

"Get dressed," my father says in a voice far too crisp for this early.

I sit up, blinking, the wooden base of my bed rattling. "I have school."

"I'll get you there on time." He steps into the doorway far enough for me to see he already has his suit on. "Just wear something warm over the uniform."

I clear bits of sleep from the inner corners of my eyes. By habit, I check my fingertips for flecks of silver, even though I know the mirror shard is too deep to blink out anymore.

My heart takes the weight of remembering the day before, the little pieces drifting out into the air like snow.

I check the clock. "I have to go help Tía with the first rush."

"I called her," he says. "She doesn't need you."

"Dad." I throw off my comforter.

"When you get to the end of your life, what are you going to say?" My father hands me my favorite mug, the brown ceramic warm against my palms. "'I wish I'd done more homework'?"

"We're already thinking about the end of my life?" I pull on a pair of fluffy socks. "There's a heartwarming thought first thing in the morning. What exactly happened on Mamá's telenovelas last night?"

He ignores me and goes on. "Or are you gonna say"—he sits down on the edge of my bed, ignoring the wooden rattling—"'I wish I'd seen the ocean more'?"

I try not to smile.

But even in the dim room he sees it. I can tell by his grin.

I'm considering it, and he knows it. He just doesn't know why. He doesn't know that these kinds of mornings have been what's been keeping me upright for months. And he doesn't know that right now, I need something that helps me forget the mirrored glass in my closet, and the little shards of it I let out into the world.

"Give me five minutes," I say.

My dad goes back toward the door. "We ride at dawn."

Half an hour later my dad and I stand on the rocks behind the ocean institute, the best place for watching waves crash in. They break against the jagged gray below and burst into soap-bubble foam.

"See?" my father asks. "Worth it or worth it?"

The spume off the waves sprays us. The cold smell of the sea soaks into my hair.

"It definitely beats the time you took me to a driving range," I say.

"Hey," he says. "Some people find golf very relaxing."

"Gringos find golf relaxing. And personally, I could never find golf as relaxing as not-golfing." I peer down into the foam-fluffy water.

The tide pools below are off-limits unless you work at the institute. But my father got us a trip down there thanks to him being friends with one of the marine biologists studying sea anemones and water salinity. Those feathery rounds looked like animals a mermaid would keep as pets. Whenever the minnows brushed their tentacles, they flinched shut. The tide-smoothed sand they rooted in seemed like the best floor in the world.

Even though we can't see all that from up here, every time my dad brings me out to the rocks I think of it, the marine biologist taking us down in a moment of the water staying almost still, my father's wonder as thick in the air as mine.

My father leans against the railing. The sea-soaked metal dampens the cuffs of his suit.

"Here's the thing, mija." He looks out into the gray morning, white-gold light breaking through the cloud cover and touching the farthest part of the ocean we can see.

"Every moment of our life," he says, "it goes with us. It lives forever. And a lot of those moments you don't have much say over. So the ones you do, you've got to do everything with them. So that what lives forever is something you want to live with."

I slump against the railing alongside him and focus on that far patch of light. "No pressure."

He fluffs my ponytail. His hair may be thinning, but it's still obvious how alike his and mine are. Brown-black instead of my mother's almost blue-black. Coarser than hers too. *I gave you my hair*, he says sometimes, running a hand over his widening bald spot. *Quite literally, huh?*

I look toward the faint silhouettes of Catalina and San Clemente.

The gulls and pelicans sweep by in arcs of white and brown.

Their wings fan the smell of the horizon toward us. It's not just the wax and dirt of their feathers. It's the bright scent of deep sea and far-off sky, what the ocean smells like when light breaks through the clouds.

Three minutes before first bell, my dad drops me off in front of the school. I've never asked him or my mother to drop me off half a block up like Brigid did before she got her car. I may not always like my parents, but chances are if you don't like them, you won't like me either, so I've never seen the point of trying to hide them.

I shut the passenger door.

"Go take over the world," I say through the open window.

My father laughs. "Yes, an empire shall rise from my extensive collection of actuarial tables." He laughs again, but this time, it's a clenched-fist movie-villain peal so spectacular that a few of my classmates stare. Some sneer. A freshman girl smiles like it's the best thing she's ever witnessed.

I wave as he drives off.

Then my whole body sinks into a slouch. I brace for another day of dodging Victoria and Brigid, PJ and Chris. The four people who have become the whole school to me because they were the ones in those two different rooms.

When I push through the right side of the double doors, the halls are vibrating in one frequency, the way that only ever happens when everyone is talking about the same thing.

Traffic is thin near the lockers. I follow to where it thickens.

A crowd packs the hall that leads to the gym.

The door to the boys' locker room is open.

My stomach kicks. I don't know why yet, except that so little good happens in locker rooms.

Everyone who can crowd around the open door does. I shove as close as I can get, grateful for both the width of my hips and the rumors that make everyone else back away from me.

The crowd between me and the locker room door is still two or three deep, but the sight of inflated latex stops me.

Condom balloons, hundreds of them, float above the empty locker room. They bump up against the ceiling.

Rage and nausea whirl inside me.

They couldn't let it go.

They have nothing better to do than try to break this boy down.

And I probably gave them the idea. Brigid probably saw us inflating them in class.

Principal Whitcomb shame-walks Lock Thomas down the hall. A completely unnecessary gesture, an Astin School flourish.

Principal Whitcomb probably wants him to hang his head with appropriate remorse.

Lock has his hands in his pockets, but he isn't hanging his head. He owes all of us watching nothing, and he knows it.

I can't quite pin it down, but there's something harder about him. The look he had before, the one that made him seem both sweet and settled, is gone. The air around him feels jagged, agitated, like he's realized the world is sharper and uglier than he thought and he's angry it took him this long to notice.

Instead of ashamed, or even nervous, he seems resigned, like he's said what he needed to say.

And that, the way he looks straight down the hall, is a fuck-you so perfect I almost envy it. Or I would envy it, if my understanding of how stupid this boy is wasn't settling deep in my stomach. It brings the unsteady, nauseous feeling of drinking something cold right after drinking something hot.

The needling feeling comes back, prickling through my hip.

PJ and Chris didn't fill the locker room with helium-inflated condoms.

Lock did. Because he has no idea what he's doing.

Maybe where he used to go to school would have let this slide, dismissed it as a prank. But Astin is a place where skirt checks are as built into the schedule as the class bells. Leah Voss once had an old film from East Berlin in her bag that she was referencing for a paper, and she got called into the office to make sure she wasn't getting indoctrinated with— not kidding—"European communism." Jess and I got pulled off the winter formal dance floor because we were dancing in a way "unbecoming to young ladies," one of a hundred little reminders that our brown, queer bodies would always be measured against pale, freckled ones.

If PJ or Chris did this, they could survive it. Their parents have built science labs, bought new bleachers, refloored the stage in the auditorium. As of next year, the gym will have PJ's last name on it. Either one of them would get a solemn, level-voiced lecture about school decorum, probably have to write an essay that was half apology, half morality tale, and maybe—*maybe*—have to publish it in the school newspaper.

But Lock? A boy whose scholarship status is written across his used books, his shoes, the secondhand tie he wore to first assembly? (Probably no one else noticed that last one, but I did, the slight fraying that showed on the underside.) A boy who, as far as the donors are concerned, exists to remind them of their own generosity? They'll make an example of him, because he was supposed to be the kind of boy they could show off at fundraisers.

Lock probably hasn't thought that far. He probably hasn't even realized that PJ and Chris and Brigid and Victoria don't have to wreck his chances here.

They just got him to do it for them.

Lock turns his head, just a little. He's not looking at me. But that change in angle is enough for me to catch a tiny flash of silver at the corner of his eye.

The prickling along my hip bone turns to a feeling like touching dry ice, a searing cold.

The shards that flew out my window not only found someone, they found Lock. That glint of silver has burrowed into him enough to make him reckless and stupid.

The mirrored glass is my fault. How it flew out my window is my fault. The fact that it got into Lock, and that he's probably about to get suspended, is my fault.

My father's voice gets in my head.

Every moment of our life, it goes with us. It lives forever.

The dread of responsibility falls on me, like remembering that I promised to help clean out the garage, or be my cousin's date to a school dance, or hold up the star in the church nativity. Only much, much worse.

I sigh. "Dammit, Dad."

The freshman girl from outside school turns. "What?" she asks.

I shake my head. "Nothing."

My father's words, together with that swirling hot and cold on my hip, shoves me forward.

Before I can consider what a truly bad idea this is, I'm doing it. I'm following Lock and Principal Whitcomb down the hall.

No Good Deed

I catch up to them just before the door of the principal's office.

"Principal Whitcomb," I say, following him in.

"Graciela." He gives an uneasy glance toward the hall. "Louise will be happy to book you an appointment."

Translation: *I'm busy. Get away from my office.*

Lock stares at me, eyes narrowed, gauging, as he stands between Principal Whitcomb's desk and a bookshelf of doorstoppers on adolescent psychology.

Jess got Principal Whitcomb right on the first try. A pretty boy (her words) who can't be older than thirty, dressed in better suits than any school administrator could ever afford, he is a walking anti-advertisement for nepotism. We still don't know whose nephew he is, but we do know that Mrs. Anders—*Louise*, as Principal Whitcomb likes calling her—would've been a better pick twice over.

School looks like a different place without Jess, all hard edges and fluorescent gleam. And a principal who never much noticed me but who is now staring at me.

He hasn't thrown me out of his office yet, so now's my chance.

"I . . ." I try to choke out the words. "He"—I look at Lock—"he didn't do it." I look back at Principal Whitcomb. "I did."

Principal Whitcomb studies me.

My heart feels like it's throwing itself against my chest plate.

"The condom balloons," I say, as though he could have forgotten. "I made them. I put them in the locker room."

Lock shakes his head at the floor. "No, she didn't."

"Yes, I did," I say. "And I can prove it." I never thought I'd think this but, thank you, PJ and Chris and their stupid jokes. "There are condoms in my locker. You can check."

"What are you doing?" Lock asks.

I ignore him and talk only to Principal Whitcomb. "I can't let someone else get blamed for something I did." I keep my voice so serious that Principal Whitcomb won't have a choice but to believe me. I am overdoing neither my remorse nor my indignation. I aim for the careful tone of someone confessing and unburdening her soul. "Especially not someone who's new to our school community."

That last part's good enough to be in one of our brochures. I can tell it's what gets Principal Whitcomb, what will make him believe me instead of Lock.

"Why are you doing this?" Lock asks me, his hands twitchy, like he's about to rake his fingers through his hair or pull at his uniform sweater.

"Yes," Principal Whitcomb says, looking at me now. "Why did you do this?"

"I didn't—" Lock tries to protest Principal Whitcomb misinterpreting his question.

I cut him off. "It was a protest," I say.

"Of what?" Principal Whitcomb says.

Principal Whitcomb and Lock are both staring at me.

My face gets hot enough to make me say the first lie I can

think of. I'm on my period, new stash of tampons and pads in my bag, so of course, that's where my brain goes.

"How girls have to attend twice as many sex ed sessions as boys at this school," I say.

Principal Whitcomb looks between me and Lock again.

Lock is staring me down.

No, not staring.

Lock Thomas is *glaring* at me.

I'm helping him, and he's glaring.

Principal Whitcomb sighs like he picked a bad day to wear his favorite tie. "I don't know which of you did this," he says. "Or if it was both of you. But whoever did, I think you know this is not the way to respect your school or yourselves. So I'm holding you both responsible. And that responsibility starts"—he opens his office door—"with you both cleaning up the mess."

He walks us down the hall and throws open the door to the boys' locker room.

Most of the condom balloons still bob against the ceiling. A few have drifted to the floor or are clinging by static to the lockers.

"What is wrong with you?" I ask as soon as Principal Whitcomb is out of earshot.

Lock shrugs. "There were about a hundred condoms on my windshield after last period yesterday. Thought I should do something with them. Thanks for the idea, by the way."

Perfect. I tried to help him survive here, and somehow it turned into a prank that has him on the bad side of the administration on day two.

"So what is it?" He unzips his backpack. "Did you need a

new community service project or something?" He blinks, and it comes with a tiny point of silver. I wonder if he can feel it.

I set my book bag down, making the last-minute decision to drop it loud enough to make a point. "I was trying to help."

He takes out a crochet hook. Green this time. How many of those things does he have?

I get close enough to get in his face, but all it does is make me feel short. "You were about to get suspended."

"For this?" He pops one of the condom balloons. "Seriously?"

"You really have no idea how things work around here, do you?" I ask.

The disciplinary code at Astin is unofficially based on who the school wants to come down hard on and whose transgressions they want to make disappear. Donors' sons get warnings when they're caught selling their sisters' medication, but Jules Kempner got suspended for three days for showing her friends nude photographs her artist older sister took. They weren't of Jules, or of anyone we knew; the models were all twenty-five or thirty, and they weren't even doing anything. They were just lounging on sofas looking bored, or flipping through crates of vinyl, or talking on princess phones that weren't plugged in, all while wearing nothing but red and green socks.

Three days, for artsy photos. Jules Kempner gets the same partial scholarship I do. How much harder are they going to be on a boy with a full scholarship and a locker room of condom balloons?

I jump up on the wooden bench and grabbed one of the balloons clinging to the wall. "If you'd let me take the blame for this, we both would've been fine. Around here, they come down harder on girls for swearing and short skirts, and they're harder on guys for pranks and fights. This was a prank. Whitcomb would've written it off as PMS."

"And why would you want that?" Lock gets up on the opposite side of the bench and pops one of the balloons hovering under the ceiling. "The new kid sound like a good charity to you?"

I will not yell at him. I will not yell at him. I think it over and over, reminding myself that the mirror shard in him has left him raw and cruel.

So I just stand there. Blinking at him. Caught between annoyance and the understanding that I crossed a line. In Mrs. Vanderlinden's class I made him laugh. But in Principal Whitcomb's office, I got in the middle of him showing the whole school his teeth. By trying to save him, I took something away from him.

I understand this. But understanding it doesn't make me any less annoyed with him. And it doesn't solve the fact that a tiny shard of mirror is making him careless.

"Guess you did your good deed," he says, voice hard as he pops three more balloons. "So congratulations."

Pan Fino

I t's like he *wants* to get kicked out." I pull on oven mitts.

Jess marks down numbers on an inventory sheet. One of many things my tía loves about her. No one else keeps better track of when we're running low on cake flour or piloncillo.

"Ever hear the one about the drowning man?" Jess asks.

I slide a tray of pajaritos from the oven, the pan dulce we shape to look a little like swallows. "What?"

Jess continues marking. "It's incredibly dangerous to try to save someone who's drowning. People flail and fight and they make it harder, and often, both people end up drowning."

"You should teach Sunday school," I say.

"I'm serious." She puts a hand on my shoulder.

I try not to flinch.

"It's stupid to try to save someone drowning," she says. "Noble, but stupid."

"We have a crowd, ladies." My tía herds us toward the front. "Ahora."

When we get to the register, the smell of sugary cocktails rushes at me. The restaurants down the street must be having a happy hour. We usually don't have this kind of crowd later than 6:00 P.M.

"Speaking of drowning"—I open a few wax sleeves while the men read off the placards in horrible Spanish pronunciation and the women wobble on their heels—"how's class?"

Jess gives me a world-weary sigh. "It'll be fine, I told my mom. Of course I can do eighteen credits. What could go wrong?"

"What's an oreja?" a woman in a silky top asks, pronouncing the *j* hard enough to make me cringe.

"That looks like corn," one of the men says, pointing at the sugared elotes.

"It's supposed to," I say under my breath.

"Is that a Danish?" another one of them asks.

Jess claps her hands. "Who's ready?" she tries to call above their chatter.

This group of slightly drunk, probably overpaid young professionals is crowding close enough to the register that I can tell lemon drops were on special tonight. They laugh how *This place is so cute*, and *I didn't even know this was here.*

A tired-looking family tries to crowd in behind them.

Something familiar brushes my hip, like the outer feathers of a bird's wing. It lands. Its slight weight settles, and I place it: that sense that's been catching me in the halls at school and in the pastelería. It's a needling feeling that tells me to do things. Help Lock hold it together during class. Suggest a gallina to a lovesick woman. Walk into the principal's office.

And now it's telling me to cut through the noise in the pastelería.

"Okay," I say.

My voice is loud enough that everyone goes quiet.

"Two cochitos"—I point at one of the men, because I have

a feeling that he loves animals, and that he'll like cinnamon dough in the shape of little pigs—"a coyota"—the woman with the braided trim on her bag and belt will appreciate the braided trim on the coyotas—"three niños envueltos"—I point at a couple who I'm pretty sure will love the strawberry and coconut, eating one each and sharing the third.

"Is she telling our fortunes?" one of the women whispers.

"Two leos and two piernas," I say, pointing to the two men who I think will appreciate the straightforward artistry of the pan fino. They want each other, though neither of them seems to know it, and I'm hoping sharing the piernas and leos might make them realize.

"I heard about this," one of the other men says. "She tells you what you'll like."

"So she just decides for us?" the woman asks.

Jess rings them up while I slip everything into wax sleeves.

"If I'm wrong," I say, handing them each their pan dulce, "come back tomorrow and I'll give you something else."

Jess and I watch them leave bigger tips than they'd probably ever leave sober.

The kind of tips La Bruja de los Pasteles used to get.

Jess nods to me. "Nice."

I wait for the happy hour crowd to filter out so the rest of the line can come up.

Jess eyes me like she's sizing me up, even as she pulls pan dulce for the next order. "What's going on with you?"

The shiver of hot and cold deepens in my hip. The chill of ice and flush of hot water swirls over el escaramujo, like different colors of light.

I piece it all together. The feeling when I gave the blond

girl una gallina matches the one when I made Lock laugh in Mrs. Vanderlinden's class. The shudder of heat through my hip now matches the one that needled me toward Principal Whitcomb's office.

I am responsible for a boy I left alone at the hospital and who now has a sliver of mirror in him because of me. Helping him is the only thing that's brought back a little of my bisabuela's magic.

That feeling shimmering over the rose hip hasn't just been telling me what to do; It's been brightening like a coil of light, telling me how to get back what I've lost.

The Pastry Witch of
San Juan Capistrano

I walk home, and with every block it comes into sharper focus.

I helped Lock not break down on the first day, and then I guessed that the blond girl with the book bag would want the fluffy, powdered-sugared dough of a gallina.

I stopped Principal Whitcomb from coming down on Lock, and then I knew what a bakery full of drunk twenty- and thirty-somethings wanted better than they did.

The mirror shard in Lock's eye is my fault. It turned him from a boy trying to hide at this school to a boy who almost got suspended from it. I have to look out for him, and I have to make sure the mirrored glass doesn't touch anyone else. And maybe if I do that, I'll get back the thread of magic that made me La Bruja de los Pasteles, a girl who speaks the language of vanilla-glazed espejos. A girl worthy of my great-grandmother's trust, instead of a girl with a mirror shard for a heart.

"Ciela," my mother calls from the kitchen when she hears me come in. "You'll come have something with me?"

My hand goes to the side of my neck, scratching the place that prickles whenever I hear my name echo across the house.

God love my mother, but the way she asks certain questions

that aren't really questions makes me want to rip a hole in my sweater.

You'll stuff the bolillos for the church picnic?

You'll dust the baseboards for me?

You'll prune back the morning glories?

You'll come to my book club with me? They'd love to see you.

You'll make yourself some scrambled eggs, and you'll eat them?

Like she's already told me, I've already agreed, and she's just reminding me.

My mother stands at the kitchen counter, cutting open avocados in the way she always asks me not to slice bagels, the fruit in her hand as she spins it across the knife's blade.

"You told me that's how people end up needing stitches," I say.

She whips the knife through and then twists the fruit open. "But I have forty-five years of experience."

"You started halving avocados from birth? Impressive."

She makes crosshatch cuts in each half and then turns them inside out, like she does with mangos, and spills the pieces into the molcajete.

"I got a call from your principal," she says.

Heat crawls up my neck.

She opens her mouth to speak again, but then pauses, considering me. "You don't wear lipstick anymore, mija?"

I shrug.

"Whatever the question," my mother says, "red lipstick is the answer."

I almost smile thinking of saying it in unison with Jess.

Then I catch the glinting silver behind my mother.

The hierbas in little clay pots on the windowsill, the cilantro and pápalo and rue, each have a sprig of leaves that have turned to mirrored glass.

I will my mother not to turn around, to keep her absolute focus on the avocado, or on my lack of lipstick, anything but the windowsill.

My mother shakes her head like she just remembered the topic at hand.

"So good news for you," she says. "You won't be suspended. This won't go on your record. But it sounds like Whitcomb's got some painful penance in store for you and that boy."

I would sink to the floor in relief, for me, and for Lock and his reckless ass. But any relief I feel is sheared away by hoping my mother does not turn around.

"If I had to guess, you'll be scrubbing gym mats or cleaning windows or polishing the chapel pews," my mother says. "Or shining the chrome on his halteras."

Is it just me or does she sound more amused than angry?

"You're not mad?" I ask, trying not to let her see that I'm looking past her, not at her.

My mother's gaze might actually wear a hole in me. "Condom balloons?"

I cringe harder. "Yes."

"Why?"

"Art installation gone wrong. It was a thing I was doing with some of Jess's friends." Sorry, Jess, but invoking your name instantly puts mothers at ease, especially mine. "It was all a big misunderstanding." I dig through my bag. "But I need you to sign this form saying you understand my depraved soul is in danger if I continue on this path."

My mother salts the avocado. "Blue or black ink?"

I'm wondering if I can convince her there are no pens in the whole kitchen, that we have to go to the living room, when I hear my father come in.

My mother goes to the garage, and I steal the sprigs of mirrored leaves so fast they cut my hands. I rush upstairs and open my closet only the crack it takes to throw them in. I'm not letting any more of that glass out.

I shut the door, collapsing with relief so heavy I barely feel the threads of blood on my fingers.

Strange Season

Pull over, okay?" I ask my dad when we're a few blocks from school.

"Have we reached that point in your adolescence?" He brakes next to the sidewalk. "You're afraid to be seen with your old dad dropping you off?"

"No." I roll my eyes at him. "Look."

Mrs. Peters's lily magnolia tree has disappeared. The whole thing. Even the stump. All that's left is a confetti of withering petals.

Mrs. Peters is out on the lawn, ranting. "It was right here!"

I see her audience. Dr. Emmott is out in his own front yard, near where his property meets the Peterses' but not daring to set his foot over the line. A line which is exceedingly obvious since Dr. Emmott has a front yard full of stones and low desert plants, an unintentional indictment of the Peterses' plush, water-sucking sod.

"Who would steal an entire tree?" she thunders.

I almost call out to ask why she cares. She's the one who wanted it gone anyway. We all saw the removal notice tacked to its trunk.

Then I see why. It's not just the tree that's gone. The root ball went with it. In its place is a hollow deep enough that I can see it from the car. The earth seems to have opened up in the Peterses' perfect front lawn.

Dr. Emmott keeps his voice low, trying to calm Mrs. Peters. Dr. Emmott is one of the most soft-spoken men I've ever met, something no one expects when they see the tattoos sleeving his arms and winding over his shaved head. Strangers cross the street away from him, and the look on their face when they hear his mild voice for the first time never gets old.

As Mrs. Peters goes on with "Who would do this?" and "What is this neighborhood turning into?" I don't realize Dr. Emmott sees me until he casts me and my dad a forlorn smile across the street. It's a look of *run, save yourself*.

"Do you know what this is?" Mrs. Peters points a finger down like she might drive it into the lawn. "Vandalism. This is an act of vandalism."

I make a mental note to bring Dr. Emmott and his husband some strong coffee and a box of galletas covered in sprinkles. They're going to be hearing Mrs. Peters rant for days.

My father pulls away from the curb. "Strange season, mija," he says. "No Santa Anas. Trees vanishing right out of front yards."

"You sound like Tía," I say.

"It's not good when the Santa Anas don't come," he says, turning right. "It's like the wind holding its breath."

He pulls up to the school, dropping me off early so I can make the time Principal Whitcomb told Lock and me to be at his office. "No more modern art, okay?"

I raise my right hand. "Lo prometo."

When I pass Victoria in the hall, I give her a lot of space. But then I hear her inhale, and I know she's going to talk to me anyway.

I brace for it.

"Big mistake," Victoria says.

The words sound like a threat, a warning.

But Victoria's not looking at me like she's threatening me. She's looking at me almost sympathetically.

"Trying to help the new guy," she says. "He's just going to drag you down. Lost cause. And trust me"—now her words harden, and she's looking me over—"I know all about lost causes."

"What?" I ask before I can stop myself.

"Just some friendly advice." Victoria keeps walking.

Lost cause. I'm still turning Victoria's words over in my brain—and the look she gave me with them—as Lock and I sit in Principal Whitcomb's office. Mrs. Anders let us in, and now we're waiting for the man of the hour to appear.

Lock is barely looking at me, and somehow he's still managing to glare at me. He's looping together Principal Whitcomb's paper clips like I used to do at my father's office.

"What are you, five?" I whisper at him.

I'm being bitchy, and I know it. And I cannot be bitchy with a boy who still has a glint of silver in the corner of his eye. I can see it at certain angles. Why isn't he trying to blink it out? Can't he feel it?

I literally fold my tongue in my mouth, like my grandmother taught me and my primos to do when we were angry. *Don't bite it. Biting just gets you blood*, she used to say.

"Good news," Principal Whitcomb says when he enters. "I've found the perfect project for you to work on together."

"What do you mean 'together'?" Lock asks, with unveiled dread.

Principal Whitcomb summons us to a room across the hall.

"These"—he points to two cardboard boxes sitting on a Formica table—"are our newest educational pamphlets. For students, parents, assemblies, and to bring out into the community. They just came in, and you two"—he picks up one glossy, color-printed sheet and presses it into thirds—"get the job of folding them."

He goes over the folds to make them crisp and sets it down.

The title beams from the front panel.

The Gift You Can Only Give Once.

Of course Lock and I get stuck with the abstinence-only brochures.

"I'll see you both after school to get started," he says. "And I expect you to bring the same energy you brought to defacing our locker room."

I look over at Lock, hoping he realizes how easily we're getting off. There must be hundreds in those two boxes, but this could be so much worse. If Lock decides to just sit here and sulk, I could probably do this all myself.

"Where do you want them when we're done?" I ask.

Principal Whitcomb lets out what might be the first genuine laugh I've ever heard from him.

"I wouldn't worry about that just yet." He opens a door I'm only now realizing is a supply closet.

It holds a tower of identical cardboard boxes almost as tall as me.

Lock's stare crawls over to me. His look, somewhere between *you've got to be kidding* and *nice going*, is barely contained.

Wrong Tree

I would give up coffee and chiles rellenos for the rest of high school if it meant I would never have another paper cut from *You Can Never Get It Back* or *Our Greatest Treasure*. Shiny leaflets meant to tell us that sex is a precious gift best left unopened.

A couple of girls slow as they pass the door. Lock and I have been folding in complete silence, so their whispers and laughs startle me.

Not Brigid or Victoria, not who Lock has probably already figured out are the ones who unzipped his jeans that night. But these are two of the girls who mimic the way Brigid and Victoria wear clusters of bracelets and twirl their hair into buns in the middle of class.

"Is that for a club or something?" one of them asks.

"No, he has to," the other one says. "Because of all the condoms."

The first one doesn't lower her voice as much as she probably thinks she does when she says, "Does he even know what to do with one?"

The second one stares at Lock like we can't see them. "I heard they had to show him how to do everything."

Lock flinches anyway.

I tilt my head up from the pamphlets and stare right at these two girls.

They look startled, and I wonder if they really thought we couldn't hear them.

At first I think it's because I'm a grade older than them. But their stricken faces tell me it's more than that. Maybe this is the effect of the rumors about me, the result of everyone thinking I'm the girl who willingly went into a room with PJ and Chris at the same time.

I don't blink.

They scramble down the hall.

I watch them scurry away, these girls who want to be Victoria and Brigid, whose boyfriends will probably follow them around like PJ and Chris. Then I wonder how much Victoria and Brigid and PJ and Chris even remember about that night. If it was just something they think happened after Victoria made out with Chris but before Brigid figured out that vodka and back-of-the-pantry Orange Crush is just as bad of an idea as it sounds.

Lock looks like he wants to kick the door shut as much as I do. But we're supposed to keep it cracked so Principal Whitcomb can check our progress.

The halls are almost empty by the time Lock and I are done. Not done with the pamphlets. Not even close. Just done for the day. We both walk toward the parking lot, not talking, on opposite sides of the hallway.

When Chris Bernard passes us, he walks between us. Lock and I are hugging opposite walls so closely that Chris has to take the middle.

"Wrong tree, Thomas," Chris says.

Lock blinks, uncomprehending. He catches himself almost

instantly, closing off his expression like he didn't even hear. But it's too late. He's already given Chris the opening.

"You know about her, right?" Chris eyes me and then looks back at Lock. "Your girl there, she doesn't like dick."

I freeze, one foot on one linoleum square, the other on the next.

A bitter taste rises in my throat.

Any other way Chris could have put it. Any other way, and I could pretend I didn't hear him.

She doesn't like dick. With four words, Chris just jammed together the fact that I resisted, that I tried to fight back that night, with the fact that I've had a girlfriend. To him, there's no nuance, no use explaining that I've gone out with girls and boys, and even less use explaining that I've gone out with people whose identities are more complex than either of those words. Trying to make him understand this would be like trying to explain sexuality and gender identity to a case of beer.

To him, the fact that I fought blends together perfectly with what little he knows about me.

To him, I am nothing but what he assumes from my resistance.

For months, I have tried to keep that night far from who I am, who I like, who I want.

But Chris Bernard has just forced them together.

"Trust me, don't bother," Chris says. "She won't even swallow."

The acid taste of bile reaches up my throat.

My feet are already responding.

I push out one side of a double door, and the rush of cooler air settles my stomach, but just for a minute. I barely make it to the hedges along the parking lot.

In this moment, I am not at school. I am back in that night, before I decide to leave Lock alone at the hospital. I am running from the ER waiting room not because I have decided to leave him. I haven't made that decision yet. But because acid is rising in my stomach.

As I slip down the hospital hall, the heat of watching eyes lands on me. Not in the curious or admiring or interested way I'm used to when I'm behind the counter at the pastelería. More like they're afraid I might hurl on them.

I can't blame them. Right now it's a distinct possibility.

I spot the gray lettering on the white square—WOMEN—below that skirted figure. But I don't make it to the bathroom.

The nausea drags me down to the linoleum, down to my hands and knees. The waistband of my jeans bites into my stomach, and I start retching into the tiny plastic trash can next to the water fountain.

First, I taste Diet Coke, the caramel coloring made sour with my stomach acid. Odd, since that's the first thing I drank, hours ago.

Then grenadine, watered down with Fresca but still sugary.

Next comes the salt taste at the back of my throat, the one that brings the feeling of hands gripping my hair. And that feeling, hot on my scalp, makes me start heaving harder.

The ribbon of sticky white comes up last.

A nervous, young-looking nurse stops over me.

For a second, I see us both as though I'm up near the fluorescents, a balloon caught under the ceiling. I see a nurse in scrubs as pink as her cheeks. And me, La Bruja de los Pasteles, bracing her hands on the floor, wondering why her stomach is still bucking even though it's emptied out.

The nurse speaks with more concern than disgust when she asks, "Honey, are you okay?"

There, on the floor, with grenadine staining my mouth, that's when I decide.

I decide that tonight did not happen. If I ever want to get up off this floor, tonight has to never have happened. And just like that, it all gets wrapped up together, so I don't even know which one has to come first.

If I want tonight to have never happened, I have to get up off this floor, now, before this nurse asks me what's really wrong. Before I tell her.

The pavement of the school parking lot is the first thing to bring me back to now. It dimples its rough pattern into my knees, bare because I'm wearing my uniform skirt.

The air around me feels stagnant, heavy. The swallows' wings don't stir the air. The Santa Anas don't sweep the sky clean or blow the shard of mirrored glass from my heart. The vanishing trees mean the air is a little less sugared with their blossoms, so I can't forget the smell of that night months ago, the grenadine and salt and that ribbon of white.

When I'm done getting sick, when I've wiped the bile-sour saliva off with the back of my hand, I get up. I have to get up. Just like I had to get up from the hospital floor that night.

When I get up, Lock is standing there. Not close. Not watching. Waiting.

I wipe my mouth again on the back of my sleeve.

He hands me a cup of water. Paper, printed with daisies. From the school office.

I take it.

Lock steps back.

"Thank you," I say, both for the water, and the distance he's giving me.

He nods at me, once. It's fast and slight, an acknowledgment.

Lock has just heard Chris talking, and just seen me hurl into the bushes, and I wonder if he has figured something out about me. If he's heard the rumors, and is piecing it together. *She won't even swallow.* That it was part of someone else's body forced into my mouth.

I sip the water, and I hope not. I hope that he's not that perceptive, that he hasn't figured out that in one room, he was violated, a girl's mouth on him when he didn't want it, and in another room, I was, part of another body in my mouth when I didn't want it. I hope he hasn't put all this together, this thing we have in common that he can't remember and I can't forget.

La Educación Sexual

The first cake I frost the next morning, I write *Happy Anniversary*.

I am sure I write *Happy Anniversary*, in green icing, just like the order slip says.

But the words piped on the smooth cream top of the cake are not *Happy Anniversary*.

The words on the cake are *You Only Have It to Give Away Once*.

"No one asked you," I say. With one flick of a cake spatula, I smooth the words into a green blur. I'll pretend frosting gradients are my new signature flourish.

I look up, disconcerted to see a blurred image of my own face.

One of my tía's paper flowers has turned from a fluffy ball of pink tissue paper to a hard ripple of silver glass.

I make sure no one's watching, and I pluck it from among its still-soft, still-colorful mates. I shove it into my book bag so fast I almost knock over a stack of boxes.

My aunt strolls back to the kitchen. "What's wrong, mijita?"

I kick the book bag under the counter. The glass is probably going to be in pieces when I get home. Maybe I'll just pull out my books and throw the bag into the closet? Do I still have my backpack from a couple years ago?

"It's nothing," I say.

She frowns at me, her *I know you're lying* face.

"The stupid pamphlets are getting to me," I say. "I'm going to be able to recite them by the time we're done."

"Sexual education," my tía says in the inexplicably posh British accent she uses for all Astin-related topics. "Yes, we must enlighten the youth, mustn't we?"

I shake my head, trying not to smile, trying not to draw attention to the fact that I am re-frosting a cake. "It's not really sexual education. We're folding five million pamphlets that all say *don't do it*."

"If only"—my tía leans wistfully against the metal counter—"you had something that could make your dear principal as uncomfortable as he's making you."

I glance at her sideways. "What are you plotting?"

"Just a little something your prima sent me after one of her feminismo workshops."

"Why do we call it *feminismo*?" I follow her as she saunters across the kitchen. "If it's feminism, shouldn't it be *feminisma*?"

"Hey, how much of English makes sense?" Pilar calls as she comes back from the front counter. "*Through. Rough. Wednesday. February*. Don't argue with Spanish."

"And don't argue with me," my tía says, gesturing me toward the tiny office where she keeps the books and takes phone orders. "Because I have something that will scare los pantalones off your principal."

"There's a mental image I need to bleach from my brain," I say.

My tía turns around. "Do you want my help or not?"

Her desk is a mess of supply catalogs and pink invoices for our regular orders. She puts a shipping box down on all of it. The postage label is still on the top flap.

"Your principal wants you to learn about la educación sexual?" my aunt asks, unlatching the overlapped flaps of the box. "How about you return the favor?"

I peer inside. The sight is so unnerving and so glorious that I swear the fuzzy mariachi music coming from the speakers is the sound of angels.

My tía grins.

Valentina

I'm the first one to Mrs. Vanderlinden's class the next morning. Lock Thomas is the second.

He gives me a wry, weary smile, an *of course* smile.

He takes his now-assigned seat next to me. He probably regrets his first-day choice now. Once the seating chart gets made, you're there for the whole year.

I ignore him in a way so pointed that my back is almost to him.

But not so much that I can't sense him looking into my tote bag. Not my usual one, the seahorse-printed one that matches the starfish one Jess has. No, this is the giant one I borrowed from my mother to fit all my books and the new friend my tía lent me.

"What is that?" he says, leaning to get a better look.

I keep my back three-quarters to him. "Nothing."

"No. Seriously." Now he's studying it, half hanging out of his desk. "It looks like a flower and a stuffed animal had a baby and you brought it to school."

"I brought some visual inspiration for our pamphlet folding." I sweep the bloom of stuffed velour petals out of my bag and slip my hand into the slick polyester of the puppet's hollow. "Meet

Valentina la Vagina." I pronounce her whole name in Spanish, to give the full effect of the rhyme.

Lock stares, taking in what must, at first, look like the plush version of a mauve-brown and deep pink rose, but is in fact an anatomically accurate plush rendering of a vagina. But with two googly eyes and a puppet mouth.

I watch the understanding break across his face. How the petals are not meant to be petals, but inner and outer labia. How the little bud at the center is not a bud but a clitoris.

How it's a stuffed-animal version of my own concha.

I wait for his shocked expression, wait to be satisfied by how a puppet interpretation of a human vagina makes him shudder.

But there's no shuddering, no unnerved glance toward the door.

"That"—he says, pausing—"is one of the most magnificent works of art I've ever seen."

"Then just wait until you see Whitcomb's face when I make her talk." I open and close my hand so Valentina is speaking my words.

He looks not terrified, but awed.

"Where did you even get this?" he asks.

"My cousin went to a workshop." I open and close my hand again. Valentina's googly eyes make her look like the spirited head cheerleader of talking vaginas. "And now she makes them."

"Why are you doing this?"

He said these same words in Principal Whitcomb's office.

But now he sounds less exasperated and more amused.

"Because if Whitcomb is trying to educate us," I say in the

high-pitched, perky voice I have just now assigned to Valentina, "we should return the favor."

Lock laughs and slips his usual crocheting out of his bag. Blue, again, a different shade this time, like my dad's favorite shirt. "But what are you going to say if he accuses you of bringing lewd art to the school, or some other violation of the student handbook I don't know about?"

"Lewd art?" I blink at him. "You mean my *flower* puppet?"

Lock smiles. "Oh, I can't wait to watch this."

PJ and Chris pause at the door to Mrs. Vanderlinden's room. They're not in this class.

They're stopping to stare at Valentina la Vagina.

A shiver traces the length of my back.

Then a little of my old nerve, the same nerve that made me do something when a drunk guy no one knew was stumbling around a party, comes back. It travels up my arm, shocking my puppet hand to life.

I open Valentina la Vagina's mouth, and roar.

Loudly.

PJ and Chris are so alarmed at the talking vagina that they skitter away, like I've set a snake loose.

I cackle, not caring if everyone in the hall switching their books hears.

Lock crochets a ring of stitches. He dips his head like he's conceding a point in a duel. "You make it really hard to hate you."

I slip Valentina back in my bag. "Then stop trying."

Amanita Muscaria

Principal Whitcomb weathers the sight of Valentina better than I hoped. He does a double take, and then moves on to inspecting our folding, says to make sure we run our thumbs along the creases one last time to set them. It's not nearly the reaction Valentina la Vagina deserves.

At least Lock Thomas appreciates the effort. He talks to me, no more than a few sentences about assignments in our overlapping classes, but it's something. And when a couple more of those girls, the ones who wear the same shoes and perfumes as Victoria and Brigid, stare at us on their way by, Lock doesn't seem to notice.

The next morning, I know which customers should bring bisquetes to their estranged siblings and secret loves. I know who needs a dozen donas de azucar for a birthday party instead of cake. I know what flavor mantecadas a mother should bring to her children who are home sick; I can tell by the love she has for them what they'd like, even though they're not in the bakery with her.

I recognize the blond girl with the book bag by the fact that she needs another gallina, even before I recognize her face.

She's still in love. I want to ask her if she's made her move yet. And if not, I hope the cinnamon spurs her on. I make a mental note to stir up a batch with a heavier sprinkling, in case she stops in again.

La Bruja de los Pasteles comes back, one novia and sol y sombra at a time. Enough that I don't even mind the thought of another afternoon folding *You Can Never Get It Back*.

The next day after school, Valentina la Vagina sits where I left her, staring right toward Principal Whitcomb's office. Except she isn't alone. Next to her sits what looks a little like a storybook mushroom—lighter stem, contrasting top, even a few polka dots. The kind you'd see in an illustration with fairies. Two googly eyes are stuck on, like the ones on Valentina. And like Valentina, it looks both like something you might find on a forest floor, and like an artistic rendering of a body part.

Except instead of suggesting a vagina like Valentina, this mushroom is distinctly phallic. And instead of being made of velvet, the mushroom is knitted.

No. Not knitted.

Crocheted.

I know this from the smile Lock is trying to hide as he folds pamphlets.

"What have you done?" I ask, a laugh breaking up my try at a dramatic tone.

"Oh, that?" Lock goes over a fold with his thumbnail, exactly like Principal Whitcomb asked us to. "Just something I threw together last night. Why?"

"It's a crocheted penis," I whisper, trying not to collapse completely into laughter.

"My mushroom puppet?" Lock blinks at me. "Honestly," he says in the voice of an offended Sunday school teacher. "I don't know what kind of suggestive thinking would get you to see anything else. It's a creative interpretation of the species amanita muscaria. Get your mind out of the gutter."

"Where did you get the eyes?" I ask, just now noticing that they're mismatched, two different sizes.

"My little sister's four. You'd be amazed what kind of craft supplies end up around the living room."

The glint of silver flashes in his eye, like the wink of a star. It still hasn't gone into him then. Maybe he could still blink it out.

Principal Whitcomb comes in. "Mrs. Anders tells me you're both . . ."

He stops cold when he sees Valentina and the Mushroom Penis.

He apparently needed the context of the mushroom puppet to grasp the full vaginal glory of Valentina.

"What are those?" Principal Whitcomb asks.

"Puppets," Lock says like it's obvious.

"For what?" Principal Whitcomb asks, and I know from the near accusation in his voice that I need to nail the innocent tone in the next thing I say. No overdoing it. No seeming like I'm mocking him.

"Botany club presentation," I say.

"On the soil chemistry interactions between wild roses and poisonous mushrooms," Lock adds.

Very nice, I mouth at him.

"Oh." Principal Whitcomb looks both satisfied and bothered by being satisfied. "Good."

On the way back to his office, he double-takes three more times about Valentina and the Mushroom Penis, like he's trying to figure out if he's seeing things. "I look forward to both of you blossoming into fully participating members of your school."

I have to clench my whole body to stay quiet.

When Principal Whitcomb's office door closes, I grab Valentina.

The laughter breaks out of me so hard that pain pinches my side.

"Hear that?" I nudge Lock's shoulder with Valentina's outer petals. "He wants us to blossom."

Lock clenches his jaw to keep from laughing, hard enough that I notice it. "Did you see his face? He's never gonna look at a flower the same way."

"Or a mushroom." I reach for Valentina's new crocheted friend.

At first, I wonder how we can joke about this, about anything even remotely related to sex. But we both know what it is to have that weight dragging you to the floor, to try to keep your shoulders up and straight enough that no one sees it. Sometimes that means you have to laugh about blowing air into condoms or vagina puppets or crocheted penises.

I turn over the mushroom puppet. "You are a genius."

Lock gives a small bow and finishes another pamphlet. "I'm a man of a few mostly useless talents."

"Oh yeah?" I ask. "What are the other ones?"

Lock checks to make sure Principal Whitcomb's door is still shut.

He folds one of the pamphlets diagonally.

"Is that *Why We Wait* or *You Can Only Give It Away Once*?" I ask.

Lock folds it into a paper airplane and tosses it toward the closet. "Oops. Lost it." The plane sails into the carpet. "There goes abstinence-only education."

"Stop," I say. "I'm crying."

Lock picks up the paper airplane and shoves it into his backpack. "So, I want to do something nice for you, but I'd kind of need your help with it."

I fold another pamphlet. "Okay."

"I want to buy you dinner, to apologize for being an ass. But I don't know anywhere around here, and I don't know what you like, so you'd need to pick someplace."

"Fair enough," I say, puppeting the words with Valentina.

I can see him trying not to lose it again.

"And, you know," he says, "I'd need you to say yes."

I shrug, even though I'm lighting up with the possibility that if I can get close to this boy, maybe I can help him get the shard of mirrored glass out of his eye. "I might."

"Yeah?"

The hope and light in his voice is like a hot coin, burning a clear round in a frosted-over window. For a second, it gives me the smallest glimpse of who I used to be, La Bruja de los Pasteles, instead of a girl carrying a slice of mirror in her heart.

I set Valentina alongside the mushroom. "Guess you'll have to find out."

Swallows

When Lock offers his hand to help me down from his truck, I take it. (*Feminismo*, my mother says, *means both being allowed to open your own door if you like and knowing you are fantastic enough for a man to open it for you.*)

We get up to the counter inside, greet Daniela as she shakes tortilla chips out of the fryer basket, and we order.

Lock tries to pay.

I try to stop him. The least I can do for this boy is pay for our burritos and Jarritos.

He swears under his breath. "I know how poor I probably look compared to your friends, but I can buy you dinner, okay?"

Daniela gives me a *Where'd you get this one?* look.

Something inside me cracks in two, brittle as an icicle. Whatever affection I've grown for Lock this afternoon, he just used it up.

It's not even the assumption that we are completely different kinds of Astin students, that he doesn't realize I have a scholarship and my own curled-corner used books too. It's the rest of it. *Compared to your friends.* That handful of syllables reminds me that my best friend graduated early last year, and everyone else at the lunch table I sat with most of freshman year is now afraid of me because of what they think I did in a room with PJ and Chris.

"I'm gonna go," I say.

Lock catches me before the door. "Wait."

I stop.

"I'm sorry," he says.

"I wasn't gonna buy you dinner because I think you're poor," I say, the smallest anger sliding into my voice. "I was gonna buy you dinner because this was kind of my fault."

"What was?" he asks.

We move aside to let a family order.

"Us having to fold thousands of pamphlets about 'our most precious treasure,'" I say.

He shudders, but almost laughs. "Never say that phrase again."

"Sorry. It's etched into my brain."

"And that's kind of my fault," he says. "So, yeah, I'm buying."

"After you just bitched me out like that?" I say. "You definitely are."

We wait in line, order again. Daniela sets a number down and gives me a look of deepest sympathy for having to deal with this gringo.

"So you're not gonna walk out again?" he asks.

I take our number. "You're lucky you're cute."

We both go still.

I want to pull back the words I just said without thinking.

The echo of months ago buckles through me.

You're lucky you're cute.

Words I said when I saw him stumbling around the party, and brought him upstairs, thinking he was drunk.

You're lucky you're cute.

I said it when he was so sloppy I could barely get him up the plush-carpeted steps.

The echo reverberates through both of us.

His pupils are taking over half the brown in his eyes.

"Have I met you before?" he asks.

My throat tenses.

I slip back into the first time I saw him, before we ended up in those two rooms.

"The party," Lock says.

My pulse goes cold in my neck.

"You were there," he says. "Weren't you?"

I nod, because even if my mouth can lie, my body can't.

"Sorry." He holds his jaw tight and looks down at the patterned tile on the table. "I don't remember much about that night."

I hate myself for it, but just for a second, I envy him, the oblivion, the not knowing. Then I wonder how I'd feel if it was the other way around. How would I feel, if I'd woken up in a hospital with some nameless boy's spit on the insides of my thighs? Would I really want that blank in my memory, the loss of a night that hollowed me out when I wasn't even awake enough to know it was happening?

We each probably think we want the opposite of what we have. The knowing-nothing or the knowing-everything.

"I'm sorry," I say.

He shrugs. "Not your fault."

Except it kind of is. He just doesn't know it.

"I don't know that I'd want to remember it anyway," he says. "I wish I could forget getting my stomach pumped, that's for sure." He tries to laugh. "Hard to sleep through that."

I pick my favorite table, under the papel picado in pinks and oranges and greens, colors that always remind me of my bisabuela's rose hips. I choose it out of habit before cringing, remembering the papel picado I had to steal from the bakery because it had turned as hard and silver as a frozen pond.

Lock takes out his blue-yarn crocheting.

I want to make him laugh so badly that I don't even think through what I'm going to say, and I land on, "Making a pair of testicles to go with the mushroom?"

I want to crawl under the table as soon as I say it. *That's* what I came up with?

But he doesn't flinch. "Blue balls?" he says, continuing his stitch. "Nah, I think I'm good."

I almost spit out my Jarritos.

"So I've met you twice, apparently," he says, "and I still don't know your last name."

"Cristales," I say. "And if you want to make sure you never forget it I can tell you how."

"Please do."

"My first name is Graciela, but everyone calls me Ciela, which is almost 'sky' in Spanish, and my last name means 'crystals,' so we all know what my porn name would be."

"Sky Crystals?"

I tip my head down, holding his gaze. "Crystal Sky."

"Oh." He cringe-laughs. "That's even worse."

"Thank my best friend for that one." I give a tiny bow,

and it's there again, that feeling that wherever I am with this boy is the only safe place to joke about sex. Here, in the air between our jumpy, nervous bodies that we pretend are not jumpy and nervous, sex is ours to make funny when we need it to be.

"Is it true?" I ask, stalling on the rest of the question with another sip of Jarritos. "What they said about you? That you're saving yourself?"

"Yes and no. I wanted the first time to mean something."

"I think a lot people do," I say.

"That's what I thought, but I guess if you admit it, if you actually say it, it's weird."

"I don't think it's weird," I say.

"Thanks." He loops through a few more stitches. "You are one of the few."

A blush of heat lights the rose hip under my skirt, the feeling I've come to think of as my bisabuela's gift coming back to life in me.

Daniela brings our food, says, "Enjoy," and flashes me a *buena suerte* look on her way back to the kitchen.

Lock puts away his crocheting. "Now can I ask *you* something?"

"Seems fair." I break open my burrito with my fork, the same way my dad does. Steam rushes out.

Lock does the same, and I wonder if he's imitating me, if he's never eaten a burrito before. "When did it happen?"

"What?" I ask.

"What happened to you," he says. "When did it happen?"

I have the unsteady, flying feeling of tripping forward.

"What makes you think something happened to me?" I ask.

"Why would you help me like you did if you didn't know something about . . ."

He can't even say it.

I can't even say it.

"I could just be a nice person." *Who didn't want to see the Astin shark tank leave nothing behind but your bones and your blank transcript.*

"You might be," he says. "But you also have that look."

I freeze, a piece of calabaza on my fork, wondering if *that look* is something I can remove, like a piece of epazote in my teeth. "What look?"

"The look I learned a lot about in group. Most of us have it in one form or another. No matter how different we are, no matter how different whatever happened to each of us is, we have it."

I take another bite of my burrito, pretending I have no idea what he's talking about.

But then I ask. Of course I ask.

"What kind of look is it?"

"The something-happened look," he says.

"And what does that look like?"

He seems to think about it for a second. "Like you don't know if tonight is a night you're gonna be able to sleep or one where you can't."

"I've mostly figured that part out," I say. Except for the nightmares in which I'm icicles cracking apart or pan dulce crumbling into sugar.

"Really," Lock says. "What's your secret?"

"Dolls."

He laughs. "No, really."

"Yes, really. I have these two little felted dolls." I show him my hands to make a point of their size, how their bodies mostly fit in my palms. "And I sort of alternate hands squeezing each one a little, and that helps me fall asleep."

His eyes close a little, like he's considering me. "Who taught you that?"

"Nobody," I say. "I just stopped knowing what to do with my hands when I was trying to sleep, which I know doesn't make a lot of sense, because you're not really supposed to be doing anything with your hands when you're sleeping, right? But I had to do something with mine."

"That's a thing," he says. "You know that, right? The alternating thing?"

"Really?"

"Yeah. They told me a lot of stuff about bilateral stimulation or bilateral processing or something, I don't remember what it was called. It made no sense to me at first, and some of it still doesn't. But apparently it was part of making me a functioning human being again. I'm officially impressed you got there on your own."

The fine hairs on my arms prickle, and the way he looks at me makes me feel bared not in the way of my clothes being gone, but in a way more like my dreams, when my skin turns to ice or glass, clear enough to see through.

I land on a subject change.

"What group?" I ask.

"Group therapy."

"You went into a room full of people and talked about"—now I'm the one who can't say it—"that?"

"Yeah." He shrugs. "It helped, actually. Probably the only reason I could show up for this semester."

My envy flares again. It's illogical, and petty, and point-less, and I know it. But I wish I'd had a summer to get to where he is, and not one in which I had to make polite con-versation every time PJ and Chris came into the pastelería, both of them acting either like nothing happened or like I invited it.

"Is that why you asked me to go out with you?" I sound far more bitter than I mean to. "Because you wanted a friend who's the same kind of sad as you?"

Go out with you. Wrong phrasing. Worst phrasing. I try to figure out how to correct it, how to tell him I didn't mean it that way, that I didn't interpret any of this that way. But he talks first.

"No," he says carefully. "I asked you out because I like being around you."

Asked you out. I can't figure out if he just made this better or worse.

He studies his burrito as intently as my tía does when she's figuring out what spices are in something, but I can tell he's doing it so he doesn't look at me.

I stall by eating a piece of calabaza out of mine. It dissolves on my tongue.

"It was a really long time ago," I say, because I have to believe it. I have to put more than a summer between me and the sound of their laughs. How their laughs, braided together, made a noise so strange it didn't seem human.

"A long time ago is supposed to make it better?" Lock asks. "Because in my admittedly limited experience, it hasn't yet."

He's given up my fork method and picks up half the burrito. Smart. I use a fork because I never liked getting lipstick on the

88

tortilla. It seemed like sacrilege to both color and burrito. I'm not wearing lipstick right now, but the habit sticks.

"Do you know who did it?" he asks.

I stab another piece of calabaza with my fork. "Yes."

He has the decency not to ask the follow-up questions. If I was awake for it, or if I found out later. If I remember it, or if I had to piece it together after. He doesn't ask any of the questions I'm dreading. He seems to know that I'll tell him if I want to, and I don't want to. I wonder if he's following some code between people like us, a code he knows and I don't, because he sat in a room with a bunch of other guys who'd been through it.

We sit in silence for a minute before he says, about the burrito, "This is amazing."

"One of the cheapest, best, and most underrated places around here," I say, satisfied that I've introduced him to the way they use the sweet earth of cumin, the round-edged green of orégano, the cilantro brightened with lemon and chile. "Just don't ask my dad about it. He thinks the place that used to be across the street is better, and he's just wrong."

"I wouldn't know," Lock says. "I've never had anything like this before."

"They don't have Mexican food where you're from?"

"No, they do. But my family's idea of a burrito is American cheese and bologna wrapped in a refrigerated tortilla."

"Stop," I say.

"With mayonnaise."

"You're actually hurting me."

"We have many talents in my family. Cooking just doesn't happen to be one of them."

He eats another quarter of his burrito, and I take nervous sips of soda in between bites.

"Did you report?" he asks. It sounds less appraising than curious. If his tone were a millimeter off, I'd tell him to mind his own business.

"No." I take up a fork full of black beans. "Because I knew it wouldn't do anything. It would've been my word against theirs, and theirs tends to get believed a lot more than mine."

I'm still angrier than I should be over the fact that, in grade school, the skinny, blond gringas could blame me for making too much noise in the girls' room or writing in the class books. The teachers, with the exception of Mrs. Gomez, would usually believe them.

It seems like once there are bigger things to be angry about, those smaller things should just drop off. Getting blamed for boobs drawn on a chalkboard or for las rubias yelling Bloody Mary because they thought they'd see a ghost in the bathroom mirror. Instead they just add to the pile.

If no one believed me on things that small, why would they about anything this big?

"I get it," Lock says. "I really do."

I should tell him no, he doesn't. He's a gringo, and a boy. What would he know about being a brown girl? But the way PJ and Chris stuck all those condoms on his locker, in his backpack, on his windshield, the way Victoria made fun of his clothes without blinking, makes me think he understands more than any other gringo boy at our school.

"Except it's a little different, I guess," he says. He's looking down at his food, not at me. "Because what happened to me was kind of my fault."

"Your fault?" I ask. "What do you mean?"

"Come on." Now he looks up. "You know what happened. I'm pretty sure half the school does."

"I still don't understand what you mean by it being your fault."

He takes a deep breath, takes a drink from his Jarritos. Tamarindo, the same one I got and the one I made him get because it's the best and because gringos almost never order it on their own.

He looks down at the patterned tile between our plates. "I let myself get drugged at that party."

"Let yourself?" I ask. "Getting drugged isn't really something you let yourself do. Someone does it *to* you."

"I didn't mean that anyone who gets drugged lets themselves, I just . . ." He sets his elbows on the table. "Wow, I'm really doing well today, aren't I?" He runs his hands through his hair. "I just meant . . . I have to believe there was something I could have done to stop it. You think I'm blaming myself, but it's not that. I have to think something I did mattered. Otherwise it's just worse. It all feels worse."

I shake my head. "You don't have to tell me any of this."

"Do you not want to hear it?" He looks right at me, in a way so still, so settled, I can't flinch away.

"I didn't say that."

"I just asked you a pretty invasive question," he said, "and I probably shouldn't have, so I figure I owe you answering the same one."

"You don't owe me anything."

He fidgets with the fork he's not using anymore. "What if I want to see what happens if I say it out loud?"

"You haven't?"

He shakes his head. "Not even in group. Not all of it. I was really more of a listener."

"And you want to?" I ask.

"I want to try. But only if you want to hear it. It costs something to listen to someone else's story. People forget that sometimes. So I get it if you don't want to hear mine."

I will never tell him that his story brushes up against mine, that he got broken open at the same time I did. Him in one room, me in another, our classmates doing two awful things at once and probably finding it all the more hilarious for the symmetry.

I will never tell him any of this.

But I can listen. I owe him that, to hear what I couldn't stop from happening, to hear what only happened because of a mistake I made earlier that night. I owe him this, because maybe if he says it all out loud, he'll cry out the fleck of mirrored glass in his eye. The one in me burrowed in too deep, and it's too late for me to cry it out. But I can still see the glint of silver when Lock turns his head a certain way and the light catches it. I might not even notice it if I didn't know to look for it, but it's there, I can still find it, so it's not too late.

If I let him talk, if I let him cry, his own tears could draw it out of him.

Then something in me pulls back, and he becomes someone I never knew before he walked into Mrs. Vanderlinden's classroom.

He becomes a boy I listen to not because I owe it to him, not because I want him to cry hard enough to wash the mirror fleck out, but because I want to hear him. I want him to be heard.

"If you want to tell me," I say, "I want to listen."

Lock takes another sip of his drink. The hitch in the back of his throat is either hesitation or the carbonated jump of the soda.

"While I was out cold," he says, "I guess some girl thought it'd be funny to, like"—his jaw goes hard, and he shakes his head at the orange and blue flowers painted on the tile—"blow me."

He shudders so slowly, it's like he's caught in a flinch. The tension shows in his shoulders. He's trying to shrug something off but it's too heavy, so it stays.

"Okay, I said it." Lock looks at the front window of the restaurant, and I'm trying to figure out what to say—what would I want someone to say?—when he adds, "And now I could really use a subject change, so you know, if you've got any ideas . . ."

I can feel in my own body how much he means it, because that's probably what I'd want too, the chance to say what happened but not to live there, to have someone know but not feel the bristling of them wondering what they should say back, to move on from talking about it even if I can't move on from thinking about it.

I follow his stare to the bird silhouette printed onto the front window glass. "Anyone tell you about the swallows yet?"

"The what?" he asks.

Something in me lights up.

He can tell.

"What?" he asks, wary but smiling now.

"I know where we're going next."

Dolls

You seen any of those little light brown birds flying around here?" I ask.

Lock nods. He goes with me through the wild grass, the green gilded with last light. "They're sparrows, right?"

"Cliff swallows," I say. "Las golondrinas. You can tell when they're flying, they have a pretty distinctive shape." I think of the clouds of wings that descend right around my dad's birthday. "And when they're still, you can tell them from sparrows by their vientres."

"Vientres?" Lock asks.

"Underbellies," I say. "They're white when they're young, and orange when they're grown. Don't believe any of the tourist traps around here. All the merchandise uses pictures of barn swallows."

"Wow. That's a little sad."

"Don't get me started."

We stop at the old railroad overpass that shadows the creek.

"If you look really closely"—I point at the underside of the old bridge, coated in rust—"you can see their nests." Blooms of papery mud spread over the walls of the support pillars. In the falling light, both water below and nests above are just barely visible.

"Those puffy things?" Lock asks.

"Exactly," I say. "This is one of the few places you can still spot cliff swallows around here. We don't see many of them anymore."

"Why not?" he asks, and I can tell he's looking for the flutter of wings.

"You'd never know it under all the landscaping, but it's coastal plain around here. Over the last, I don't, hundred years, this place has gotten so built up that the swallows really don't come here much anymore. They don't work with the habitat around here."

"I know the feeling," he says, then pauses. "But if they're cliff swallows, why are they here?" He looks out toward the hills, where the land turns to wilderness preserve. "Aren't there plenty of cliffs to choose from?"

"They seem to like bridges better. They're more protected." I watch for flickers of motion around the nests. "And they reuse nests, so having them under overhangs gives them a better chance of not falling off in winter."

"How do you know all this?" Lock asks.

"My best friend went through an ornithologist phase." In the time I've known her, Jess has also insisted she would be a physicist, a dramaturge, an archaeologist, a psychologist, and a florist.

"And if anyone tells you about La Noche de las Golondrinas, they're either true romantics, or they're trying to see how gullible you are," I say.

"What's La Noche de las Golondrinas?" he asks.

"It's this old story," I say. "According to lore, if you spot one out at night on a certain day of the year, you'll be lucky for the rest of the year, or lucky in love for the rest of your life, or something like that."

For decades, girls from in town and out of town have worn pretty dresses to Swallows' Night. Nobody really believes the superstition about how the flicker of wings makes it a little easier to draw your beloved's eye, the stories about love catching the wind and taking off. But they figure it can't hurt, and it's fun, so it's a kitschy bit of recent history that hangs on. A lot of tourists' daughters, a few locals, even a handful of girls from school show up in vintage lace and tulle they've either borrowed from their grandmothers or bought to look like it.

I've never been one of them. Every year on La Noche de las Golondrinas, I'm too busy selling pan dulce with my tía.

"The dolls I told you about," I say, "the ones I hold when I sleep, they're sort of meant to be girls on La Noche de las Golondrinas."

"What do you mean?" Lock asks. "Are they birds?"

"No. They're girls in these fluffy dresses. That's how a lot of people show up to La Noche de las Golondrinas. It's kind of a tradition. But when I was little, there was this one lady who'd sell tiny dolls like that, girls in their fancy skirts. Except none of them ever looked like me. They were blond, or redheads, sometimes brunettes with really pale skin."

"That's messed up."

"Yeah," I say. "So my abuela made me my own, ones with black hair and brown skin, and their own fluffy dresses."

"Sounds like you have a good grandmother."

"Had," I say.

"Sorry," he says.

"Don't be." I think of my abuela noticing how I looked

for myself among the pale dolls. I never told her how much it made me feel like if there was no doll like me, there was no me. She just knew. "She was a good grandmother," I say.

Even if right now she'd tell me that I wasn't careful enough with the gift her mother left me.

Lock watches something in the grass, and I wonder if he's catching the film of dragonflies' wings, drawn by the standing water.

"Do you believe it?" he asks.

"Believe what?"

"The luck thing."

I shrug. "Kind of irrelevant. Our signature bird is hard enough to spot during the day."

And this year, so much is vanishing. Trees. Swallows. Even the Santa Ana winds.

"It's no more fiction than the rest of the talk about the swallows," I say. "The brochures around here announce their return on March 19 every year and their departure on October 23."

Lock stares at me. "Like they're consulting a calendar?"

"You can joke, but a lot of people think that. I mean, I guess it's around the same time that the first one gets here and the last one takes off, but it's never the same days."

I think I see something, the stretch of a wing on the underside of the old bridge, but it's just light flashing off the bolts.

"I can tell you something about them that is true, though," I say.

"Is there going to be a quiz?"

"Yes, why aren't you taking notes?" I say. "Swallows are supposed to be one of the most social land birds. They even build their nests touching."

"Good for them. I don't like anyone that much."

I laugh. "They're also really tolerant of disturbance. The trains don't use this bridge anymore, but even if they did, the swallows would still nest under here. They'll nest in highway culverts. They're shockingly unbothered by human activity."

"Tolerant of disturbance. Don't mind human activity." Lock stares into the bridge's shadows, crossing his arms. "I have a lot to learn from these guys." He looks back at me. "Thank you. For this."

"For telling you facts about birds you rarely see?" I ask.

"For teaching me stuff about this very strange place where I now apparently live."

"Welcome to San Juan Capistrano."

He smiles like I just said something true, like this really is the first he knows of this place. "Thanks."

He looks harder at the grass, takes a few steps, crouches down to it.

It's only when he picks it up that I see the flash of silver.

Lock gets back to standing. "Look." He holds it out to me, a leaf of mirrored glass. As the shape resolves, I find the faint etching along its surface and match it to what it once was. A swallow feather, turned to a scrap of mirror.

I have to get it away from him. If he takes it home, it could splinter apart, and another shard could get into him. One could get into his parents, or the little sister who's the reason he could find plastic googly eyes in his living room.

I breathe enough to settle these thoughts so they're not whirring in me. I can't sound desperate right now.

"Can I have it?" I ask, in my best flirting voice, quiet but focused, like I'm asking to borrow his favorite pen or take a sip of his soda.

The way he looks at me, the way he lifts his head a little to toss his hair out of his eyes, tells me I succeeded.

"Yeah, you can have it," he says, keeping his eyes on mine as he sets it in my hand.

Notice

Lock pulls onto my street.

"Where did you get this thing?" I pet the dashboard so the truck knows I mean no offense. "It's older than both of us combined."

"This guy who owned a peach orchard sold it to me," he says. "I was working at his favorite liquor store, and he liked me, so he gave me a really good deal."

"You worked at a liquor store?" I ask.

"Yeah," he says. "A drive-through."

"Drive-through liquor stores are legal?"

He tilts a hand back and forth. "This one was legal-ish?"

"Are *you* legal to work at a liquor store?"

"Not even a little," he says. "Paid under the table. That was one of the best parts."

"Only one of the best parts?"

"The other was shaking up the twelve packs of anyone who was rude to the cashier."

"No."

"Oh yes. You could hear them swearing from their car."

"They opened it while they were still driving?"

"All the time. I consider what I did to be both justice and

public service announcement." He shakes his head like he's remembering. "Sometimes I miss home."

"Where's home?"

"Olivedale," he says.

"Olivedale," I repeat, like that's going to give me a better picture of it.

"You have no clue where I'm talking about, do you?"

"Not even a little," I say. "Never been there."

"I mean, you could go, but why would you want to?"

"Town motto?"

His laugh is sudden but warm and full, a downpour when it's sunny. Lock has a great laugh, especially when he's not expecting to laugh. It has an almost clicking sound to it, like crickets. "No, at a population of 1,349, I believe the unofficial town motto is 'Would it kill you to live here?'"

Now it's me laughing, so hard and quickly that I feel it in my ribs.

"Wow," he says when I point out my house, the brightest one on the street. "Your family really likes color."

"My *mom* really likes color," I say. "And my dad really loves her."

Mamá was smug for months about finding all the colors on clearance at the paint store, mixing mistakes that were off tint and therefore rejected. Apple-red base, trim on the windows alternating between butter-yellow and deep blue.

Lock pulls up to the curb and opens his side.

"You don't have to get out," I say.

"I'm short, I know what a pain this is." He jumps down. "And you're even shorter than me."

He meets me at the passenger side door and helps me down.

"Just so you know," I say as he gets me onto the grass. "I'm the tallest of my cousins."

"Noted," he says.

The smell of the grass, damp with early evening, climbs up my legs.

In my peripheral vision, a slip of bleached yellow looks like it's floating.

Then I place it.

The familiar size and trim of a removal notice.

It's tacked to a tree across the street, the one that looks like its blossoms are made of snow.

"Sorry," I say, talking to Lock but not looking at him. "I have to go."

I run around the back of his truck, each step loud on the asphalt.

"Should I ask?" Lock says when I'm halfway across the street.

I turn around in the middle of the road. "Go home."

I bang on what was once the McKinleys' front door.

A woman answers. Newly manicured nails, freshly highlighted hair, recent spray tan. And the kind of crisp white shirt women only wear around the house if they never have to do anything dirty.

The woman gives a pointed sigh. "Yes?"

I point to the snow tree, and the notice on the bark. "Do you know how many resources it takes to establish a tree like that?"

She gives three slow blinks. "I'm sorry?"

"There's a city ordinance that doesn't allow the removal of healthy, functioning trees without a hearing."

She shuts the door in my face.

"And I'm going to show up to that boring-ass city council meeting," I yell at the door. "With a strongly worded letter."

I cringe. *A strongly worded letter.* I'm sure she's trembling in her Chanel flats.

"And then I'm going to . . ."

In the corner of my vision, the light in my bedroom window comes on.

I look across my street and follow a familiar silhouette.

My mother is in my room, and she's going toward my closet.

I race across the street, through the front door. I get to the top of the stairs and into my room just in time to put myself between my mother and the one door hiding a world of mirrored glass.

"Oh," my mother says. "Good. You're here." She unfurls a strapless dress with a full, tea-length skirt.

As I catch my breath from running, she shows it off. The fabric is softened with age, and it has the smell of having been in an attic a few years. But the color is antique silver, like moon glow and candlelight mixing together, like how champagne looks under crystal chandeliers in movies about the 1900s.

"Where did you get this?" I ask.

"Goodwill," she says. "Do you think you got your skill at thrift shopping on your own? Por supuesto que no. It's genetic." She displays it, the tulle of the skirt flaring. "Tell me this isn't you."

It is. At least, it would have been, months ago.

This was exactly the kind of dress I would have worn to homecoming or winter formal. La Bruja de los Pasteles would have worn it. She would have reveled in how the softened silver looked against her brown skin, how the skirt would flow out from her hips.

But it feels like a kind of magic I haven't earned back yet.

I miss loving my body that much. I miss matching my lace-trimmed underwear to my makeup, even though no one would know but me. I miss my cute bras in melon colors. I miss putting on pink and aqua nightgowns that matched my room and clung to my soft body.

But missing something doesn't pull it any closer to you.

"Do you love it?" my mother says with the gravitas of one of her telenovela stars.

The thin threads of silver embroidery wink at me. "It doesn't matter if I love it," I say. "I'm not the kind of girl who wears dresses like this."

"Because you don't want to be?"

"Because I'm just not." I don't look like the little dolls they used to sell at La Noche de las Golondrinas, with their peach felt skin and strawberry-blond hair, their mint-green tulle skirts and eyes embroidered with bright blue thread.

"You know what you need?" my mother asks.

"A dress I can't wear anywhere?"

She taps a finger at the air like a fairy godmother with a wand. "A new lipstick."

I groan. "Mom."

"Whatever the question, red lipstick . . ."

"Mom." I say it hard enough that she actually stops talking. "I don't wear lipstick anymore, okay?"

Her face falls into that awful wounded look when she's just gotten her feelings hurt but doesn't want me to know. It's so much worse than when she guilts me on purpose. She lowers the hanger, and the dress sinks.

I am the worst daughter in the world.

My mother is the one who told me my curvas were worth celebrating. Every day growing up, I came home to a family where hips and thighs meant health and beauty, and it saved me from thinking there was something immodest and shameful about my body.

My mother has always known how to remind me I am beautiful. The least I can do is meet her halfway to this beautiful, ridiculous dress.

"What would I wear it to?" I ask. I'm not going to winter formal. Why give PJ and Chris and Victoria and Brigid more of a chance to gawk at me?

"La Noche de Los Golondrinas," my mother says.

"Swallows' Night is me and Jess and Tía and Pilar selling cuernos to superstitious tourists," I remind her.

"I think it's sweet," my mother says. "The stories. The girls in their pretty dresses." She waves the hanger.

"You really want me to wear that to sell pan dulce?" I lift a corner of the skirt. "It'll be covered in powdered sugar by the end of the night."

"Just think about it." My mother hands me the dress. "You're whatever kind of girl you decide you are."

I almost say, *Yeah, I'll needlepoint that on my next pillow*, but then I press my lips together to shut myself up.

The mirrored glass has taken enough. It's turned me into a girl who's always searching the world for the glint of silver.

I'm not letting it turn me into a girl who breaks her mother's heart.

Cold Spell

In my dreams, I'm freezing. I'm covered in cold water that soaks my hair and my shirt and then turns to a coat of ice on my skin.

I gasp, like I did that night. It shocks through me and rattles my rib cage. It comes as a shuddering, the feeling of ice getting down into my bones.

I wake up shivering and sweating, and it takes me a minute to realize what's woken me up.

Not my dream.

Rustling outside.

I go to the window and see a figure across the street. Blue duck cloth jacket, jeans, baseball cap. He's crouching at the roots of the snow tree, like he's figuring out the best way to tear it down right now.

Rage rises out of my sleepiness.

The lingering panic from my nightmare blurs together with the fact that I am about to lose the deep brown of the snow tree's branches and the pale tissue paper of its blossoms.

My lecture on city ordinances has backfired so spectacularly that the woman is having the snow tree ripped out in the middle of the night.

This is, apparently, the year I pick ridiculous hills to die on, because here I am, slipping out of the house so quietly my parents won't hear, and then flying into the street. The worn cream of my grandmother's old slip floats out behind me.

I have no plan, so I try to come up with one in the seconds it takes to cross the street. Scare this guy off with facts about public hearings? Bang on the neighbor's door? Attach myself to the tree in protest?

"What the hell are you doing?" I say before I've even gotten to the opposite sidewalk.

The guy goes still, like he's scared of me. Did the neighbors give him a primer? Did they tell him about la loquita in the house across the street?

"You're in violation of a city code," I say. It's as pathetic of a threat as I've ever come up with. Right up there with the strongly worded letter. "You know that, right?"

I see his silhouette coming toward me, but he stumbles, tripping over a root.

Good. At least he's not pretending he doesn't hear me.

I've stormed halfway across the street when a glint of silver stops me.

It blinks bright from the corner of this stranger's eye. I recognize that tiny flash of cold light before I recognize the rest of him.

I stop at the sidewalk. "Lock?"

The Forest Thief

What were you doing with my tree?" I ask.

Lock eyes me across the front seat. "*Your* tree?"

"You wanted me to get in the truck, I'm in the truck. Now answer my questions. What were you doing?"

Lock rests his palms on the steering wheel.

"Did that lady in that house hire you?" I ask.

"What?" he asks. "No."

"Then what were you doing?"

He sets his forehead against the steering wheel.

"Lock," I say.

"I was gonna take it," he says without lifting his head.

I blink at him. "You were what?"

He sits up a little. "I was gonna take it, okay?"

"Why?"

"It's a long story."

Understanding floats through my brain. It wafts like a leaf before settling.

Then it lands.

"You." I almost shout it at him. "You're the tree thief!"

"I'm not a thief."

"You took the wild lilac on Los Rios."

He doesn't look at me. "They were gonna rip it out."

"And the lily magnolia!"

"They were gonna cut it down." His cheeks are taking on a flush that seems more worked up than embarrassed. "I saved them the trouble."

"Why?" I ask.

"It's a long story."

"You don't get to use that excuse! I am in your truck in my nightgown!"

"Yeah." He clears his throat. "I noticed." He flushes deeper. This time it's embarrassment.

I cross my arms. "What do you do with them?"

He takes off his hat so he can look straight at me, no shadowing. "You really want to know? Because you're going to need to put your seat belt on."

I buckle up, not breaking eye contact the whole time. If this is a bluff, I'm calling it.

He takes off his jacket and hands it to me.

"Here." He clears his throat again. "You know, in case you're cold."

His awkwardness makes me want to screw with him, but he's nearly cringing into the steering wheel. Plus, I am cold.

"There's nothing wrong with them, you know," Lock says as he pulls away from the curb.

I shrug on one sleeve. "What?"

"The trees," he says. "People just didn't want them there. They don't fit in with their *landscaping vision.*"

I am too annoyed to tell him I've thought the same thing. Una maldición on that stupid remodeling show.

"Where are we going?" I ask.

"Not far. Right near my family's apartment."

"How does that help?" I ask. "I don't know where you live."

"You mean we're *not* required to memorize the student directory?" he asks with feigned offense. "Well, that's thirty hours of my summer I'll never get back."

I glare at him while slipping into the other sleeve of his jacket. It smells like tree bark and wet earth, falling leaves and the metal of the shovels clattering in the truck bed. All the exact things I'd expect a tree thief's clothes to smell like.

We drive past the city college, the mall, the freeway onramps and off-ramps, until we're into the wilderness park.

"Are you about to show me where you've buried PJ and Chris?" I ask.

He stares straight ahead and deadpans, "The less you know, the better."

He pulls to the shoulder, where a row of wild trees screens the land from the road.

"Okay." He jumps out on his side and comes over to mine. "Just remember, you wanted to know."

He leads me through that screen of trees.

I expect raw brush and low scrub.

But the night opens to a world of branches.

The purple spears of chaste tree. The icicle wisps of fringe tree. Lichen-laced plum and apple trees. The silver-blue rounds of smoke bush leaves, and its clouds of maroon cotton-candy fluff. The sloe-thorn, studded with fruit as round as the moon and as dark as the night itself. The sugarplum fuchsia of redbud that I always thought made the branches look like fairy wands.

The puffs of periwinkle flowers I recognize as the wild lilac from Los Rios.

The pink petaled cups of the lily magnolia.

In the thin light of the moon, against the blue-washed hills in the distance, it's a secret forest. It's small magic, packed into this corner of the wilderness park, where la llorona is holding her breath.

"Lock." My voice holds my wonder, my marveling, at all these branches.

I find him behind me in the dark. "How did you do all this?"

There's a damp ring around the base of a few trees, evidence of new planting.

"I dig out the root balls and haul them into the back of my truck," he says. "Means I can only go for the smaller trees, but that's how it is. If I wear work clothes, you'd be shocked how little people pay attention. I pick a time the owners are out, and as long as I act like I belong there, the neighbors write me off as a gardener or a city employee."

I think of how my mother is one of the few people on my block who greets the gardeners parking their trucks on Fridays. My neighbors pay so little attention to Raúl and Luis that they could probably knock down a retaining wall without anyone noticing.

"How do you even know how to do this?" I ask.

"Before the liquor store, I worked at a garden supply," Lock says.

That explains the Carhartts, the duck cloth jacket I'm borrowing right now.

"I was mostly hauling sod and chip bark," he says. "But I picked up a few things about watering, vitamins, root balls, replanting shock, all that."

"You stole every one of these?" I ask.

"I prefer the term 'relocated,'" he says. "It's not like they didn't want them all gone anyway. And I didn't take every one of them. There are some that people gave me." He touches the bark of one of the plum trees. "This lady near where I live, her brother died a few years ago. She gave out seedlings at his funeral, and she kept one and had it in a pot on her apartment balcony. It got big enough that she wanted it planted."

I can't help the part of me that gives at that, this woman putting this small tree, this living memory of her brother, into this boy's careful hands.

"Part of why I've got to come out here every day," he says. "Can't skip watering this one while it's still taking." He stands back and regards the screen of trees at the road's edge. "I think I'm gonna have to cut back those hemlocks though. Let it get more sun."

A single cliff swallow, with its sienna belly and indigo head, flits through the redbud branches. The bird flutters away, the moon catching the veins of its feathers.

Lock turns to me.

"So there you go," he says. "A forest out of what everyone else gave up on."

"So," I say, "the crepe myrtle on my street."

He puts his hands in the pockets of his Carhartts. "I thought I could save it for you."

"You wanted to bring my tree here?" I ask.

He looks at the ground. "You seemed kind of attached."

My heart feels soft as the sugar shell on a concha.

I glance at each of these trees, sizing them up. My snow tree has a wider root system than any of these.

"You were gonna get the crepe myrtle by yourself?" I ask.

He shrugs. "It was a stretch, but I thought it was worth a try."

It happens fast and then fades. But just for that second, the last of the ice I dreamed about, the frost covering, breaks away. Just for a second, the mirror shards are as harmless as snow globe glitter.

For a second, Lock is not the boy whose life got wrecked alongside mine. He is not a boy one room away, the wall between us so thin I can hear his jeans being unzipped.

He is a boy who cares enough about these unwanted trees to pull them out of the ground and bring them to a secret forest somewhere off Ortega highway.

I'm breathing hard, not because I'm trying to catch my breath but because I'm finally catching it. All the damage I've caused, at least this wasn't part of it. The vanishing trees weren't my fault. They were the careful, unseen work of this boy.

I only realize I've said something when Lock asks, "What wasn't your fault?" I didn't even feel the vibration of speaking at the back of my throat.

"Nothing." I can't look at him, so I look at the flickering leaves and late blossoms of the secret forest. "It's beautiful. All of it."

Instead of watching me like I'm fragile, or frightening, he looks strangely touched as he says, "Thanks."

Polaroid

Between classes, Brigid and I pass each other in the halls. I know she's going to say something before she opens her mouth. She has that considering look, tinted with disdain, that she learned from Victoria.

"You look better," she says.

I stop, not so much because of the words but because of her voice. It's almost encouraging.

"The blush, the lipstick." She swirls a hand at my face. "You look like you're feeling better."

You look like you're feeling better.

Like I had a cold.

"Good for you," she says.

She keeps walking.

That rage in me turns. It blazes inside me.

"I didn't ask you," I say.

Now she stops, looks back. "Excuse me?"

"I didn't ask you how I look," I say, landing hard on each word.

Brigid presses her lips together like she's trying to laugh. "I know you don't want friends. You made that really clear. But I wouldn't go out of your way to make enemies."

"What does that mean?" I ask.

"Everyone liked Jess," she says. "Nobody likes you. Except us. We liked you. But you've done a great job of showing you don't give a shit. Victoria may still be nice to you, but she's not going to forget what you did."

"What *I* did?"

"What, do you not remember? You didn't seem wasted, but I guess . . ." She finishes the thought with a shrug.

"What do you mean what *I* did?" I'm so lost as to what she's talking about that I can't help pressing her for an answer.

Brigid squints at me. "Do you seriously not remember?"

My throat tightens. "I remember everything about that night."

"Then you know what I'm talking about."

"No, I don't."

"Cut the doe-eyed shit. It doesn't work on someone like you."

Someone like me? Someone brown? Queer? Someone with hips and an ass?

"Victoria doesn't forget things," Brigid says. "And neither do I. Even if PJ and Chris's drunk asses forget the next morning. And trust me, if you really want this to get uncomfortable, it can."

She knocks my shoulder on the way by.

The force rattles through me.

What the hell is she talking about?

How is it not already uncomfortable?

Brigid and Victoria can't seriously be mad at me for what PJ and Chris did with me. They have to know it wasn't my choice.

Don't they?

Or is that why they hate me so much? Is that what they've held against me ever since that night?

The question is still buzzing through my brain—*they have to know, don't they?*—after last period.

When I open my locker, a heavy, white-bordered square falls out.

For a second I can't make sense of this square, what it is or what it contains.

What it is comes to me first.

A square of film. A Polaroid—the kind that are graying out in my family's old albums because of the acid in the film. They come from the sort of camera that usually appears out of someone's dad's garage.

While I'm still trying to comprehend the square in front of me, I remember Victoria and Brigid's fascination with their family's old stuff. Last winter formal, Victoria got bored with the racks of holiday dresses and trotted out one of her grandmother's wool skirts (she wore it with a white tank top that cost more than my desk). For half of freshman year, Brigid's wrists clicked with acrylic bangles from the 1970s, her hundred-dollar-perfume wafting out from underneath.

My eyes try to understand the dark image within the white border, as though the picture is developing in front of me.

It's the blur of my hair over my face. I recognize the moment it was taken, the wince of me resisting. But how the camera catches me, the way I'm showing my teeth almost looks like I'm smiling.

This is a picture of a girl who looks drunk enough that everyone would expect her to go into a room with two laughing boys.

The memory of that night reaches its hands out, trying to drag me back.

Who took this? *When* did they even take it? It shows so little of the background that it could have been anytime that night. It doesn't even show enough of my shirt to make me sure it *was* that night. They could have snapped it at any party, and then pulled it out now, the image made new with the implication that it's from the night I went into a room with PJ and Chris.

This picture not only makes me look drunk, it makes me look willing. I never would have been willing even if I was drunk, but somewhere like Astin, it's somehow your fault for drinking, not the fault of the pendejos who take it as permission.

This picture is a threat as sharp and as clear as broken glass.

Brigid and Victoria and PJ and Chris have already made the whole school think what they want. If I piss them off enough, they can show them this.

Rumors are one thing. But the thought that Jess, that my tía, that my mother, could see this, makes my body feel as brittle as frost. No matter if they believed the truth or what this picture shows them, it would break their hearts, and it would break my world open.

Brigid passes my locker, giving me a pinched little smile on her way by.

Las Hadas

Frost the pink cakes. Stock the front display cases. Make another batch of galletas de gragea, coat the sugar cookies in tiny rainbow nonpareils. Anything I can do to get my tía in a good mood, because I need her in a good mood.

I even work on the piñatas—hollowing out cake halves, filling them with bright candy, frosting them back together. As fast as my hands can work, I cover them with sugar-paste ruffles or coconut to look like the tiny paper flags on a piñata.

Usually, I love our piñata cakes as much as our customers, with their brilliant colors and surprise candy hearts. But right now I cringe at the thought of how, as soon as they get cut open, all of their insides spill out.

Especially because I can't stop thinking about that photo.

"Mira," my aunt says in wonder when she comes in. "Las hadas have come in the night and done half our work for us." She kisses the top of my head before slipping on her hairnet. "Thank you, mija."

I turn around, squinting to the dawn outside the windows.

"My motives are not entirely pure," I say.

"Qué intriga," my tía says. "I'm interested."

I press my lips together. "Could I ask you for something?"

"You're wearing blush and standing up straight." She points

at my apricot-shimmered cheeks. "You could ask me for the moon."

"So you know my mom and dad have their big anniversary coming up."

"Mierda," she says. "Good you reminded me." She goes to her desk and finds her datebook. "I need to get them something."

I stand in the doorway between the kitchen and her office. "So they're supposed to have their anniversary trip next week."

"Lo sé." My aunt writes in the paper datebook she still swears by.

I slump against the frame. "And I don't think they're gonna go."

She flips the datebook back to today. "Why?"

"Because they don't think they can leave me alone."

She glances up at me. "Why not?"

I feel like I'm having a conversation with my youngest primo. Antonio's *why* questions tire out all but the most intrepid of us older cousins.

"Because they think I'm not okay," I say.

"Are you okay?"

"I'm better than I've been in a while," I say.

I'll really be better if I can not be that girl listening on the stairs, knowing she's a weight keeping her parents hundreds of miles and thousands of feet down from all those bright balloons.

My aunt stands up straight.

She studies me. That blush on my cheeks. My washed hair, the curl in my ponytail, even though it's going right into the thin mesh of my hairnet. My jeans that show off my Cristales hips.

My tía purses her lips. "You let me talk to them."

I hope, so sharply I can almost see my parents floating among those five hundred painted balloons. "Really?"

"You watch." She gives a final nod. "I'm a big sister. I have my ways."

The bell announces a customer up front.

"I'll get it," I say. "Jess is due in any minute. I can cover the front until then."

I'm tightening the bow on my apron when I see him, the boy whose features are becoming as familiar to me in real life as they are in my nightmares.

Only now he's in the pastelería, where I've never seen him, and my nightmares have never taken him.

A little girl wearing a plastic tiara charges in front of him, like a cat getting underfoot. He dodges without startling.

"Careful, Vi," he says.

"Make me taller," the little girl says when she gets to the bakery cases.

Lock picks her up and she settles onto his hip.

She tries to put her plastic tiara on his head.

When his eyes land on me, he blinks—I count—five times.

"Oh," he says, placing me, registering me out of my school uniform and in my robin's-egg-blue apron. "Hi."

The *Hi* is more wary than friendly. He had no idea I worked here. He was probably expecting the señoras with their hair as pale as powdered sugar.

"Hi," I say, and he can probably hear in my voice how much I'm enjoying seeing him in a pink plastic tiara.

"Vi," he says, "this is Ciela. Ciela, Violet."

The little girl extends her hand in a way that makes me think she's hosted a lot of tea parties.

I let her give my fingers a brief shake.

My bisabuela's magic doesn't let me down. It bubbles up with a clear whisper.

"You don't like frosting," I say.

The delight on her face tells me I'm right.

"How did you know that?" Lock asks.

I weigh the best response. *Lucky guess*? Or borrow from my tía, *I have my ways*?

I take long enough to decide that I just end up shrugging.

"Her preschool does this thing where the summer birthdays bring stuff in on weeks no one else has a birthday," Lock says. "She's a June birthday, so she's up."

I'm already reaching for the most colorful sugar cookies we have. This girl could take or leave the pink frosting of los cortadillos, but I am pretty sure she has a strong commitment to rainbow sprinkles.

"And, as you've already established," Lock says, "she's a bit of a hard sell."

"You and my aunt would get along," I tell Violet. "She doesn't like frosting either." My tía considers it a necessary evil, the cost of doing business.

I take a galleta gragea from the glass case. I am getting back the ribbon of magic that lets me know exactly which kind of bread or sweet a customer needs to feel calmer or braver or a little more hopeful.

"How about you try this?" I hand her the round sugar cookie, so coated in sprinkles you can't see the dough.

Violet considers la galleta, inspecting the cookie's front and back, while I consider Lock.

The fact that my bisabuela's gift hasn't come back enough for me to read this boy, the fact that I can't guess what pan dulce would light up the corners of his heart when he's standing right here in the pastelería, unnerves me. It sticks to me, like when I can't get a recipe right, when the dough doesn't bloom as it proofs, or when the spices are a little off.

"Do you like coconut?" I ask Lock.

"No, he doesn't," Violet answers for him.

"Does he like frosting?" I ask Violet.

Now he answers, shrugging, "I can take it or leave it." He smiles like he just figured something out. "Wait. Are you trying to guess with me like you did with her?"

I try not to eye the bakery cases.

"No," I say.

"You totally are," he says.

"I am not."

At least Violet is giving a nod of approval that tells me I'm right about her.

I fill a bakery box with rainbow sprinkle cookies.

"Let me know when you figure it out," he says. He's enjoying this too much.

"Oh my God." Jess's voice pulls all our attention to the kitchen door. She looks at Lock. "Plaid flannel?"

"Huh?" Lock asks, because right now he's not wearing any.

"What's he doing here?" Jess asks. She seems delighted, and that's my fault, because I never told her what Brigid and Victoria did to him or about the mirror shard.

She only remembers the first hours of the party.

"Are you two . . ." Jess looks between me and Lock.

Violet's eyes follow Jess's.

It had been Jess who'd first noticed me looking at a boy that night, a boy whose name I did not yet know.

You like him, Jess needled me as we claimed a sofa. *You've been staring at him all night.* She lifted her Diet-Coke-and-grenadine in his direction.

Don't look at him. I tried burrowing into the sofa cushions. *He's going to know we're talking about him.*

Since you're clearly oblivious, it's my duty to tell you he's been staring right back whenever he thinks you won't notice. Jess pinched my arm in a way that made me yelp more for effect than out of pain. *Carajo, just go talk to him.* She shoved me off the sofa. *Go. Anda al Plaid Flannel.*

By the time I started talking to him, he was already loose in a way I thought meant he was a drink or two in. I had no idea that something had gone into his Dr Pepper.

If I'd known him, maybe I would have known.

If I'd known better, maybe I would have known what was coming. Maybe I would have known how to stop it, how to keep us out of those rooms.

By the time I come back to the pastelería, Jess has stepped in, ringing him up, and a look of blank terror is breaking over his face.

He recognizes me now.

Not just as a girl he met at the party.

He remembers something. Maybe not just the hazy memory of my face, but the truth of me that night. The details. High-waisted jeans. My favorite yellow sweater. A fishtail braid my mother spent half an hour on.

Now he's backing away from it, from me, and toward the door, Violet still on his hip.

"Hey, don't forget your food." Jess shoves the bakery box into his free hand.

He takes it but keeps backing away.

Violet watches us both over Lock's shoulder.

Just before he turns, I see it, the fleck of silver in his eye. It brightens and then vanishes, like a green flash at sunset.

He flinches like he feels it going into him.

That's how I know.

Right there.

That fast.

The mirror shard gets so deep into him, he can never cry it out.

Pendejos

hat was that all about?" Jess asks.

I turn to her. "Did you really have to do that?"

"What?" Jess asks. "You liked him. And now he's stopping by to see you, and you didn't even tell me?"

"He wasn't here to see me."

"Bullshit. Is that where you disappeared to that night?" she asks, sounding more interested than accusing. "Were you with him?"

"Just drop it, okay?" I say low enough that my tía and Pilar won't hear us over the whir of the mixers and the convection oven fans.

"You know what?" Jess says. "Fine. Don't tell me anything. That's what you've been doing all summer."

"Jess."

"No. I'm tired of acting like things haven't been shitty between us since I went to Laurel. Are you mad at me for graduating early? Do you feel like I abandoned you or something? Is that what this is?"

"No. Of course not."

"Then what is it with you and me? I don't know anything about what's going on with you, and frankly, you don't know anything that's going on with me."

"That's not true."

"Oh yeah? How many times have you been to my dorm?"

"I don't know. A few?"

Maybe once since I helped her move in.

"What building do I live in?" she asks.

I open my mouth without realizing I don't have an answer.

Jess moving out of her house and into the dorms was a fight with her parents, since she can commute, and clearly does for her shifts at the pastelería. Sunday dinners with her family are enough for her, especially with her sister, the buffer during holidays, living halfway across the country.

It's been weeks since I've asked how she's doing with any of this.

"Who's the girl I like in my comp lit class?" Jess asks.

"There's a girl?"

"Yeah," Jess says. She sounds almost sad about it. "You'd like her. Loud laugh. Collection of stuffed animals that covers half her bed. Great chef but can't bake. Makes her appreciate a good dessert even more. She's been in here before, and maybe if you'd been paying attention, you'd have noticed. She usually has half the library with her."

"Wait." Something between Jess's description and my memory clicks. I think of a girl who's come into the pastelería a couple of times. A book bag heavy enough that my shoulder hurt just looking at it. The scent of las gallinas, of vanilla and cinnamon and cream.

"Is she blond?" I ask.

She sighs. "You always think light brown hair is blond hair."

"Okay, fine, then would *I* think she's blond?" I ask.

"Probably."

"She's in love," I blurt out.

"What?" Jess asks.

I nod.

"With me?" Jess asks.

"I don't know. I just know that's why she needed the gallinas."

Jess looks more forlorn than I think I've ever seen her. She really likes this girl, and she's right, I haven't even noticed.

"I want to meet her," I say. "Officially, not just over a cash register."

"Forget it," Jess says.

"I mean it. I'm sorry. I want to know what's going on with you."

"And I want to know what's been going on with you all summer."

Jess gives me that look, not demanding exactly, but questioning and patient, like she'll stand around all day waiting for my answer if that's what it takes.

Jess always said we were meant to be amantes so we could become hermanas. But after that night, my hermana heart snapped shut along with every other version of my heart. Jess was the one who sat with me when I got my tattoo, staying the whole time at the Dr. Emmott–approved shop, not even flinching when the artist putting in the color pulled up blood. We told each other about crushes, books we love and hated, yeast infections and bad cramps.

But I couldn't tell her any of what happened after we lost track of each other at the party.

When Jess and I were together, we'd been soft and careful and anxious with each other in bed. How could I tell her that the next time I was on a bed with anyone else was because I'd been forced down on it?

But now, if I don't tell her, I'll lose her. I can see it in the hard sheen on her eyes.

"Something happened that night," I say. The words are threadbare as they come from my clenched throat.

"What night?" Jess asks.

"At the party."

I can almost see the cloud passing over her eyes. "What do you mean 'something'?"

The knot in my throat gets harder. The muscles in my throat that let me swallow tense and lock up.

Jess and I were beautiful as amantes and beautiful as hermanas and I thought we would lose all of it if she knew how broken I am. That I would shrink from being hermana to hermanita, a little sister to be pitied and guarded.

Or worse, she'd notice the handful of frost that was my heart, the broken glass inside me. She knew me so well I thought she'd see through my skin, and know that how I got hurt, and how the boy in the next room got hurt, was my fault.

But I can't keep telling no one anymore.

"I mean something bad." I say it fast. Then I grab the glass cleaner and spray the bakery cases. I can't stand still, watching her while she realizes what I'm saying. "That's when I stopped being able to do what I could always do with the pan dulce."

"Wait." She rushes next to me, following my path with the Windex. "Did that guy who was just in here hurt you? Is *that* what happened?"

"No."

But she's still getting worked up. "Because if he did, I will take his gringo ass down."

"Don't take him down," I say. "I've been trying to help him."

"Help him how?"

"With the pendejos at school. They just won't let up on him."

"But why is it your job to help him?" It's not a screw-everyone, let-him-fend-for-himself question. It's a question like she knows there are pieces she's missing, because I'm not giving them to her.

I can't help sighing, not because my best friend doesn't deserve an explanation but because I don't know how to reduce everything down to one that makes sense. "That night's when I lost my bisabuela's magic"—as I say it out loud, *lost* makes it sound like a sweater or a necklace, something I left someplace—"but when I started helping him, that's when I started getting it back."

"What if that has nothing to do with you helping him?" Jess asks.

"What do you mean?"

"What if it's because you're actually standing up to the aforementioned pendejos?" Jess says. "I know who you're talking about. I went to that school too. Victoria's been making you feel like nothing since your first semester. And I've never seen you fight back before."

The thought lands as a slight weight. But I only get a few seconds with it before she starts in again.

"And you swear he didn't hurt you?" Jess asks.

"He didn't."

"Really? Because if some girl I couldn't stop eyeing at a random party was suddenly at my school, I'd be happy about it, and you weren't happy about him, and the only sense I can make out of what you're telling me is that he hurt you, and you hoped you'd never see him again, and when you did, you panicked."

"Jess," I say.

But she's not done. "And you don't want to tell me, because you know that if he did, whatever the trust-fund kids are doing to him is nothing compared to what I'm going to—"

"Jess." I cut her off, finally, with the help of dropping the Windex and the cloth on the counter. "It was both of us. Something happened to him too."

She stares at me. Blinks at me before saying, "What?"

I try to relax my throat enough to talk.

"They had me in one room," I say, anger sharpening my voice even as I keep it low, teeth clenched, because months later I'm still afraid if I open my mouth too much, I'll scream. "And him in the other and he doesn't remember and I do and I wish I didn't."

It all comes out in one breath, and for a second I'm there, in both rooms. The one I was in, bright with white bedspreads and curtains and expensive lamps. The one he was in, dark, with all the lights off.

Jess doesn't try to hug me, or touch me at all.

She doesn't ask me why I didn't report. She knows as well as I do that it would have meant going up against families whose names are on classrooms and sports fields.

She just shakes her head at the floor, and says the best thing she could possibly say right now:

"What the fuck?"

It's not a question of disbelief. It's not even a question she's asking me. She's not looking at me.

It's a question she seems to be asking the whole world.

What the fuck.

Her saying it out loud lets me breathe out. It's the question some corner of my heart has been asking for months.

Verdad

Please tell me this is the last one." I haul another of mi madre's matching suitcases downstairs.

"You know how much it takes to look like I rolled out of bed like this." My mother gives her own face a game-show assistant's wave. "Speaking of which." She turns the wave on me now. "You'll fix this?"

I look down at my pajama pants. "Fix what?"

She gives a long-suffering sigh. "At least wash your hair."

"This from the woman who taught me the cinnamon-as-dry-shampoo trick?" I say. I'm still deeply skeptical of this method, and my tía considers it a sacrilegious waste of canela. But that never stops my mother from chasing me with a pinch of it between her fingers.

"I'm not asking for Miss America evening gown," my mother says. "Just"—she gets the look that makes other people think she's trying to find a delicate way to put something; she's usually not—"a step or two above boys' gym class."

She pricks her fingers in the air, that fairy godmother move again, as though she might be able to sparkle me into a Cinderella version of myself, complete with lip gloss.

"I'll take a shower and turn my sweatshirt inside out," I say.

"Estupendo," my father says as he walks by. "We like hygiene around here."

I would probably put on the fluffy tulle dress my mother brought home from the Goodwill and prance around on the sidewalk if it would convince them to make their flight. Getting my parents off on their trip is one thing I've managed not to screw up.

My aunt gives a little beep-beep of her horn outside, and my dad, then my mom, hug me goodbye.

"Your tía's gonna look in on you." My mother pulls out of our hug. "So don't get any ideas about crazy parties."

"Does that mean I should cancel the male strippers?" I ask.

"No more than three," my mother says, "or it's just tacky."

"You are so wise."

"You'll record my shows, ¿sí?" she asks.

"You set it to record, Mamá," I say.

"Well, make sure it works," she says, getting into my tía's car. "Clara and Evelina are gonna find out they're sisters any day."

My tía pulls away from the curb, and I wave at them until they turn off our street. It's only once they're out of sight that I notice a familiar truck, and a familiar boy getting out of it.

My stomach drops.

Lock crosses the street. "I came to look for you at the bakery, and your friend Jess said I should come here." He puts his hands in his pockets. "Actually, what she said was that if I already knew you well enough to know your address I should come here, and if I didn't, then I don't know you well enough to show up at your place of work looking for you, and I should—direct quote—kindly go screw myself."

"Sounds like Jess."

His voice is casual enough that I wonder if I imagined the recognition dawning in his face.

I hitch a thumb at my parents' red-blue-and-yellow house. "How'd you find the place?" I deadpan.

He gives a good try at a laugh but doesn't get all the way there.

"Can we talk?" he asks.

I look toward my house. "Do you want to come in?"

"No."

Wake Up

That's when I know.

He knows everything.

He knows it was my fault.

He knows that if I hadn't misjudged, if I hadn't made the mistakes I made that night, I could have saved us both.

I assumed Lock was drunk. Not drunk enough that we needed to call someone, but enough that it wasn't safe for him to wander around a party where no one knew him, in a house he'd never been in. Because I thought that, I brought him upstairs to one of the Kinkopfs' five hundred guest rooms, and I told him to sleep it off while I found my keys and a bottle of water to get into him.

That was the moment that decided it for him. I put him in the room where the worst thing to ever happen to him happened.

Then I came back upstairs to make sure he was okay, to check if he was still on his side where I'd left him, to see if he could tell me where he lived or where he was staying so I could get him home.

That's the moment that decided it for me.

I didn't get to him. Victoria and Brigid got to him first. And PJ and Chris got to me.

Those two mistakes put us in those two rooms, his as dark as the ocean at night, mine so pale that white decor still leaves me nauseous.

I know that right now I am in the front seat of Lock's truck. But every time I blink, I am back in that night, in the moment after. PJ and Chris have left me. Victoria and Brigid have left Lock, whose name I don't yet know. I lie still, throat tight as the muscles in my shoulders, eyes shut until I don't hear anything else upstairs, and I know they're really gone.

Then I find Lock.

They left him on the bed, his jeans undone, and before I zip up his fly again, I try cleaning him up. I don't want him waking up and finding rings of lipstick on the raw skin of his penis. But when I try using the damp hem of my shirt, he groans in his sleep, so hard and with such pain that I think his teeth are going to cut his tongue. So I just set his boxers and jeans back in place.

I take him by the shoulders and say, "Wake up."

His body flops under my hold.

I shake him harder, pleading with him.

He doesn't move, except taking the impact of my hands.

"Wake up," I say again, the crying at the back of my throat shredding my voice.

If any of that night is loud enough to have reached him, it's probably this, me almost screaming at him to *Wake up, just wake up*.

Or what I do next.

I look around the room, trying to figure out what I might be able to wake him up with that won't hurt him. I have to wake him up. I have to get him out of here.

Then I see the cups on the dresser. One I already know is

empty rests on a marble coaster. The other one, clearly still full and holding melting ice, sits in a puddle of condensation. Brigid's, no doubt. Victoria knows better than to mess with the lacquer on her parents' furniture, and because her parents are going to give her hell about the water stains, she's going to give Brigid hell.

No. I can't do this to him. I can't throw ice and watered-down vodka onto this boy during what is probably the worst night of his life. But I hear voices and footsteps downstairs, and if I don't get him out of here, Victoria and Brigid might come back to mess with him more. They might bring other girls up here as a kind of test, using their reactions to weed out who's worth their time and who not to bother with. After tonight, I don't put it past them to make a game out of how many lipstick shades they can put on an unconscious boy.

I grab the cup from its ring of condensation. Before I can rethink it, I throw it on him.

The ice hits him. The thinned-out vodka soaks his sleeve. He gasps, a grunt catching at the back of his throat. He doesn't wake up all the way, but he's stirring.

Whatever they gave him tries to pull him under again. I can almost see its hands in the dark.

"No." I clutch his arm. "You're getting up. Now."

He's not awake. But he's responsive enough that I can get him standing as long as he's leaning on me.

That's the Lock who exists to me if I think too hard about that night, if I stay too long. He's messed up, and scared, and half-conscious, and I'm the bitch who's forcing him to his feet and forward.

Lock's voice pulls me back to now. It lifts me out of the

smell of my own sweat and PJ's and Chris's aftershave and Victoria's and Brigid's perfume, and puts me back among the bending branches of the road I grew up on.

The moment between Lock speaking and me understanding what he just said feels like when I used to walk along the low cement wall outside my abuela's apartment, that endless moment of knowing I was about to fall off, trying to get my balance anyway.

"You brought me to the hospital," he says.

I come all the way back to right now, to Lock's truck, on my street.

Lock blinks at the windshield. He's not looking at me. He's got one forearm against the steering wheel, and he's staring straight ahead.

I keep looking for a flash of silver, that tiny fleck of mirrored glass in his eye. If I can still see it, then it hasn't really gone all the way into him. It hasn't gotten so deep that it can't be drawn out.

But there's nothing except the sheen of his eyes.

"You saved my life," he says, soft as the sound of the leaves blowing across the street.

"No, I didn't," I say.

"Ask the nurses if you don't believe me," Now he does look at me. "I don't know what would have happened if you'd left me there, and neither do they."

I braced so hard for his anger that this catches me off balance, like I'm losing my own center of gravity.

I don't deserve this. What I deserve is him hating me. What I deserve is me hating myself. Because those mistakes, me misgauging, me calling it wrong that night, added up to everything we've had to live with ever since.

I should tell him the truth, that the same night destroyed us both, and that it was my fault.

But I can't say it. I can't say all this to a boy who is still pulling himself up off the floor.

"Why didn't you tell me?" he asks.

Before I answer, I can taste the words on my tongue. This is something true I can tell him:

"Because I didn't want to remember it," I say.

He nods. "Thank you. For"—he takes a breath in—"for what you did."

I'm about to tell him not to thank me when he keeps talking.

"But I can't be around you anymore," he says.

The shard of mirrored glass in my heart shifts. "What?"

"What you just said, about not wanting to remember. I don't either. I can't. And that means I can't be around you right now."

A coin of heat presses into my collarbone.

My bisabuela's magic is settling back over me, one wing at a time. Lock is finding his way around school. We're done with Principal Whitcomb's endless pamphlets. And the sliver of mirror in Lock's eye has gone so deep he can't cry it out or blink it away. It's gone to his heart, the same as mine. There's nothing else I can do about it. If the best way I can look out for him is to stay away from him, that's the least I can do.

I nod, feeling the prickle of salt at the corners of my eyes.

There's no reason I need him, or that he needs me. All I can do now is try to keep the mirrored glass from getting into anyone else.

"I'm sorry," he says.

"No, I get it," I say, trying to pass off clearing my throat as allergies or coughing. "I really do get it."

I spent the summer trying to get back who I was before that night. A girl steady enough to walk in high heels. A girl fearless enough to put on winged eyeliner in the passenger side mirror of her father's car. A girl who wore V-neck shirts low enough to show the shadow of her boobs, instead of layering camisoles under everything and sweatshirts over everything like I do now.

That girl grew up being able to hold a morita chile on her tongue longer than any of her primos. That girl would lick mole rojo off her fingers without caring if anyone thought she was unladylike.

Lock must have an equivalent, a part of himself he's been trying to get back. And if he has to be around me, a girl who saw him passed out on that bed, with lipstick staining the fly of his jeans, he'll lose that part of himself for good, the same way I almost lost my bisabuela's magic forever.

I open the passenger side door. The wind stirs the air, like the Santa Anas are still considering whether they might sweep the sky clean.

"Ciela," Lock says.

I turn to him, door half open.

"Thank you," he says.

I nod.

I don't look back again.

This Is Not a Taquería

Right before closing, I get a call from a woman who's stuck in traffic, late picking up her sister's thirtieth birthday cake. She's a regular who orders often and tips well, so I stay.

Every time I'm in the pastelería, I get a little more of my bisabuela's magic back. Maybe it's not as instant and certain as it used to be, when I could tell a bride exactly what kind of pasteles de boda she would want before she even saw our list of flavors. But even with Lock and me falling away from each other, it's still coming back, like remembering the words to a song I knew as a little girl. I get back the language of las orejas, with their flaky swirls of pastry, and the sugar-sparkled flair of los abanicos, and the swirled, dyed dough of las almejas.

I go out to the front to clean off the glass cases. Then I mop with the orange-scented stuff my tía mixes from dollar-store floor cleaner and citrus oil. Out of instinct, I don't let the mop head near my feet, the same way Pilar doesn't let me get broom bristles anywhere close to my toes.

I'm so deep in the work, and in thinking of Pilar's voice—*Never, mija, not if you want to get married*—that when the wink of silver flashes at the corner of my eye, it takes me a second to place it. It takes that second for me to remember, and for the dread to let itself in.

In the jars of rock candy, where the sparkling rods of pink and blue and yellow used to be, are sticks covered in jagged silver. They have the same geode-like crystals as the candy before them, but now with the sharper look of glass, like they've been made from a shattered mirror.

The smell of the orange oil turns flat and heavy in the air.

When I go toward the jars, it's more compulsion than decision. I have to know if I'm seeing what I think I'm seeing or if it's some trick of the light.

It could be sugar. I need it to be sugar. I need the mirrored glass not to have followed me so deeply into the pastelería that it turned all my prima's rock candy at once.

And the glass is already in shards. Yes, the pieces are clinging to the flimsy wood of the rock candy sticks, but if anyone takes a lid off a canister, those pieces could so easily fly off and into the world. This is not the smooth curve of a mirror flower or the flat glass of papel picado turned to an etched mirror.

This is glass that's already broken.

I'm going to have to take them all, even the jars. I'm going to have to shove them into my closet, and tell my tía I'm sorry, but I was clumsy with the mop, and I broke the jars, yes, all of them. And that I had to throw the rock candy out with the cracked glass, there was no saving it.

The bell on the door rings.

I set the mop handle against the wall, take off my cleaning gloves. I reach for the pastel box on top of the bakery case so I can ring up the woman's cake.

But it's PJ and Chris, tripping across the threshold.

They bring the familiar smell of almost every Astin party—a mix of cheap and expensive booze, weird flavors of chips that go in and out of favor.

"We're closed," I say, gripping the mop handle again.

PJ looks around. "You make tacos here?"

"We don't make anything right now," I say. "We're closed."

"You make Mexican food and you don't make tacos?" PJ keeps turning his head, perplexed.

"This is a pastelería," I say. "Not a taquería. There's a taquería down the street."

I instantly feel bad that I might have just made them the Delgados' problem. I wonder if I should call ahead to tell Miranda not to let them near the sangria, to take another look at their IDs, the good fakes they've been using since ninth grade.

For the sake of everyone on the road, I hope to God they're not driving.

I go back to mopping. I need them to decide I'm too boring to bother with. I need to get them out of here before they see the sugar crystals that have turned to mirror shards. I need to get the candy jars home where they can't hurt anyone, especially not my tía, and Jess, and Pilar.

"Hey," Chris says.

I splash the mop back into the bucket.

"You could be a little friendlier, you know." Chris grabs the back of my arm.

That hand helped cover a boy's locker in condoms.

That hand helped leave me as brittle as a shell of ice.

For once, I am too angry to be afraid.

I swing the mop. The soaked head hits the middle of Chris's chest. The splash gets PJ.

Chris steps back, recoiling from the sight of his floor-mop-soaked shirt.

"If you two don't get the hell away from me," I say, clutching the handle, "I will talk. I will tell everything that happened that night."

Chris's face is still, almost placid, when he says, "No, you won't."

He says it not like a threat, but a fact.

I lower the mop head.

PJ and Chris know I can't say anything. Their parents' names are on plaques in hospital wings and theater lobbies. Next to them, my word weighs nothing.

"You're lucky Vic's not here," Chris says. "Brigid too."

My hands go tighter on the mop handle. "Why am I lucky they're not here? It's the two of you . . ." I lose the end of the sentence. I can't even say what they did, not without getting pulled back into that night.

Chris shoves PJ toward the door.

"If you don't know that," Chris says on his way out, and he sounds almost sorry for me, "you're even dumber than I thought."

Gay as a Picnic Basket

I expect to wake up from a nightmare that night, another dream of my body dissolving like sugar or ice, or maybe the jagged glass that looks like candy cutting my tongue.

But instead, I wake up with the little felted dolls in my hands and my best friend's voice in my head. Her question, about whether I'm finding this lost thread of magic not because of Lock, but because I'm fighting back, is as bright as the pink blushing the sky.

Maybe I'll only ever be La Bruja de los Pasteles again if I refuse to let them fit me into a Polaroid frame. They can only ever make good on that threat once, and if they do, then fine, I'm a slut, I was asking for it, I was drunk, I deserved it, whatever they want to make everyone believe. But if I let them hold that threat close to me, if I only move as much as that square of film lets me, my life will only ever be that one night.

So I don't stay curled in my bed, pillow squished over my ears like it can stop Chris's and PJ's laughs ringing through me. I get up. I go back in to the pastelería. I apologize for the candy jars I pretend I broke, and accept my tía's compliments about how good a job I did cleaning it all up.

Then I fill gallinas with cream, as the idea I woke up with

swirls into place. It gets louder with the smell of cinnamon and vanilla.

There's nothing I can do for Lock. If he needs distance from me from now until we graduate, the least I can do is give it to him. I helped him, just like I was supposed to, and now the best way I can help him is to let him go.

But I can still do something for my best friend.

So I knead lavender into dough for swallow bread, pressing the little buds in and willing the smell to loosen the knot of my heart.

While the pan dulce bakes, filling the air with sugar, I call her mother. I write down exactly what dorm Jess lives in. Then, that afternoon, I find the familiar building.

When she answers the door, she's wearing her reading glasses and periodic table of the elements shirt. If I didn't know she'd been studying, the sound of her white noise machine would tell me. The smell of her favorite hand cream mixes with the different fruity shower gels wafting through the hall.

I hold up a basket. "I made you a picnic."

"Wow." She stares. "In case you weren't queer enough already."

"Hey, this is my mom's." I put it into her hands. "So be nice to it."

She takes it. "You didn't have to do this."

"Yeah, I did. Because I've been such a shitty friend, I didn't even know you were in love."

"I'm not in love."

"Not yet."

"And you had a good excuse for being a shitty friend."

"I don't want an excuse," I say. "I want to show you I care about your life."

She gives me a sigh but also a very best-friend smile. "And where do you want to go with this gayest of receptacles?"

"Oh, that's not for me and you," I say. "It's a date in a box. Just add girl with book bag."

"Her name is Liz."

"Just add Liz."

"You're not serious."

"Completely." I lift the edge of the basket. "Please appreciate the romance theme we have going here. Novias, besos, conchas."

"You're way too pleased with yourself right now."

I ignore her—she loves this, I can hear it in her voice—and continue showing off the different kinds of pan dulce. "And not quite as on-theme, but equally important: gallinas, her favorite."

"I'd be so creeped out that you know that if you weren't you."

"And of course, pajaritos." I point to the wrapped pan dulce. "Can't go see the swallows without swallow bread."

"See the swallows?" Jess asks. "Thanks to suburban sprawl, there *are* no swallows."

"Well, maybe not on Camino Capistrano." I set one of the maps from the chamber of commerce on top. "But you're not going there. You're going to take her out to the old bridges. That's where most of them are this year anyway."

"You think going out to the middle of nowhere is going to sweep her off her feet?"

"I think you telling her about La Noche will. Tell her about how if you see a swallow at night, your heart will be lucky."

"That's just an old story," Jess says.

"Then why are you smiling?"

We laugh.

Jess doesn't look at me differently. Even with what I told her, she doesn't look at me like I'm broken, or breaking. It's a relief like a thousand swallows taking off at once.

"Oh, I almost forgot." I slide a rose-bead bracelet off my wrist. "Here." I slip it over Jess' left hand. "Wear this. I've never had a bad date when I've been wearing it."

I don't tell her I've never worn it on a date and that's why I've never had a bad date wearing it, but I consider this lie justified. Jess really likes this girl. I can tell by that smile. She needs all the confidence that I and the perfect pan dulce can give her. And I need to know I've done something else right.

Piedras y Coronas

After the last rush of the day, I slide mantecadas into the oven, a batch for my mother's church group.

"Why don't you go home?" I ask my aunt, watching the heat spread the sugar tops over the muffins. "Spend some time with Tío."

The curly hairs around my forehead have gotten frizzy under my hairnet. The dry heat in the kitchen has evaporated the tiny bit of mascara I put on this morning. But something about the sun going down while I'm molding sugar makes my brain still and quiet.

"You're a good girl, mija." My aunt packs up a few roles de canela and marranitos. My uncle's kids always visit on weekends, and those are their favorites.

"Go," I say. "I've got it here."

I start preparing sugar paste for the loudest pan dulce we make. In the kitchen, my tía refers to this kind as las conchas de sirena, because the round, puffy dough gets a sugar top in the colors of a mermaid queen's tail or some magic corner of the sea. They sell out every weekend.

I work the color into each metal bowl of sugar paste. Blues like the ocean at the horizon. Greens like seaweed. Purples like the sea urchins and anemones my dad and I saw in the tide pools.

As I press the heels of my gloved hands into the bowls, I shut my eyes, and I am almost La Bruja de los Pasteles again. I remember all the times I knew exactly what kind of sugared dough someone needed. Sometimes, if I was around someone enough, I didn't even have to be in the pastelería to know. Sometimes I could guess who needed the curled pastry of an oreja or the sugared crescents of cuernos. I brought a lab partner un beso after a bad breakup, because I thought the lift of the dough would tell her she could do better. I gave my cousin the whirl of a novia right before he proposed to his boyfriend, and I like to think maybe the spiral of sugared dough helped him get up the nerve to do it.

And when Jess was having a rough night studying for her slate of advanced classes, I came armed with a delivery of donas de azucar, because—her words—"even cell mitosis looks better with donuts."

Jess. For once, I'm not just thinking of this summer, when there was so much I didn't tell her as we dipped French fries into milkshakes or painted our nails rainbow for Pride. I'm not even thinking of what I told her. Right now, I'm just hoping the right pan dulce and the lore of night swallows is helping her and the girl she's out with.

The bell on the customer door rings.

I go to the front, tensing at the thought of PJ and Chris coming back. But the air is so calm I know it's just one person, and not either of them.

The light turns the painted walls from sky blue to teal and gilds the papel picado. I can still picture the missing panels I had to take when they turned to silver glass. The one with the delicate cutouts of swallows, the one with the tiered pastel de boda, the orange flowers. But there are still pink hearts and green rabbits and purple hummingbirds, and right now they're fluttering from the door opening.

Lock hesitates a couple steps in, wearing a not-quite-matched jean jacket and jeans combination that Victoria would rip apart even worse than the plaid flannel and that he looks annoyingly cute in.

Seeing him here again catches me off guard, enough that it feels like the air outside is holding its breath along with me.

He looks around, in a way he didn't the last time he was in here. He studies the photos on the walls. Tías abuelas lighting luminarias for Las Posadas. The dust-covered road just outside my great-grandfather's village. My abuela at my age, clipping wild blue mejorana.

"Sorry." Lock dips his head. A little of his hair falls in his face. "Are you closed?"

I shake my head. "Just winding down. What can I get you?"

It comes out so formal I shudder. But we're not friends. He made that decision, and I'm honoring it. So he's a customer, and I'm La Bruja de los Pasteles.

He stands there, hands in his pockets like they always are unless he's holding a crochet needle. "Okay, look. I'm sorry. You were my friend when I had literally no friends here, and I just bailed on you."

"Lock."

"Please," he says. "Just let me finish." He breathes out. "I didn't know how to handle the fact that you saw me like that."

"I get it," I say.

If he'd seen me after, if he'd been awake enough to register how I was breathing and how my body was trembling even as I made him get to his feet, I'd feel the same way.

"It freaked me out," he says. "Not just because we're friends but because"—he looks around before looking at me—"I really like you."

I can almost feel how this would feel if that night had never happened. I can imagine the fizziness that would bubble up in me when this boy, with his secret forest and his laugh like crickets late at night, told me he liked me. But that night broke down whatever that feeling might have been. It turned it to glass, and then splintered it apart.

"And I know how this is probably supposed to go," he says. "I'm probably supposed to just come in the door and kiss you instead of talking about it, right? But I don't work like that. I don't know if I ever did, and I definitely don't now. Not after—"

He doesn't finish the sentence.

The word *after* stands on its own.

"And I don't want to do anything you don't want me to do," he says. "And I didn't know how to say any of that, so"—he shrugs—"I'm saying it now."

Since Lock showed up, I've gotten back the magic I thought I had lost forever. I know whether a customer would like the sugared twist of las corbatas, or the star shape of a rehilete, or the wreath of a rol de canela, the cinnamon dough softening in strong coffee.

But I still can't guess with him. I haven't been able to figure it out. When I'm around him, it's like a flicker of light wavering at the corner of my vision. A few glowing points swim, slow, like fireflies or falling stars. But when I turn to catch it, it's gone. I can't pin him down enough to guess what kind of pan dulce would tell him what he needs to hear.

So I just start talking, like I do around him whenever I don't know what to say.

"It's bullshit anyway," I tell him.

He looks surprised. "What?"

"The show-up, get-the-girl thing. If any guy walked in here unannounced and tried to kiss me, I'd hit him with a mixing bowl."

"Good to know," Lock says.

I'm still trying to guess. The red of colorados? Piedras, bread that looks like the stones in the wilderness park? Coronas? No, but I swear I'm getting closer.

"Is that what you came here for?" I ask. "To say all that?"

"No, I'm here on an errand," he says. "My mom asked me to pick up something for Nate. He's gonna be at work until about midnight tonight, and he really likes desserts, and my mom wants to greet him with something better than boxed cake mix."

I try not to cringe.

"Hey, I told you, we're not chefs in my family," he says.

"And Nate is . . ."

"Sorry," he says. "My stepdad. Violet's dad."

I go behind the counter. "And what does he like?"

"He's not a big fan of frosting."

"So that's where your little sister gets it."

"Good memory," Lock says.

How awkward he is makes me more awkward.

"There are other bakeries, Lock," I say, and until I say it I don't realize it's going to be half question, half calling him on this. "You could have gone somewhere else."

He's not awkward now, doesn't flinch, doesn't look away when he says, "I didn't want to go somewhere else."

I will not smile. I will not smile. I will think of folding a thousand abstinence-only pamphlets so I will not smile.

My thoughts don't stick there though. They float to the kitchen, to bowls of sugar dough, the colors against the shine of the metal.

Maybe PJ and Chris and Victoria and Brigid took something from us, that match-flare light between us. But I'm not letting them take this, the small, bright possibility that we could still be friends.

So I ask, "You got somewhere to be?"

Pansexuality and Pan Dulce

"Y ou might want to rethink this," Lock says, taking in the metal counters and pallets of flour in the pastelería kitchen. "I once set a stack of coffee filters on fire trying to *sauté* something. I didn't even know what *sauté* meant, I just heard it on TV and I really wanted to try it. Trust me, you do not want to teach me."

"I like a challenge." I hand him a hairnet and gloves.

"Okay." He puts both on without comment. "But I warned you."

"Wow," I say.

"What?" he asks.

"You're pretty secure in your masculinity."

"Thanks?"

"I mean it. Most guys aren't man enough to put on a hairnet."

"My mom used to work in a school cafeteria." He stands next to me at the metal counter. "I take food safety pretty seriously."

Before knowing Lock, I had no idea it was possible to look this earnest and this cocky at the same time.

I pick the most proofed of the base doughs, show him how to shape it into rounds.

"How are you not babysitting right now?" I say.

"What do you mean?" he asks.

"I mean"—I hand him a stainless steel cutter—"you have a little sister, and you're not on a sibling-watching shift. I had to look after my younger primos all the time, and they're not even my brothers and sisters."

"She's with her grandparents." He makes even cuts to divide the dough, a perfect copy of the first balls I made. So far, so good. No coffee filters bursting into flames. "One of the few convenient things about us moving here. We're a lot closer to them."

"They live around here?" I ask.

"About a half hour, forty-five minutes." He keeps looking at the rounds I made, trying to copy them. "They love her, so they do the drive a lot."

"That's nice of them," I say.

He pushes on the sides of one round. "Yeah."

I look up from the one I'm shaping. "That was a loaded *yeah*."

He sighs. "Yeah."

I stare at him until he buckles.

"Violet's grandparents don't really like my mom and me," he says. "They"—he hesitates—"kind of think my stepdad married beneath him."

"Wow."

"Yeah," he says. "At Christmas, you can almost hear how hard they're working to tolerate us. So I think they like getting Violet away from soap operas and Velveeta."

"*That's* the big bad influence they're so afraid of?" I ask.

"Well, hearing how my mom named me didn't help."

"How did she name you?" I ask, going back to shaping another round.

"She named me Lock because everyone was giving her a hard time for getting pregnant and not being married."

I stop. "What?"

"I told you this." He squints at me. "I know I told you this."

"You definitely didn't. What does her not being married have to do with your name?"

He laughs, more to himself than me. "They really liked using the phrase 'out of wedlock' so this was kind of her screw-you."

"Out of wedlock?" I ask. "When were you born, 1910?"

"It kind of seemed like it sometimes."

I finish shaping one of the rounds. "For whatever it's worth, Violet clearly adores you." I remember him picking her up in the bakery. "She did floppy arms with you."

"What?" he asks, with the half laugh of having no idea what I'm talking about.

"You know," I say. "Floppy arms."

"What's floppy arms?"

"That thing kids do where you're holding them but they're not really holding on to you, because they know they don't need to." I think of an old picture of me doing that with my tía, on my third birthday. Pieces of pink and yellow paper fluff from the piñata de estrella are in my hair, and I am playing with her earrings, unconcerned about her dropping me. "If they're scared of you they tense up, and if they're not scared of you, but they don't know if they can totally trust you yet, they hold on. But if they feel safe with you, they just sorta flop around and do whatever they want. Because they know you have them."

Lock's smile is sad, but holds a light, like something glowing at its center. "Thanks."

He works at the dough.

I put my hands over the backs of his. "The pan dulce can't talk, so I'm speaking for it. Ease up. You've got to let the yeast spring back."

"Sorry."

I guide his hands to fluff up the dough again, the plastic of our gloves crinkling against each other. I show him how to blend together the different colors, how to cut the shell whirl of the sugar topping and lay it on each round. What racks to put them on.

The pan dulce bakes, the sugar smell filling the kitchen, and Lock starts washing dishes in one side of the enormous metal sink.

"You don't have to do that," I say.

He laughs. "Yeah, I do. Don't pretend like I've been helping you back here. I'm slowing you down, and I know it."

He turns the water off between dishes, soaping one up and then turning on the tap. It's the habit of a boy who grew up knowing his mother would have to pay the water bill, or knowing his county was in a drought. Probably both. After he told me where he'd grown up, I found Olivedale on a map, and it's smack in the middle of the Central Valley. We have a distant cousin who grew up in and out of that area, one who supposedly ran away with the circus or from it, or something, and according to her it's a place where most of the water rations go to the almond orchards.

"By the way." I lean against the edge of the sink's other side and watch him spray water into the bowls. "You can tell your step-grandparents that Velveeta is one of the wonders of the modern American grocery store. And I'm Mexican. So that's high praise."

"Huh," he says, like he's wondering. "Guess I'm a better chef than I think."

"Oh yeah?" I ask.

"My shells and cheese does get four stars from the four-year-old."

I pull the first batch of conchas out of the oven, and move them to the cooling racks, fingers lightly helping them onto the spatula.

"Isn't that burning your hands?" Lock asks.

"I'm used to it," I say, holding up one hand as though he can see the tiny calluses on my fingertips through the plastic glove. "Besides, you can't leave them on there. The metal's still hot, they'll keep cooking."

I stand back and look at them on the gridded racks, the colors blurring together on each top like a painting.

"See?" I catch Lock's eye. "You're going to take a box of these back to your family, and they're going to be really impressed."

"They're not going to believe I had anything to do with this. I once tried to make macaroni with Kraft Singles."

"Before you mastered Velveeta?"

He rinses the last bowl and sets it on the drying rack. "Exactly."

I hand him one of the bowls I just dried. "Put that up there for me, will you?"

He slides it onto a high shelf, and I am too busy staring at how good his ass looks in his Carhartts to tell him he just put it in the wrong spot.

What is wrong with me? I couldn't summon a flirty smile for any of my dates this summer, and I am checking out the last boy in the world I should be looking at this way.

I need my mother or my tía—or Abuela, come back from the dead—to slap me on the hairnet and tell me to stop, just stop.

"Okay," I say when the pan dulce is cool. "Time to try your work."

He looks worried.

"Hey," I object. "I made the dough before you even got here."

"And I'm pretty sure the mere act of me touching it magically ruined it."

"Eh." I shrug. "You were wearing gloves." I hand him one of the conchas. "Cuts down the chances."

We each break one open. Vanilla-and-clove steam wisps from the dough.

He tries it. "That's really good."

He sounds surprised. Does he really think he could have made one of the pastelería's signature recipes taste like Kraft Singles just by being near it?

"This particular color palette was my aunt's idea," I say. "She likes to think of it as a mermaid concha."

He looks at me. Blankly.

"Concha is the type of pan dulce this is," I say, "the round kind with the sugar crown on it. Kind of the queen of pan dulce."

He's actually eating it now, without caution.

Time to strike.

"You know," I say, because he makes me feel off balance enough that right now I want to return the favor. "In some regions, *concha* is another word for . . ."

"For what?" he asks.

"You know," I say. "The same part of the body as Valentina."

He looks at me. "How stupid do you think I am?"

"It's true," I say. "Ask anyone. Ask my mother. She'll tell you I'm right."

"Okay," he says. "Sorry. I stand corrected."

I wait a second before saying, "So depending on who you ask, you're kind of eating a mermaid vagina right now."

He almost chokes on the pan dulce.

I fill a glass from the agua fresca dispenser, trying not to laugh at him.

He coughs into his sleeve. "You waited until exactly the right moment to tell me that, didn't you?"

"Yeah." I hand him the glass. "I really did."

He swallows from it and finishes coughing.

"Sorry." I can't stop laughing. "It was too easy."

"Glad I can amuse you," he says.

I assemble one of the pastelería's bakery boxes.

"So." I pull off his hairnet, then mine. "You moved all the way here for Astin," I say, and then transition into the posh accent my tía always reads the school brochures in. "Has our academic rigor lived up to your expectations?"

He laughs. "They have a lot more advanced math classes than my last school, so yeah."

I drop back into my normal voice. "So now the real question."

"Okay." He takes another drink off the agua fresca, wary.

"Was it worth it?"

I can't catch everything that flits across his face. The night he doesn't remember. The flashes of it he does.

His expression settles, and he looks straight at me. "Yes."

My heart catches, like the gravity–not-gravity feeling at the top of La Medusa, my mother's favorite roller coaster.

I started all this, trying to help Lock, because I wanted to get back the gift my bisabuela trusted me with, and because I knew that fleck of silver in him was my fault.

But now I want things I can't have. I want to know what we would be if so many awful things didn't float, unseen, between us.

"I'm sorry I didn't tell you," I say. "About bringing you in."

"Oh, I get why you didn't. There's literally no good time to bring something like that up." He sets the agua fresca down and wipes his condensation-damp hand on his jeans.

"And sorry about Jess, earlier," I say. "It wasn't her fault. It was mine. I didn't tell her about you." I pause. "Well, I did, but not that you were the guy from the party."

"The guy from the party?" he asks. "What does that mean?" His voice carries an apprehension I can read instantly. He thinks *the guy from the party* means *the guy who was blacked-out enough that I had to drive him to Ortega Hospital*.

"It means she was trying to get me to talk to you," I say. "Jess and I may have been not meant to be as girlfriends, but we're meant to be as best friends and wingwomen."

"You and Jess went out?" He seems neither surprised nor bothered, like I've just said *quantum physics postulates that you can't know the exact position and velocity of an object at the same time*.

I already know Lock doesn't consider me damaged or broken for having survived something I can barely talk about. If he considers me odd or—as my mother would say—*out there* because I don't date any single gender, then I want to know

now, because if he does, he can promptly disqualify himself from both my life and my tía's kitchen.

"That's what Chris was talking about," I say. "When he said I don't like . . ."

I can't repeat the words.

But I don't have to. Comprehension breaks over Lock's face.

"Got it," Lock says, with a slow nod. "Wow, what an asshole."

"So if you have a problem with that, with what I am," I say, trailing the end of the sentence, giving him the opening.

"I don't. But if you don't like guys, then I'm"—he cringes— "I'm really sorry, and I really hope we can forget everything I said earlier, or at least have a good laugh about it, because you might be the only friend I have at school right now, and I really hope I haven't just blown that by being oblivious."

He's rambling. Híjole, he's cute when he's rambling.

"In addition to putting it in the worst way possible," I tell him, "Chris put it in just about the most inaccurate way possible too. It's not about me not liking—" I still can't say the word Chris said.

I try another way. I will not let Chris Bernard reduce this to a conversation about anatomy.

"I don't *not* like guys," I say.

He laughs. "That's a weird way to put it."

"Maybe," I say. "But it's the best way I know how to explain it." Unless I want to tell him how Jess describes me: I'm so queer even my dulce is pan. "I don't *not* like any gender or gender identity or gender expression. Everybody has things in people they're attracted to. I do too. It's just that for me, they don't really come with specifics about gender."

Lock can't meet my eyes, and I'm pretty sure it's not about how queer I am, but about what's still going unaddressed between us.

"Then I guess the question is whether you like me," he says. He tries to make it sound like a joke, like there's nothing riding on it for him.

He fails.

The way he's looking at me, his eyes dark as piloncillo sugar, makes me want to fidget with my apron strings. And in the space of that look, it shifts. Something in me shifts. I like this boy, even if the worst thing that happened to each of us happened one room apart. I like him, and admitting it means I get to take something back from PJ and Chris and Victoria and Brigid.

"Lock," I say.

"Yeah?"

The inside of me feels bubbly as Jarritos.

"If you tried to kiss me right now," I say, "I would not hit you with a mixing bowl."

His laugh is soft, almost a breath.

It might be the clumsiest possible way I could give consent, but there is it. I've given it, and I mean it.

A few months ago, I wanted to say no so badly it became an unspoken thing that ripped through me, like a falling star through the atmosphere. And the fact that now I not only want to say yes but don't want to say no feels as miraculous as all the swallows in the world flying into the air at once.

I don't know how to tell Lock any of that. But before I can pick it apart, before I can think of something better to say, his mouth is on mine.

It's slow, soft, less tongue than the two guys who've kissed me before. The way his lips move is certain but not aggressive. I part my lips and kiss him harder, and he matches me, waiting for the permission my mouth gives him. We break apart long enough to breathe, the thread of air between our lips deep with cinnamon and cloves and vanilla.

I kiss him again, shutting my eyes tight enough that, for just that minute, all the sugar lacing the air is swirling like a snow globe, and there is enough of me left to bring back to life.

Suburban Forestry

Lock is in his truck behind the school five minutes before I asked him to show.

When I climb in, he startles.

"Sorry," I say.

"No." He calms. "I'm sorry. I'm early."

"Yeah, so am I. I'm Mexican and queer. If I don't aim for early, I'm four hours late."

"Am I allowed to laugh at that?"

"I'm the one who made the joke, so yes."

"Okay." He faces me. "You have my attention. What can't we talk about within earshot of the responsible adults in our lives?"

"Well," I say. "I happen to know that the couple who lives across the street from me are out at some gala until dawn. So now's our chance."

"Our chance for what?" he asks.

"To take another run at that tree," I say.

He blinks at me. "You're serious?"

"You have no idea." I pull a roll of cloth from my bag and unfurl it, like snapping a flag open.

"Wow." Lock regards the coveralls.

"I think I guessed your size right." I throw it at him.

He reads the letters stenciled across the back. "Department of Suburban Forestry?"

"And I"—I pull the second set of coveralls out of my bag—"will be your lovely assistant."

His laugh is half gasp, the kind of amused wonder I've only seen in him in small degrees. Now it blooms.

"Where did you get these?" he asks.

"I don't know if you've heard this about me," I say, "but I am una aficionada of the secondhand shops around here."

Lock holds the coveralls out far enough to get a better look at the letters.

"I really don't want to be ungrateful here," he says. "But slight problem. Won't your other neighbors recognize you?"

"The ones we like are at Bible study tonight, and the rest wouldn't know me if I presented ID."

"Okay, second slight problem," he says. "What if someone who's actually from the Department of Suburban Forestry sees us wearing these?"

"Not gonna happen," I say.

"How do you know?"

"Because there is no Department of Suburban Forestry."

He sits back. "You are something else."

"I choose to take that as a compliment."

He looks at me in a way that makes the memory of kissing him shimmer up the back of my neck. "It is."

The Secret Forest

As Lock and I dig the snow tree out of the neighbors' front yard, the rose hip under my coveralls shimmers with heat. The coral and green sparks as Lock and I brush against each other, heaving the root ball into the rusted bed of his truck. The inked escaramujo feels as alive as a growing plant while I try not to laugh at the damp earth going all over us.

We brush ourselves off, get in, and Lock drives. He doesn't speed. He doesn't do anything a Suburban Forestry official wouldn't do.

But when we hit the highway, he revs the engine. I turn the hand crank for the window, and night air floods the cab.

My hair streams across my face, and I let out all the laughing I kept inside on my street. I am stealing the snow tree, and it's not only the rose hip coming alive, it's my body.

I slip from the thrill of having to stay quiet to the recklessness of laughing into the dark.

Lock smiles over at me, wary. "What's funny?"

"Everyone thought you were such a choirboy."

"I've been a choirboy, thank you very much."

"You know what I mean. A buenudo. But you're not. You're

a tree thief." I tilt my face to the night, trying to smell the sky. "Worse than that. You're a whole-forest thief."

"Hey," he says. "You just made yourself an accomplice. Whatever I am, you are too now." He checks his rearview.

In the back of the truck, the tissue-paper blossoms are shivering on the branches, a cloud of stars against the dark. A few break off and float away, constellations spinning over the highway.

It never happened.

In this moment, it never happened. Me making the wrong call, putting him in that room where I thought he could sleep it off. None of it happened.

Lock stops the truck alongside the road, deep in the hemlocks' shadows. My muscles bristle awake with the effort of helping him drag the root ball off the truck bed and into the hollow he's already dug for the crepe myrtle. As we pack the dirt down around the roots, my hands take the clean cold of the earth. The dirt under my nails looks more perfect than any manicure. My breathing brings in a smell I can't quite place, like a mix of Christmas tree and fruit-box cardboard drying in the sun.

In this secret forest Lock has created, one chaste tree and wild lilac at a time, that night never happened. As the snow tree settles into its new ground, I am helping this boy instead of wrecking him. The cut that the mirrored glass left in me is just enough for the smell of flowering branches and wild canyon to get in.

The wind trembles the white crepe myrtle, and a shower of tiny, pale flowers dots our hair like snowflakes. Under the smoke tree and lily magnolia, we have dirt on our hands and our foreheads, and the star-salted night on our skin, and our bodies are ours.

Lock pauses, studying me.

"I just realized you're wearing a hair ribbon," he says.

I touch the headband of pink satin tied in a bow at the base of my neck, the way my mother and aunts and grandmother all did when they were my age. "And?"

"You're wearing a hair ribbon with coveralls," he says.

"When I femme, I femme hard."

"That's adorable," he says, right before we both look up, feeling the faint spray of first raindrops. "We better work fast."

He bends down to check the root ball. But the particular sound of the rain stops me.

It's not the soft patter of rain on leaves.

It's the tinkling of water drops on glass.

I scan the branches until I find them, the wispy leaves that have become tiny silver knives, like hoarfrost needles.

While Lock is still bent down, while he's not looking, I pull away the blades of glass, slicked with rain. Before he sees them, I hide them deep in the pockets of my coveralls, where they can't hurt him, and where I can pretend, at least for now, that the mirrored glass hasn't reached Lock's forest.

Los Vidrios

Lock glances up at a lighted sign. "'Hell'?" he asks as the reflection of the yellow lowercase letters crosses the truck windshield.

"It used to be a Shell station," I say. "I think the sign got declared some kind of landmark, but the 'S' burned out a while ago."

He lets out a laugh, slight and wry. It's an odd feeling I can't help liking, showing someone where you've lived your whole life, how carefully they notice things you've gotten used to. The orange bellies of las golondrinas. The twitching branches of certain trees, how they look awake and alert. A burning-out sign that seems to announce Camino Capistrano as the road to the underworld.

"Turn in here," I say, pointing to the neon sign that sits in the window of my favorite half foodstand, half storefront.

Lock pulls into the small lot. "What are we doing?"

"You're getting the next lesson in your culinary education."

He parks. "My what?"

"Don't argue with guacamole fries," I say. "That's an essential part of lesson three. Do you drink coffee?"

"Coffee and fried food. I feel like I should be hungover for this."

"Says the guy who makes mayonnaise and bologna burritos."

"*I* never did that. I just had to witness it."

He is about to get out when I put a hand on his arm.

"Thank you," I say, my dirt-damp hand touching his dirt-dusted forearm. "That tree means a lot to me."

"Yeah," he says. "I kind of got that."

I set my lips against his cheek, lightly enough that it's almost not a kiss.

I don't mean it as less than a kiss. I mean it as a thank-you he can't brush away with a smile.

He shuts his eyes for the few seconds it takes me to press my mouth to his skin, and then draw away.

The smallest shiver goes through him, and I realize that sometime while driving he shrugged out of his coveralls. He's still wearing the coverall pants, but the upper part hangs around his hips. His undershirt is all he has on top.

I wish I didn't notice the path of that vein from his elbow to his wrist, or the way the blue and red neon traces that particular muscle in his arm.

But noticing, thinking of his body like this instead of passed out on that bed, it makes me feel a little like the girl I was before this year. A girl who saw mirrors as nothing but a place to check my lipstick.

I trace a line of blue neon along his sleeve. "I'm getting this one, don't argue."

"Come on," he says. "I got you into this."

"Because you wanted to save my snow tree." I push the door open. "Consider it a thank-you."

Another car whirs into the lot. The gleam of its finish seems to pull all the neon from the air.

"Shit," Lock says, staring past me.

Chris and Victoria spill out of the shined-up car.

"Let's go somewhere else." Lock is already reaching for the ignition.

I remember Jess, her theory that maybe this was never about Lock, this was about me fighting back.

"Like hell we're going somewhere else." I jump down, on principle and on promise of guacamole fries.

"Ciela."

"Stay here," I say, and slip to the window while PJ and Brigid are still close enough to the car that maybe, maybe they won't notice me.

The man at the window looks up from his crossword long enough to take my order. The brothers who run this place keep a TV in the upper corner of the kitchen, but never seem to watch it. One of many reasons I love it.

I bristle at the thought that my classmates have started coming here too.

I keep my head down, avoiding the light of the neon.

"Hey." Brigid tilts her chin up, as though summoning me.

Keep walking, I tell my body.

Do not stop, I tell it. *Go back to the truck and wait until Ed nods at you that your order's ready.*

But my body didn't listen to me months ago. Why would it now?

I stop walking.

I wonder if the four of them see the veins of glass, slowly filling in the broken asphalt like water.

Brigid studies the earth-darkened knees and elbows of my coveralls. "Is this your new look?"

"Be nice," Victoria says from behind her.

Be nice.

This from the girl who probably unzipped Lock's jeans or told Brigid to.

Victoria rules the four of them. She has the luxury of being—when she feels like it, when the mood strikes her—magnanimous.

Just off the counter, PJ and Chris are laughing, and the sound is so close to that crackling noise I remember that it feels like a burn on my skin. It's the breath off a gas flame.

The threads of mirror glimmer across the ground, like spilled mercury.

The truck door slams.

"Sorry to interrupt." Lock appears, his coverall sleeves hanging alongside his legs. "But if you're going to try to get us to do your book reports, you'll have to catch us during business hours."

Brigid casts a sneer toward the comet trails of dirt on his forehead.

But Victoria studies him as though she's impressed by how he looks in an undershirt.

She glances at me, wanting me to notice that she's noticing.

Something proprietary rises up in me. Not jealousy. To feel jealousy you have to think, at least a little, that someone is more likely to steal a person you care about than to hurt them.

Protectiveness.

"You two make a nice couple," Victoria says, as coolly as the fog off the ocean. "Guess you should be thanking us."

My heart turns to dry ice. Not glittering like a handful of snow. But something that both sears and freezes. Something that evaporates instead of melting.

Then the hard shell of my rage holds it together, keeps it from vanishing into nothing.

Victoria and Brigid and PJ and Chris can't claim Lock and me. They don't own the small thing sparking between us. Them breaking us both down has nothing to do with him and me being together. I think of Jess saying how much we were looking at each other early in the party, before either of us ended up in those rooms.

Lock doesn't seem to register Victoria's words, or the silver glass snaking through the rough patches in the rain-wet asphalt.

Ed calls our number. Lock goes to the window, picks up our food, and is back, in one fluid motion. He moves fast, even while holding two lidded paper coffee cups on top of the take-out container.

He is trying to take me with him, to draw me into his gravity.

This time, it works. My body wants to, and I let it, and it does, putting distance between me and the parking lot that no one yet notices is glinting. The veins of glass are moving like a tide coming in, but the rain-damp shine of the parking lot hides it.

"You know she's gay, right?" PJ says.

Lock pauses, stares PJ down.

Gay is a word Jess wears as proudly and comfortably as a favorite jacket. But it never fit me right. I never felt gay any more than I felt straight. I've had crushes on girls, on boys, on friends who identify as both, as neither, as outside those words entirely.

It's not that I mind being mistaken for gay, or for a lesbian. It happened all the time when I went anywhere holding hands with Jess, and it never got to me. I liked both words. I still do. They're beautiful and true in themselves even if they aren't quite true about me, because they're true for people I love. My oldest prima, una lesbiana, with her girlfriend. Dr. Emmott and his husband, who both call themselves gay.

But somehow, in PJ's mouth, a word I didn't mind, a word Jess wears so proudly, becomes a slur.

The sick feeling comes back, rising in my stomach. It has the same color and texture as when Chris spat those words at Lock. *She doesn't like dick.*

Lock stares at PJ long enough that PJ gets uncomfortable and talks first.

"She likes girls," PJ says, as though Lock might not know the meaning of the word PJ just pinned to me.

Lock inclines forward enough that for a second I worry he's about to go at PJ. My hand is already twitching, ready to grab his arm. As much as I appreciate this boy caring what labels get shoved at me, PJ is not worth it. None of them are.

I'm about to throw my palm to Lock's forearm to stop him when he looks at me in exaggerated surprise.

"You're kidding," he says. "You like girls? I like girls too." He makes a good show of it, the sarcastic wonder.

If I could like this boy any more than I already did, in this moment, I do.

"That's amazing!" He gapes at me like this is a revelation, like finding out we were born on the same day. "We have so much in common."

I laugh, at first because I can't help it, and then because I don't want to help it. I want the four of them to see us laughing, right in front of them, as though they're not here.

Victoria rolls her eyes. PJ seems puzzled by what he must regard as Lock's utter stupidity.

Thank you, I mouth at Lock.

It's me pulling him toward the truck now. We're done here. Whatever they think of us, we leave it on the asphalt.

Our backs are to them when Chris calls out, "Guess that means you still got your flower, huh, Thomas?"

Lock stops, as though the pavement has ended and he's at the edge of a pier. I swear I can almost see into his heart, the glint of mirror silvering his blood. The shift in him, the hardening in him, is the same kind of look he had in Principal Whitcomb's office. It's a look of the mirrored glass making him reckless, confrontational.

"Go fuck yourself," he says without turning around.

"Guess we have our answer," PJ says.

"Come on." Now I'm trying to draw Lock into my orbit. I'm the one keeping our path.

We get in the truck. Lock puts the takeout container on the dashboard and the coffee into the makeshift cup holders, coils of wire that either he or the owner before him added. I stare at the rusted metal so that my eyes won't drift out of the car.

Don't look over, I tell myself.

I play with the lids on the coffee cups, pretending I'm making sure they're closed.

Don't look at them.

But I do.

At first it's not as bad as I think. PJ and Chris are still waiting for their order. Victoria is pulling at a thread on Chris's shirt like she can't decide whether she wants to trim it or unravel the whole thing. I even get the small satisfaction of seeing PJ stumble on a wider band of glass and look around like he's wondering who tripped him.

But Brigid is still watching me, the side of her face and half her blond hair lit neon blue. She is watching me so intently that she doesn't notice the silver glass filling in the cracks in the damp pavement.

Veins of glass smooth over the tiny parking lot and then crawl out toward the sidewalk. It shines over the asphalt, catching the glow of the neon.

But Brigid doesn't see it either. She watches me with an almost-satisfied expression. She holds her mouth in a closed-lip smile, like she's just figured something out.

I should look away. I tell my eyes to look away, my face to turn.

But her stare catches me, and in that second I know what she's figured out. It breaks in me, a dropped plate that seems to fall forever before shattering on the floor.

She knows Lock doesn't remember, and that I haven't told him what I know.

And now she's afraid I will. She thinks I'm going to tell him, definitively, that it was them who thought it would be funny for him to wake up with lipstick on him. She has marked me as a threat, in the same way she would notice a new girl in our class with shinier hair or better nails.

A twitch of movement comes next to me. That turns me away from Brigid, toward Lock.

He stares across the street, the stoplight going green and yellow and red for cars that aren't there, not this late.

His casual bluster is gone. PJ and Chris stripped it away.

He has a hand to his mouth, and he's doing something I can't quite figure out. He's not biting his nails. He's not sucking on his fingers like a child.

He's biting his fingertips. He goes at them like he wants to scar away his fingerprints with his teeth. But I can tell there's no such intention, or any intention, behind it. He does it absently, with the sense of familiar, distracted dread that marks a nervous habit.

The question of whether he has always done this or if he started last spring is too heavy and too sad for me to hold right now.

They couldn't let us win. Not even once.

Chris couldn't have Lock getting a single good shot in at PJ.

"Lock," I say as gently as I can.

He comes back, startling a little. He stops biting, drops his hand, settles into my touch.

"It's not you," I tell him. "It's because you're with me. If you were out with any other girl at school, you'd be fine."

"What are you talking about?" Lock asks.

How do I even explain this to him? How do I explain that a girl like me, with the same hips as my mother and my abuela, is expected to try to hide them, not wear the same tight jeans as any flaca in my class? I eat and I love food more than an Astin girl is supposed to, reveling in the spice of mole and the color of sugar shells dyed as bright as sunsets. And I never kissed Jess in front of the guys at school, not even when they told us to, especially if they told us to.

"You know," I say. "I'm almost like them but not quite. I'm like a Kirkland Signature Astin girl."

An untempered lack of comprehension breaks across his face. "What?"

"You know," I say. "Kirkland Signature. The brand at Costco that's like the real brand but not quite."

"I know what it is." His face turns.

He looks not quite angry, but serious, in a way I've never seen. I've seen angry. And a minute ago I saw afraid, but not intense, like this.

"Never say anything like that again," he says.

"I was joking," I lie.

"It's not funny," he says. "You're"—his hand twitches a little. "I—" I try to figure out if staying quiet will make him less likely to start biting his fingers again, or if saying something will.

He stares out the window at the traffic light directing nothing. Except now it's directing PJ's car out onto the main street.

Lock hands me the takeout container and turns the ignition.

He takes a gulp of his coffee and shivers like it's a bracing wind. This place's coffee is strong enough that there's no other appropriate reaction.

"So where are we going?" he asks. I can tell he's trying to sound offhand about it, but the way he says it is uncertain, deferring. Like I can map this city neon sign by neon sign. Like he is not a boy who made a secret forest out of a corner of the wilderness park, but a boy who only ended up here because he got lost.

"Where do you want to go?" I ask. I hand him the question back, because if he doesn't decide he belongs here, they'll convince him he doesn't.

He shifts into drive. "Pretty much anywhere else."

"Go slow," I say, watching glass fill in the potholes, reflecting the light like puddles.

Lock either doesn't hear me or thinks I'm joking. He doesn't go slow. He pulls out onto the road at a speed that would be completely reasonable if it wasn't for those patches of slick ground.

"Lock," I say, a warning, right before I feel it.

One wheel catches a patch of glass. The truck fishtails, rear axle sliding right.

I register what's happening a half second before Lock does. When he's adjusting his grip to steer into the slide, I'm already pulling at the wheel.

A driver leans on their horn, flies past, almost clipping us.

Lock takes the brake down slow enough to halt the truck instead of spinning us out.

The truck skids to a stop, just short of crashing over the curb and into the splintered wood of an old telephone pole.

I don't realize I'm going forward until my forehead's about to hit the dashboard. I brace, and in the split second before it happens, I can picture how I'll crack open. I'll break apart, leaving glass and blood and whatever else I'm still made of.

Lock grabs me and pulls me back, hard enough that the impact doesn't happen.

The car is still enough that I can feel him shaking.

"Are you okay?" he asks.

I lift my head to look at him, and my mouth is close enough to his that I can feel the heat of his breath on my skin.

A hard edge presses into the back of my neck. With the chill of dread, I know what it is, instantly, and I hope Lock doesn't see the band of silvered glass in my hair.

I look around for anything to draw his attention, something other than me, and the pink ribbon turned to a strip of mirror. I can feel it breaking apart from the impact, and I have to get it off me and into my pockets or my bag before it splinters into pieces and gets into me or him or anyone else. I already feel a corner of it scratching a cut into my neck, and I dread the possibility that a shard flew off and into Lock when we stopped hard.

My best option for distraction is the takeout container, still shut but slumped forlornly against the base of the passenger side door.

I pick it up and open it to reveal the food shoved up against one side. "Seismically shifted guacamole fries?"

"Earthquake-themed food." He tries one. "I see a new trend in California cuisine."

As he starts the truck again, I run my hands through my hair, trying to catch every piece. The mirrored curves of the ribbon. The cracked loops of the bow. The band of light pink I imagined Lock pulling the end of until it came loose, but that is now two palmfuls of broken glass.

Shutter

From my window, I can see my neighbor in her mono-grammed robe, staring at her front yard. Not at her missing tree. At the hole in her perfect lawn.

I bite my lip not to smile, in case she can see me between the curtains.

From hundreds of miles away, mi madre will know if I've done what she's told me to do. Mexican mothers always know. So in addition to keeping the house clean and misting the hens and chicks plants, I get in the general galaxy of my mother's idea of *presentable*.

I start by brushing my hair, coarse like my father's, and not quite curly and not quite straight like my mother's (I use a comb identical to hers). I fluff on the peony-pink blush I've started wearing again.

Then I think, just for a second, of adding a little eyeshadow. Not peacock-blue eyeliner or gold metallic or anything else I haven't touched in months. Just a wash of peach over my eye-lids. A highlight of paler brown just below my brow bone.

My hands are out of practice, and the wash ends up sheer and nearly blended to nothing. But my face looks brighter, more awake. I look like a girl who might belong in this room, with its sugar pinks and butter yellows and hotel-pool aquas.

I will never tell my mother this, because it would mean having to endure her satisfied grin, but as I walk into school, I feel the glow of these colors I've missed. Coral and peach and pink blushing the brown of my skin. The warm, glimmering haze of it follows me as I open my locker.

When the square of white falls out, I know what it is. I almost roll my eyes in preparation for another Polaroid of me looking drunk, hair in my face like I'm stumbling forward.

I grab it by the corner, ready for the dim background, the different shades of brown that make up every image of my face.

But the glossy square isn't just brown and washed-out background. It isn't a vague shot that could be from any party.

Alongside the dark blur of my hair is the blue of jeans.

Lock's.

The sliver of glass in my heart becomes a blade of ice.

I'm not the only one caught in a square of film.

This one shows us both. In the same room.

The story I've been telling myself so that I can keep breathing crashes into the truth this photo shows, that there was no wall between what PJ and Chris did to me and what Victoria and Brigid did to Lock.

I was there, and I couldn't stop it.

The photo nearly slips from my hands.

I scramble to catch it, grab it by the corner.

The strange crackling of their laughs—PJ's and Chris's and Brigid's and Victoria's—comes into focus along with this image.

The sound, that strange, not-quite-human noise of their laugh, it wasn't just their laugh.

It was a camera shutter.

They were taking pictures.

They snapped photos with a camera so old I hadn't even recognized the sound of it going off. I'd had my eyes shut too tight, my throat clenching, my heart cracking open because of what was happening to me and what was happening to a boy I could not help. As I tried to let my brain wander away from all of it, I folded the sound of the shutter and flash into their laughter.

I still remember it, how fire-like it was.

Now it's burning up my whole world, while the inside of me turns to a screaming storm.

"You two were just adorable last night." Brigid's voice startles me so hard I almost drop the photo again.

She comes out from behind my locker door and taps the corner of the Polaroid. "You really don't want him to see the rest of these, do you?"

The threat goes into me clean but breaks open inside me. Little shards of it get everywhere.

There are more.

Of course there are more.

And of course they used Polaroids, film that doesn't record who took a picture, or when. Film that won't tell their secrets.

Just mine.

No, not just mine.

If Brigid shows them to everyone, they will not only burn up my whole world, they will burn up Lock's.

I check around, looking for an exit. I check for PJ and Chris and Victoria, and for anyone else watching.

Everyone's too busy getting their books, swapping notes, waiting around until the last minute before class.

"Nobody wants this to be a big deal." Brigid's whisper is soft as her perfume. "It was just a party. So don't get any ideas about telling crazy stories, okay?"

If my throat and my mouth could manage it right now, I would laugh.

Brigid has no idea what kind of lies I've told myself to forget exactly what happened. I had to pretend there was a wall between us to live with the fact that I couldn't save him.

What *stories* does she think I would ever want to tell?

"Just leave him alone." My voice sounds like a whisper. I'm trying to be quiet, but the words are getting choked to nothing. "He's not going to do anything."

Brigid shrugs. "Make sure he doesn't, and we're fine."

"I don't decide what he does."

"Yeah, you do." A tinkling laugh lightens Brigid's words. "If you want to. Just like me and Victoria do with PJ and Chris."

I try not to shut my eyes, because if I do, I will be there again, with Chris taking me by my hair and PJ taking me by the shoulders while, on the other side of the room, Victoria and Brigid shove Lock's slack body to make sure he's out.

I don't want to look at the photo again, but I do.

If it was just me, I could let it go. I could turn my back and leave Brigid with any lies she wants to tell.

But it's not just me.

It's a boy who will be stripped and left raw again if anyone sees this picture.

"You can't do this to him," I say, my voice small enough that Brigid has to come perfume-range close again to hear me. "You can hate me all you want, but you can't do this to him."

"Hate you?" Brigid blinks. "Why do you think we hate you?"

Her confusion is so genuine I don't know what to do with it.

"You are *way* too sensitive about all this," Brigid says. "Nobody hates you. Which you'd know if you'd taken two seconds to think about it."

I grasp each individual word. But they're not coming together.

"What?" I ask.

Brigid huffs out a breath. "Do you think we'd even bother with anyone who wasn't worth it?"

"What?" I repeat.

"It was a compliment," she says. "You're good at classes, you're Jess's friend, you're completely whatever about being into girls, and you're even sort of pretty sometimes."

Even sort of pretty.

There is so much wrong with what Brigid just said, but my brain catches on those words.

Even sort of pretty.

A reminder that my brown body is something to be excused, not celebrated.

"If you hadn't been so uptight about it," Brigid says, "we could have been friends. We wanted to be your friend."

My ribs feel brittle as glass, like if I breathe wrong, they might all crack at once.

Brigid and Victoria and PJ and Chris didn't even consider that they might be hurting me.

They meant it all as an invitation.

It was an overture to me becoming one of them, the

pretty-enough queer brown girl they'd fold into their group, some novel addition.

They thought they were bestowing some kind of honor.

"But you had to get all dramatic about it," Brigid said.

My disbelief catches in my throat, a snagged breath.

Dramatic.

Me fighting, resisting, was *dramatic.*

They probably expected me to giggle, to say a half-hearted *No* and then to smile and say *Okay, fine, I guess* so they could cheer me on.

They counted on any girl—especially a pretty-enough queer brown one—doing whatever they asked in exchange for their favor. Bearing anything, enduring anything, excusing anything.

They wrote their assumptions into the curves and colors of my body.

"And Lock?" I ask, keeping my voice low. But my teeth are so gritted it sounds like I'm spitting the words at her. "When he was crying in his sleep, you're gonna call that dramatic too?"

"Oh, lighten up, okay?" Brigid blows out a long, exasperated breath. "Your new boyfriend, he was kind of a Bible thumper if you hadn't heard."

Bible thumper. I keep catching on single words or phrases Brigid says. I don't want to, but they get their teeth in me. *Bible thumper.* It's not like I think Lock would care—I doubt he would, he's used to jabs about him being from the middle of nowhere—but because it brings into sharper focus what I already know: That anyone who wants to decide what to do with their own body, instead of letting Victoria and her friends decide for them, deserves an insult.

"He probably would have died a virgin if we hadn't loosened him up," Brigid says. "So you're welcome."

You're welcome. The words cut into me, but it takes me a second to notice the pain, like a knife slipping out of my hand.

"I tried telling them you'd be uptight about it," Brigid says. "But Vic really likes giving people chances. She's just a really beautiful soul like that."

I almost choke on the air in my throat. Is she really talking about the girl who can't give a compliment without fine print? *He's cute even with the acne. She has a pretty face even though she's a little fat.*

Except that Brigid is saying all this dead serious. Her mascaraed eyes blink with complete earnestness.

"Anyone else would've counted themselves lucky, you know." Brigid cringes like she's about to tell me I have my skirt tucked into my underwear. "You're kind of ungrateful. Maybe that's why you don't have any friends anymore. We tried to be your friends, and we all saw how that went."

Two things floating around my brain collide. This conversation, and one I had with Victoria. Lost causes. I'm a lost cause, because I wasn't the willing, flattered participant they expected me to be. I'm a lost cause, because this was their idea of extending their friendship.

I feel it, instantly, Brigid passing to me the burden of how that night escalated. If I had laughed, even nervously, and then given in, they could have always pointed to that. *You had a good time, you were laughing.* Even if that laugh had been uncomfortable, apprehensive, an anxious reaction, they could have turned it into what they wanted. But my resistance is an indictment.

It's a kind of condemnation they're not used to. I fought back in a way they found inexplicable.

I fought back, so they went in harder.

I fought back, and it set something off in them.

I fought back, and it turned their idea of a party game into a fight.

I fought back, and it started a shared chant in their heads, a rallying cheer to urge each other on. *Keep going, keep going, keep going. Make her do it.*

By fighting back, I put a crack in how their world worked. I took the gleam off the honors they bestowed.

And they still hate me for it.

PJ and Chris almost forgot about it, the way rich boys forget about everything. But seeing me with Lock must have lit the flare again.

"I think you probably have some work to do on yourself," Brigid says, just before turning back to the flow of hallway traffic. "So maybe think about that."

Freezing, Burning

It's not like it was completely untrue, that we were in two different rooms. To him, we were. Lock, under whatever they put in his drink, was in a place as dark as the ocean at night. And I was in a room bleached with white everything.

I had to imagine us in different rooms, because every time I remember what happened to him, my body feels as soft and fragile as pan dulce. I told myself there was a wall between us, because I couldn't live with what I saw, what I was in the same room for and could not stop. I couldn't carry all of it. I had to bury it in a corner of my heart dark enough that I could forget it. I had to bury the part of me that knew this boy was destroyed not just in the same moment I was but the same place. I had to bury the part of me that knew, or else there was no him, and there was no me, there was only the unfathomable force of that moment, and that room.

So this is how I've lived with it, imagining us in two different rooms, with Lock as far away from me as the dark took him.

But with that Polaroid, Brigid has shoved us back in the same space. She has ripped away the lie that lets me survive.

I don't register when Victoria comes near me after last period. I assume it's because the hallway is crowded, and she's just taking the easiest path.

A second too late, I remember that Victoria doesn't move out of the way for people. People move out of the way for her.

If she's coming near me, it's because she wants to.

I understand this at the same time she hitches the cup she's holding, and splashes ice water onto my shirt.

I gasp, my breath in sharp and stinging.

Victoria keeps walking. Her perfectly tinted and highlighted hair bounces behind her.

The cold hits me. It gets deep enough into me that I'm there again, in that room, on that night.

Victoria—the Victoria who exists in this moment, in this hallway—is walking away. But the cold still has a hard grip on me. Brigid and PJ and Chris are nowhere I can see, but somehow I am pulled back through those months, and PJ's hands are on my arms, nails digging into my skin.

I am in that room again, and they are throwing ice on me because I will not do what they want.

If I had been made of ice then, if I had been strong and flinty like La Reina de Las Nieves, I could have resisted. I could have stayed still, lips pressed together, even if they threw a whole winter's worth of snow on me.

But I wasn't, so I didn't.

The stream of my classmates parts just enough to show me a familiar boy on the other side of the hall, the boy who was on that bed months ago.

He is watching me now, with something between worry and comprehension.

It's going to happen again, right here, in the hall at school.

PJ or Chris is going to drug him, and Victoria and Brigid are going to unzip his jeans, and they are going to look around for the first girl to enter that room so that PJ and Chris can do with her what Victoria and Brigid are doing with Lock. And that girl will be me, coming to check on a boy I thought needed to sleep off one drink too many.

Everyone will just watch, backs to the lockers, and let it happen, because that's what people do. They watch and they let things happen.

When I clench my lips shut, they will throw ice water on me again, like they did that night, and I will gasp again, and my mouth will relent open.

Except they've already thrown ice water on me.

I am already gasping and shivering. I am freezing, while the memory of their fire-crackling laughs and the snap of the Polaroid is burning me.

I go for the closest doors. I cross the parking lot. Then the street.

By the time I get close to the creek bed, I'm already pinning my next breath on seeing the orange cups of the poppies, the coastal sagebrush and grasses, all the things my primas and I brushed our fingers over as children and that Jess taught me the names of.

But when I get there, I stop short. There's none of the color or soft movement I know. The poppies have gone silver. The green wands of the sagebrush look like crushed crystal. The bright green leaves and pink flowers of the mapacho plants have turned to blades of mirrored glass. Pieces of mirror have replaced the burgundy leaves of castor plants. Their clusters of coral buds and yellow flowers look carved from silver water. The little pools, muddy from their clay beds, look like age-spotted mirrors.

There's too much of the world turning to mirrored glass. I can't get it all. I can't shove it all into my closet. There's too much of it.

"Ciela."

The sound of my name, in his voice, makes my rib cage feel brittle as fallen branches.

I shrink into the Ciela I was the first time my primas and I played in this creek bed. Small, and hopeful that if I stayed still, no one would see me. My breath hitches to a stop in the hope that Lock won't see me.

"Ciela." He takes another step toward me, slowly. I can hear it in the soft give of the wild grasses. I tense with wondering if the sound will turn to the crunching of broken mirror.

The willow flycatchers are taking off from the trees, fleeing the harsh glint off the glass. The pocket mice are skittering up the creek bed, stirring the grasses. The checkerspot butterflies are flitting away.

A pair of wings goes past him, taking his eyes off me. He's been watching me so closely, and he now startles a little, like he's just noticing the flowers that look blown from mercury glass, the leaves like tiny mirrored knives.

He blinks at how the sun gilds the sharp edges, how they cast rainbows on the branches that are still branches, how the bigger pieces reflect back broken reflections of us both.

Lock's shoulders settle. "Oh," he says with a breath out.

It's not shock or revulsion. It's pure understanding. Like maybe the shard of mirrored glass in his heart recognizes the mirrored glass around us.

I cross my arms, like that will make me feel less bared to him. It's such a useless reflex that I laugh. How it sounds is the first thing that makes me realize how close I am to crying. I'm not enough in my body to feel the prickle along my eyelashes, the sting of the salt, the tightness in my throat.

He doesn't look at me like he's figured out something is my fault. He looks at me not like I'm something frightening, but like I hold something wondrous in my glass-scarred heart. He looks at me like he can already see it, like I don't need to break myself open to show him the jagged, glittering world inside me.

"Ciela." He says my name like it's perfect and sharp, something to be careful with on his tongue.

A branch trembles above him. Knives of mirrored glass shiver, throwing back the light. I catch the warning in how they move, and that threat is the only thing that makes me do what I do next: I touch Lock without asking him.

I grab him and pull him out of the way just as the cluster of mirrored blades fall. They streak down past us, and stab into the ground.

"I'm sorry," I say, an apology for touching him without asking. "I'm sorry."

"It's okay," he says. I wouldn't believe him if I didn't feel him untensing, holding on to me.

We're touching more than we did when he kept me from hitting his dashboard. We're even touching more than when he kissed me. We stand there, breathing hard, like we're both startled to realize we can be this close and still be safe.

The Wind Takes Them All

I have to tell him.

I have to tell him I was in that room, that I know exactly how it happened because I was there for all of it. And that he would know exactly what happened to me if he'd been conscious to see it.

It was all of them, PJ and Chris and Victoria and Brigid, doing what they did to us in front of each other, like some kind of performance. But why wouldn't they show it off? Why wouldn't they all want to laugh together at both of us?

Lock needs to know. I decide this as we're getting into his truck.

I decide this as he takes off his uniform sweater and polo shirt and hands them to me, without a word, because my shirt is soaked enough to show my bra, and I'm still shivering.

This boy, whose jeans were unbuttoned and unzipped without his consent, is willing to strip down to his undershirt in front of me without flinching. I have to tell him. He needs to know what I know.

"So where am I taking you?" he asks.

"Lock," I gasp out before he can start the ignition.

That stops him.

"I have to tell you something," I say.

He waits.

"I was at that party," I say.

"I know," he says. "You brought me to the hospital."

"It's not just that." My voice thins out.

I have to tell him.

"I put you in that bedroom," I choke out.

He goes still for a second, and then shakes his head. "What?"

"I thought you were drunk." My throat is going dry as I say the words. "I didn't know they'd put something in your drink. I thought you just needed to sleep it off, so I took you upstairs and I stuck you in one of the empty rooms, and then I left you there to go find my purse and find you water or something and then when I came back—" My voice cuts out. My throat feels dry as the outer bark of a tree. "I'm sorry," I say, too wrung out to cry. "I'm so sorry I put you in that room. I'm so sorry."

He gives me the oddest look, something between considering and shock.

He hates me.

I deserve it. I deserve it so much I'm not even afraid of it anymore.

"Why didn't you tell me?" he asks.

"Because I didn't know how to look at you and tell you this was my fault."

His expression shifts, not quite changing, but deepening. "You really think this is your fault?"

The smell of the snow tree still hangs in the truck cab, and in this moment, it's thickening on my tongue so much I can't say anything back.

"Listen," Lock says. "You tried to help me. What they did with it, it's not your fault." He swallows, hard enough that I can see the notch of his manzana de Adán. He shifts in the driver's seat so he faces me. "It's not on you."

The old vinyl crackles under him, and I try not to flinch at the thought of the Polaroid.

"You brought me back to life, Ciela," he says. "I don't know if you get that. And it's not even . . . what we did . . . what we've been . . ."

As he stammers, his eyes drift to the empty space between us.

No. He can't do this. He can't think I have done anything good for him.

"It's just knowing you. Knowing you get it." He looks up. "It makes me feel like, I don't know, like there's life after all this."

A familiar nausea comes back to my stomach. My body feels brittle as the sugar top of a concha.

"Lock," I say. "There's something else you need to know."

He looks down again. "Don't say it."

My stomach drops suddenly enough that for a second I can't feel the nausea. "What?"

"Don't tell me."

"Why?"

This time he looks straight at me. "Because I know what you're gonna say, and I don't want to know."

"Lock." My voice turns his name into a weak sound. "I know who did it, and I know how it happened."

"So do I," he says.

I stare at him.

"I may not know specifically," he says, "but I can narrow it down by who thinks it's funny. I can guess by who was laughing hardest when I found the condoms on my windshield.

Why would I want to know more than that? Having to walk by her every day? Knowing who thought it'd be funny to do that when I was too passed out to say no? Who thought it'd be hilarious to leave lipstick on me?"

The mirror shard in my heart turns.

He thinks the four of them know because they told each other.

He has no clue how many people were in that room.

"Knowing which guy probably had the idea?" Lock says. "How would that help me?" He's trying to keep his eyes on me. I can tell he's fighting for it. "I know enough." The sound of crying comes up through his voice, and it makes me notice the sheen on his eyes. "Whose"—his flinches, shakes his head— "mouth was on me, I don't want to know that. I know enough."

That tiny piece of mirror cuts into every corner of my heart. There is so much more he doesn't know than whose mouth was on him.

"And you know what else I know?" Lock says. "I'm not a donor's son. I'm a scholarship kid." He tosses his head toward the parking lot, where his truck sticks out among the polished chrome and silver. "My word doesn't stand a chance against theirs."

My heart falls. It's the same reason I not only didn't want to tell anyone, but knew there was no point.

"Look," he says. "I know I'm a white guy. I'm not going to pretend I know what you've been through, and I'm not going to pretend I know what it's like to be you. But I think you know exactly what I'm talking about."

"I do." My throat clenches. "But don't you at least want to know—"

He cuts me off. "Has knowing helped you?"

"Lock."

He looks up, watching me through the pieces of his hair that are falling in his eyes.

"Has it?" he asks.

For a second, there's no sound inside the truck but our breathing.

He looks so unguarded that I feel like I've walked in on him naked, and I want to tell him to cover himself, to seal himself up.

"If you tell me it has," he says, "if you tell me that knowing helped you, I will listen." He looks at me without wavering. "Did it?"

I shudder, trying to shake off the feeling of Chris's hands in my hair.

Every argument I have for telling Lock turns to a thousand crepe myrtle petals in my hands. The wind takes them all.

"No," I say.

"At all?"

"No." My voice barely breaks a whisper.

"Why not?" he asks.

I owe him the truth.

"Because I have to live with it." I hardly manage enough sound to make the words.

He gives me a sad smile. "There you go."

Don't do this. My own brain is shouting at me, at Lock. *Don't do this, don't do this, don't do this.*

Don't make me not tell you everything I know. Don't make me be the only one who knows it. I can't know it all by myself anymore.

"Lock," I say.

"Ciela," he says, and it's half plea, half warning. "I need

you to respect this." He tosses his head to get his hair out of his face. The light catches on his eyes. They glint, wet. "I do not want to know."

There's so much I know that he doesn't. But he is asking me to close the door on all of it. If he can barely live with what happened to him, I can't put on him what I know or what happened to me in the same room.

When he speaks again, each word lands with its own weight: "Let me say no."

That stops me.

There's no arguing with it. Any words I have left die in my throat.

I don't get to tell him just because I don't want to carry it around by myself anymore. I don't get to take that choice away from him.

He didn't get to say no to them that night.

And he is saying no right now, to me, to everything I want to tell him. The least I can do is honor it.

His eyes drift toward the clock on the dashboard.

"Eff," he says.

"'Eff'?" I didn't think I could laugh right now, but his censoring is so out of character, it catches me off guard. I can't help it.

"I have a four-year-old sister," Lock says. "When I'm about to go home, I switch into older brother mode. That involves 'eff' and 'dang,' and on a real bad day 'forking.'"

"Okay. So what's wrong?"

"I'm supposed to make dinner and I don't even know what I'm making."

"I thought you didn't cook."

"I do cook. I cook what I absolutely cannot screw up. If it

comes out of a box with very clear instructions, I cook, and I'm not half bad. I also make the best Kraft Singles quesadilla you've ever had."

"You are causing me psychic pain."

"Then you just add ketchup . . ."

"Now you're *trying* to annoy me."

"I know," he says. "I'm sorry. It's just too easy."

We're both almost laughing, shaking out of the almost crying.

He brushes his hair out of his eyes, and my laugh goes cold in my throat.

The way he moves shows me a rip in his sleeve, and a thread of silver that lights up for a half second before vanishing.

The little mirrored knives got him on their way down. I couldn't even get him out of their path in time. A tiny piece of mirror got into his arm, and if I don't want it to be another one that ends up deep inside him, I have to get it out.

I track back over the last thing he said, and the small flash of an idea is as bright as that thread of silver.

Glass, Cutting Light

I lead him through the mercado, in the same path I've taken with my mother since I was three. We pick out chiles from the jewel-red ristras. I ask about the nietos of the woman who grows the squash blossoms. I hear my horoscope from the man cutting queso fresco off a wheel, the crumbling edges like seed pearls.

Everyone stares at Lock, not suspiciously, more in confusion, as though he is a pale horse who has wandered through the doors.

Las viejas give me serene, closed-lip smiles, and I know this will be reported to my mother.

Lock's apartment building is the same as a half dozen others within a few miles of school. Stucco. A trickling concrete fountain in the center of the courtyard. Paint colors meant to look vaguely Spanish. And the same off-white walls and almost-pink, almost-beige carpet that must be required in Southern California, because we have it in our house too.

The frames on the walls are half photos, half art that's mostly Violet's—arcs of pink and purple finger paint, sprays of glitter—but a couple look like Lock's—watercolor trees on craft paper old enough that it's yellowing. In the kitchen, worn cookbooks lean alongside newer ones. In the living room sits what looks like a giant version of the Tupperwares my mother puts food in, filled with the bright colors of what I'm guessing are Violet's toys.

I set down the grocery bag. "You said you already had onions?"

Lock opens the cupboard and cuts a white onion from a hanging row. It takes me a minute to realize what's holding them.

"Are those . . ."

"Cheap tights," Lock says. "It keeps them from sprouting when we buy them in bulk."

They're not tights, they're nylons, but I don't correct him. My mother has expressed to me that such finer points are beyond most boys. Such finer points are probably beyond most of my classmates, gender notwithstanding. The only reason I know is because my abuela demanded my primas and I wear sheer stockings whenever we went to her church. It was both for modesty, and because my grandmother wanted us to learn early that gringos decided what "nude" meant in everything from makeup to high heels, and that it almost never matched us.

Lock carefully peels the paper shell off the onion.

I brush my fingers over his sleeve, sucking air in through my teeth like I'm just now noticing the tear, the scratch on his arm. "We should get this cleaned up."

"That?" He lifts his sleeve, inspecting the rip in the fabric more than the cut on his upper arm. "I can sew that up in two seconds."

"Of course you can sew," I say.

"What's that supposed to mean?"

"It's a compliment. Most guys at school wouldn't go anywhere near a needle and thread." I pretend not to sound too interested or concerned when I ask, "Where do you keep your rubbing alcohol?"

"Rubbing alcohol?" he asks. "For this?"

"You crochet, you sew, don't give into machismo now."

"It's a scratch."

"You're bleeding."

"Was bleeding." He looks at his arm. "I missed the bleeding entirely."

"Okay, compromise. Once we get all this on the stove, you let me clean that."

"If you can even find it by then, go ahead."

I unpack the grocery bag.

"You really didn't have to do this," he says.

"I want to," I say. "You're not nearly as much of a lost cause in the kitchen as you think."

He checks the clock and I realize he's gauging how much time we have.

"Do your parents know that I'm"—I'm saying the question as I think it, and now I wish I hadn't started—"you know, like you?"

"Like me?" he asks. "What do you mean?"

That you made a friend at school who's hurt in the same way you are.

"You know what I mean," I say.

"One of our school's illustrious scholarship students?" He gives me a look that makes me sure he's being deliberately dense.

"Lock."

"A tree thief?"

"Lock."

The laugh goes out of him, like a sheen dulling, and then he's serious. "I would never tell them that. It's not mine to tell. I probably wouldn't have even told my parents about me if I didn't have to. You know how awful that conversation is."

I take out a bag of corn. "No, I don't."

He looks at me. "You haven't told your parents?"

I fiddle with the strands of silk on the corn. "I'm pretty sure part of them looks at me and sees me at age five. I'm afraid if I tell them what someone did to me, that I'm broken like that, that's going to be the first time they've ever thought of me as a woman." I don't realize it until I say it.

He whistles softly, like he's acknowledging the weight of what I just admitted.

"Yeah," I say slowly.

"You're not broken." Lock takes out a cutting board. "You know that, right?"

"Lock," I say, a disbelieving laugh pushing up from under my voice. I think of how I layer sweatshirts over everything even when it's too warm for them. I think of Chris holding me by the roots of my hair while PJ cheers him on. I think of how I can't wear red lipstick anymore because it makes me think of Brigid and Victoria leaving Lock with his jeans unzipped.

I think of the mirror shards burrowing into both our hearts.

"Yes, I am," I say. "Aren't you?"

As soon as I ask it, I hate that I've asked it.

He gives a pained laugh. "Fair enough."

"No," I say. "I'm sorry. I shouldn't assume anything about you."

His jaw goes hard, not like he's mad, more like he's tensing. "It's not that."

"Then what is it?"

"It's just"—he starts cleaning the corn in a quick, efficient way that makes me know that this, at least, he's done before—"if I hadn't let myself get drugged, I could have stopped it."

"You've got to stop thinking that way."

"Do I?" He rips away the leaves covering the yellow ear. "Somewhere, I made a mistake. I set my drink down. I didn't watch it. I did something."

Somewhere, I made a mistake.

I try not to map the words against what I've been living with for months.

"Would you say that to me?" I ask. "Or anyone else like me? That I let it happen to me?"

He rips away a lock of corn silk. "I'm a guy."

He says it without bluster or entitlement.

He says it with shame so deep it catches in my chest.

"This happens to guys," I say. "You know that. You were in a room with them every time you went to group."

"Yeah, well." He starts prepping the next elote. "That was the first I ever heard of it. Before I went to group, I kind of thought I was the only one."

I try to slip back into the space I found with the secret forest, the space of this-never-happened.

But the proof that it happened is this boy in front of me. He has enough of a sense of humor about the things that hurt to make balloons with condoms and to crochet mushroom penises. But underneath that brittle, casual layer is a misguided chivalry, a sense that because I am a girl, I am someone who survived, but because he is a boy, he is someone who was weak and careless. Every way he declares me strong seems to come with a reverse-image judgment of himself.

As we stand in his family's kitchen, I want to fold all this into what we're making and turn it into something else. I want it to fall under the crisp scent of cilantro and sweet corn, the bite of tomatillo and chiles, the warmth of calabaza and black beans. I want to give unyielding faith to my mother's assertion that mole and squash blossoms can soften anything. That the deep garnet of ancho and guajillo chiles can put enough spice in your blood that you can face the world.

"Okay." He rolls up his sleeve. "Don't say I'm not a man of my word."

He shows me his arm, the narrow cut that held a wisp of silver. I look for it as I splash rubbing alcohol onto a cotton ball, blot it down his upper arm, hope for a tinsel-thin line of silver to come off on the white.

"I'm okay," he says. "Really." But he doesn't know what the smallest shard of mirror can do, that it left me cold enough to lose my bisabuela's magic, that it made him reckless enough to risk his place at Astin.

There's no silver, not that I can find in his arm, not on the cotton ball, not on my fingertips as I cover over the cut. My heart tenses with the hope that I brushed it out, and not that his blood has already taken it in.

"Are you?" he asks.

"Am I what?" I ask.

"Are you okay?"

In the last few months, I've gotten this question from my mother, my tía, the nurse at the hospital, strangers who bump into me at the mercado, las viejas at church who cluck their tongues when I show up on Sunday without makeup. And each time, I've lied. Each time, I've bitten back the answer I want to scream into the sky.

But now, I don't scream it.

Now, when I finally say it, I'm laughing.

"No," I say. I'm laughing over how true it is. I'm laughing in wonder at how I managed to lie, every single time, until now. "Absolutely not."

I wait for him to stare, for his eyes to widen with wondering how the hell I could laugh about this.

Instead, he laughs with me, shaking his head as he says, "Me neither."

"Why are we laughing?" I ask.

"I have no idea," he says. "It's not funny."

"It's really not," I say.

But we're still laughing, like we know we have to. Like we know there's no way to live with it except to laugh every time you remember how.

I spear calabaza onto forks.

"Moment of truth." I hand him one.

"This can't be good," he says. "You let me near something that doesn't involve a packet of powdered mix."

I blow on my fork. "You did fine with the pan dulce."

"This is different," he says. "You've taken the food out of its natural habitat and brought it into the land of grilled cheese sandwiches."

"I'll have you know it takes a lot of skill to make a perfect grilled cheese sandwich. Now quit stalling."

We try the chile-spiced cazuela. The fine grit of the corn dissolves on our tongues.

"I refuse to believe I had any part in making this," Lock says. "It's too good."

"You did. I was right here. I saw you."

The taste of las especias brightens everything.

It starts with the string of lights on the apartment balcony, the plugged-in timer flicking them on just as it gets dark.

Then it's the water beads on the dish-drying pad, glinting like drops of glass.

Then the way the scent of pápalo clings to Lock's hair and shoulders, the green smell like epazote.

You love him, sings the warmth of the spices.

He loves you, chimes the sweetness held within the bite of the chiles.

You love him, whisper las flores de calabaza and the delicate gold of their petals.

I'm still for a minute, caught in the fact that, for once, spices are talking not just to me but about me. It's more than my bisabuela's gift coming back. It's her magic blooming through my blood, putting deeper roots into me.

The front door opens.

I jump.

Lock doesn't.

"Something smells good," a man's voice says.

"All her," Lock calls toward the front door. "I just cleaned corn and cut stuff up."

Violet runs at Lock's legs.

"Hey." Lock laughs and ruffles her hair. "You have fun at Grandma and Grandpa's?"

"Grandma taught me how to cut snowflakes out of paper."

She unfurls two that have gone limp from her enthusiastic grip, but are pretty enough to cast patterns in the balcony lights.

I assume Violet won't remember me until she greets me with "Rainbow sprinkles," as though it's my name.

It's far from the worst nickname I've ever gotten, so I'm not arguing.

"These"—Lock studies the snowflakes—"are fantastic. I say we put them in your window. You'll get snowflake shadows on your wall."

Violet looks at him in wonder and then bolts down the hall.

"She's a future decorator. He knows how to speak her language." A woman I assume is Lock's mother appears in the living room. Blond, not natural, I can tell that much, but she picked a good shade. Skinny. Long, pale eyelashes. Smoking lines around her mouth, faint enough that she probably quit a while ago. Her jeans taper down to sneakers like the ones my aunt wears at the pastelería.

"Lock," she says. "Aren't you gonna introduce your friend?"

"This is Ciela." He nods at my school uniform. "You'll never guess how we know each other."

A man in a polo shirt—it has the logo of a country club where Lock told me he works—extends his hand. "Nate." He has salt-and-pepper red hair that explains Violet's strawberry blond. "Nice to meet you."

"Wait," Lock's mother cuts in. Her face lights up in a way that alarms me. "Are you the vagina-puppet girl?" She says *vagina* at half volume, presumably so Violet won't hear.

"Oh dear God," Lock says, shutting his eyes like he's actually praying, "please strike me down where I stand."

"*That*'s how you've been describing me?" I ask him.

"My fault." His mother raises her hand. "I'm bad at remembering names." His mother studies me. "She's pretty."

"She's standing right there, Mom." Lock dips his head. "And so am I until I can figure out how to tunnel under the concrete."

Lock's mother throws her purse down on the sofa. "You're staying for dinner."

I hesitate over everything I know, and everything Lock's family may or may not know. That I'm not just the vagina-puppet girl, but the girl who brought Lock to the hospital that night. That I'm not just the girl who brought him to the hospital, but who left him there alone.

Sometimes, I carry my secrets around, and I barely feel them. Sometimes, I can hold them, like the secret forest taking all of Lock's forgotten trees. Other times, I feel nothing but how that night broke me into pieces, like glass cutting light into different colors. How it made me a girl whose heart is silvered with ice and glass. How it made me a liar. How it made me both more afraid and more reckless.

"That was a statement, not an offer," Nate says.

Lock nods at me. "You'll get used to it."

Bloom

I promise the next time you come over," Lock says, pulling in front of my house, "they'll know your actual name."

"Don't bother," I say. "Rainbow Sprinkles is growing on me."

I wave at him from the door. He's like Jess, watching to make sure I get in okay.

I go upstairs and flop down on my bed, wanting to sift out the good parts of today from the bad.

Except that, for a second, I forget that my bed is a wind chime I sleep on. The wooden slats rattle as soon as I throw my weight down.

I shift, and it gets worse. Something about the sound of my own bed giving me its commentary makes me try to retaliate. I throw my weight around, as though I can tire it out.

That is how exhausted my brain is. I am getting into a fight with an assemble-yourself bed.

The doorbell rings.

I groan, get up, giving the mattress a shove to let it know this is not over, we are not done. Not even if our neighbors across the street are here to make accusations about their missing tree.

But when I open the door, it's Lock standing there.

"Hi," he says. "Sorry. I wanted to make sure you're okay."

"Yeah." I brush my hair out of my face and wonder if I still look bed-fight flushed. "Fine. Perfect. Why?"

He gives me a steady look. An *Okay, I'll wait until you give me a real answer* look. If he and Jess become friends, with this look and her equivalent, I'm never going to be able to lie to them about anything.

I slump against the front hallway wall and rub my hands over my face. "I don't know what's wrong with my bed."

"Can I take a look at it?" he asks.

"What?"

"Only if you're okay with me going in your room," he says. "If you're not, I get it."

I wave toward the stairs. "Be my guest."

I follow him up.

"Wait." I touch his shoulder.

He does that startle response I know I've done with him. It's fast, almost imperceptible, each of us settling into recognizing who's touching us within a quarter of a second. I get over being jumpy faster with him than I do with anyone else.

But I still cringe that I made that mistake. Sometimes getting comfortable around someone means you forget how to be careful with them.

"Sorry," I say.

He looks back, recovering, unbothered. I know that feeling, the way, if you feel safe enough around someone, you shrug off the momentary fear that comes from being touched.

I've learned this with Lock. I probably would have learned it with Jess by now if I had told her earlier.

"How did you even hear me?" I ask. "Weren't you driving away?"

"I was checking the street for other removal notices."

"You are so weird."

He finishes taking the stairs. "Are we talking cute weird or creepy weird?"

"Ten percent cute weird, zero percent creepy weird, ninety percent weird weird."

"I'll take it." He pauses in front of my door. I don't have to tell him which one. The string of chili pepper lights probably do it for him.

He laughs.

"What?" I ask, kicking my laundry basket in front of the closet. I doubt Lock would go opening doors without asking, but the obstacle still makes me feel better.

"IKEA, right?" he asks.

"Yeah," I say, standing in front of the closet so I'm a second obstacle. "How'd you know?"

"I have this bed," he says. "I got it at a garage sale when we moved here, so it didn't have the manual, and I didn't know the name of the bed to find it, so there was some trial and error involved." He pauses before actually going into my room. "Mind if I give it a shot?"

"Have at it," I say.

He hauls the mattress off the bed. "I made this same mistake." He grabs the linked set of wooden slats that stand in for the box spring.

He flips it over, and it rattles loudly enough to echo in the hall, then settles.

"Tell me you're joking," I say.

"Afraid not."

"That cannot be what I was missing this whole time."

"There's a curve on these things that's almost invisible unless you know to look for it." He pulls the mattress back into place. "Try it now."

"Uh-uh," I say. "You play the bed-xylophone."

This might be the first true eye roll I've ever seen from him.

"I'm serious," I say. "Get on it. You'll see what I mean."

"You want me to get on your bed?" he asks, wary.

"Yes. I want you to see I'm right."

"Fine." He sits down.

And the bed sounds like a bed. Like a mattress without a xylophone under it.

"How did you do that?" I sit next to him, flopping down hard enough to jostle the wooden slats.

The bed stays quiet, nothing but the mattress squishing under me.

Right there.

That fast.

The air turns.

I see a wisp of something glimmering through the air, like a tiny, faint Milky Way.

It tells me what the pápalo and las flores de calabaza were trying to tell me in Lock's kitchen.

Pan de yema. Anís. Vanilla. The sunrise light of the eggs from my cousins' chickens, the ones who fluff their feathers in the damp grass. I've been trying to figure it out since the first time Lock walked into the pastelería, and now I know.

For this minute, I am not a girl with a heart cut by glass. I am a girl whose heart is as wild and bright as the colors swirling in chamoyada.

"What is it?" Lock asks.

I can tell he's about to sit up.

I kiss him hard enough to pin him down, and when I'm half on top of him, he takes my waist in his hands.

He kisses me back hard enough that the air between our mouths grows a taste, sweet and spiced as dulce de leche.

I am all the way on top of him, my hands at the hem of his shirt when I stop and ask, "Do you want this?"

He brushes a piece of hair out of my face. "Yes." Even though the word is quiet, it sounds certain. "Do you?"

The way he looks at me, at my body, at the brown of my skin, the way he holds an arm across the small of my back, makes me feel as beautiful as a field of sparkling ice, a whole sky of northern lights.

"Yes," I say, and when I say it I am not afraid, of him or myself. This close to him, my heart is not scar tissue around a sliver of glass. It's a living thing, hot and luminous.

The shimmer in the air goes through our bodies, and it feels like a wind throwing us into this. I push up his shirt, kiss the center line of his chest, keeping my mouth far from the waistband of his jeans. I unzip my uniform skirt and put his hands on the pleats. I have wanted it off since it took the splash of the ice water.

His fingers brush my hip, the rose hip tattooed just below the curve of my underwear.

"Is this a press-on?" he asks

"Lick it and find out," I say.

His throat hitches in a way that tells me I've caught him off guard.

But he recovers so fast I don't realize he's actually doing it until I feel his tongue slick over my hip.

My laugh is loud and surprised. It's a sound that belongs so completely to La Bruja de los Pasteles that for a minute I wonder who it came from.

"I can't believe you just did that," I say, the words soft under my trailing-off laugh.

"Huh." He studies the tattoo, now glossed from his mouth. "What do you know? It is real." He traces the round of the escaramujo's heart. "What is it?"

"It's a rose hip," I say.

"A rose hip on your hip?" he asks. "Cute."

I reach down and swat at the same place on him.

"No, I mean it." Now he traces the wispy sprouts coming off the top of the coral bulb. "How'd you talk your parents into it?"

"How do you know they know?"

He gives me a look like he's gotten an idea about the psychic powers of Mexican mothers.

"It was my fifteenth birthday present," I say. "Without a quinceañera, they got off easy. And we have a friend with a lot of tattoos who knew where to send us." That was one of the conditions, Dr. Emmott's approval.

Lock traces the two leaves, and the shiver of his touch travels up my side. "Why'd you get it?"

The fact that he's willing to slow down enough to take an interest in these two square inches of me makes me want this boy even more.

"I wanted to remember my body is mine," I say.

An unintentional assumption hangs between us, that this is something I had written on my body after what happened to me, a kind of reclaiming. Instead of what it is, an emblem I had before it happened, one that sometimes feels anachronistic on my own skin.

I kiss him before I give myself the chance to correct him. I want to know my body can feel something other than what it has felt for months. I want to handle this boy differently than Victoria and Brigid did. I want to be gentle and careful.

And I want the chance to decide.

"Are you sure?" he whispers, his mouth alongside my ear.

I put my mouth next to his ear, and tell him the truest thing I have ever told him:

"When I'm with you, none of it happened."

I put my hands over the backs of his, pressing them into me. He takes the cue of my touch, and carefully moves his hands over me, learning the softness of my thighs and my ass.

"Lock," I say.

He stops.

"Do you happen to have several dozen condoms?" I ask.

"You know, I think I might. Let me just check my locker. Or my backpack. Or my windshield."

He winds an arm around my waist and turns me over onto my back. I laugh in a high, squealing, careless way that sounds like La Bruja de los Pasteles might have laughed the first time she took a boy to bed.

Right now, he is not the boy I could not save. Right now, he is the boy whose breath shudders in the curve of my ear as I unzip his jeans. He is the boy who grasps the band of my underwear as gently as if it were fragile.

We trade whispers so softly I can't tell who's saying what.

If you want me to stop, just say so.

Stay with me.

You're here.

You're safe.

It's not then. It's right now.

He touches me, and there is enough of me. There is enough of me as my lips brush his neck, whispering things I hope he'll feel on his skin even if he can't hear them. There is enough alive in me to grow a hundred rosebushes, a thousand blooms, a million leaves, from the single rose hip printed onto my skin.

I take this boy inside me, wanting him there, knowing he wants to be there.

I take him inside me, because this, now, is what we decide.

La Concha de Sirena

I wake up in my pajamas instead of naked.

I have the vague, half-asleep memory of Lock pulling them out from under my pillow and putting them on me. And of him getting dressed, pressing his mouth to my temple, slipping out the front door.

He made sure I didn't wake up naked, in that disoriented place of wondering where I am and where my clothes are. He doesn't know that on the worst night of my life, my clothes stayed on the whole time. But the fact that he made the effort, even thought of it, makes my heart feel soft as the sloe-thorn fruit in the secret forest.

I rub the sleep out of the corners of my eyes, squint into the pale sun coming in.

A flash of color breaks the familiar tone of my comforter and makes me sit up.

It's a whirl of yarn in green, turquoise, purple, magenta, topped with a sticky note from the pad on my desk. Written in all-caps block letters:

I MEANT TO GIVE YOU THIS LAST NIGHT BUT FORGOT. CONSIDER IT MY ARTISTIC INTERPRETATION OF A MERMAID VAGINA.

I remember almost making him choke on the concha. A laugh, hoarse with sleep, breaks out of me.

I pull the scarf to my face, smelling the smell I've come to think of as Lock. The metal of crochet needles. The rust of his truck. The branches and blossoms of stolen trees.

The window shows a day just cool enough to wear a scarf, the leaves trembling like they're thinking about turning and falling.

I wind the scarf around my neck and open my eye shadow palettes. I brush these colors onto my eyes, fuchsia and purple, peacock blue and green. It's a little messy, the colors making more of a patchwork than a gradient. But these colors are enough to steady me as I walk to the creek bed, so I can pull every petal and leaf of mirrored glass I can off the trees.

I brace for the sight of it spreading. Maybe the grasses will have turned by now too. Maybe the little pools of water will be mirrors as thick and stark as frozen ponds.

But when I get there, I stare into a world of familiar color. The poppies are orange as candle flames. The sagebrush is green and alive. The mapacho flowers have blushed back to pink. Dragonflies skim the little pools of water, and the soft clay beds sparkle with silt.

It's all coming back to life.

I run all the way to the pastelería, so full of my bisabuela's magic I feel it sparking at my fingertips. I'm getting everything back. Today I'll guess what pan dulce will make a customer notice the particular blue of the sky. I'll know who needs to eat a pajarito to regain their faith that the swallows will all come back one season. I'll guess that a pink-striped cuerno will make a girl less nervous about being a flower girl.

Maybe my tía was right about this season, and it's finally shifting. Maybe the swallows are coming, stirring the clouds with their wings. Maybe the Santa Anas are waiting at the edges of the sky.

Jess feels it too. As soon as I walk in the kitchen door, she breaks into a smile.

I know she went on another date last night; I packed a box of gallinas and a special batch of galletas in Liz's favorite shade of blue. And I know from how Jess looks at me that she knows something happened with me and Lock last night.

She and I say, at the exact same time, "Tell me everything."

Shadow Horses

With Lock's hands on my body, my world is not glass. It's stolen trees and roses as red as if they'd caught fire. It's water the sun turns to raw gold, and ground coming back to life with the heat of the stars.

But when we fall asleep in my bed, my body forgets he's there. The warmth of him can't reach me.

When I feel the nightmares coming close, I take my abuela's dolls out from under my pillow and hold their small felted bodies in my palms.

Tonight, I dream of crows, their wings turning to blades of dark glass the minute I look at them. I dream of gold palaces that pale to silver as soon as I touch their walls. I dream of horses that become nothing but shadows.

I dream of La Reina de las Nieves. But not of the Snow Queen herself. I dream of the little robber girl, the only brown-skinned girl in the story. She is careless and cruel. She keeps Gerda in her bed with an arm across her neck. In my nightmares, I hear her laughing at how easily she frightens birds and reindeer, and her laughter frightens me more, not less, when I hear how much it sounds like mine. Then the laugh is in my own throat, and I am la pequeña ladrona, the robber girl holding an unwilling body in my bed.

Then I dream of Lock, of the sounds he made in that room as he tried to surface from sleep. I dream of his low, pained noises, trying to object, to say no.

But now, those sounds come with heat in my hands. They come with the sting of cutting my fingers.

I shrug out of sleep enough to open my eyes. I squint into the lamp we left on when we fell asleep. The sight of blood shocks me the rest of the way awake. It stains my fingers. It glosses the silver of two mirror shards that fill my palms instead of the little felted dolls.

Blood, threads of it, cross Lock's pale back.

I scramble out of bed. I get the jagged glass into my closet and wash the blood from my trembling fingers.

My breath hitches as the last of the red swirls down the sink and vanishes.

Then I start checking Lock's back. I look for any sign of silver.

Lock stirs. "What are you doing?" he asks, voice heavy with sleep.

"I hurt you," I say.

He turns toward me, sits up. "What?"

"I hurt you," I say.

He must feel the sting on his back, because he looks over his shoulder. "You just scratched me. That's all."

"I hurt you," I say again.

"Ciela." He looks at me with the unbearable compassion of thinking I clawed him in my sleep, held on to him so hard I dug my nails into him. "It's really okay."

"I hurt you," I say.

He doesn't know that I could have just put more of the

mirror's silver into him. He doesn't understand that if I'd gone deeper into my nightmares, I could have mistaken him for some looming shadow, and driven a sharp edge into him.

I'm trying to tell him something, and he's not hearing me.

"I hurt you," I say again.

"Ciela." He looks at me hard enough to stop me from saying it again. "It doesn't hurt."

It Happened

We frost cooled cakes before my tía comes in. I trim a mocha cake with bulbs of pale frosting and pipe fluffy roses and heart-shaped green leaves onto the top. Jess spreads citrus pastels over lemon cake, blurring the colors like paint.

I write *Happy Anniversary* in neat letters, and set down sugar pearls to accent each one.

I write *Happy Birthday* and *Feliz Cumple* on piñata cakes and the pink-frosted tops of cortadillos.

We run through the stack of order forms until one stops me.

It's from the Delahooke family, something to celebrate water polo or early college admissions. It calls for *Congratulations* across the top.

A cake for one of the boys who held me still, while their girlfriends took pictures.

"Why don't you let me take that one?" Jess slips the order form from my hand.

I nod, my fingers shaking as I let it go.

The only reason PJ and Chris and Victoria and Brigid will leave us alone is because they know we'll stay quiet. And the only reason we'll stay quiet is because we know we can't win against their last names.

They hold those photos like something sharp against our skin. Lock probably feels it as he walks the halls every day, even if he doesn't know why.

"I don't blame you," Jess says, her voice soft in the air between us.

"What?"

She eyes the cake I'm working on.

I have not written *Here Comes the Bride* in bubbly script.

I have written, in bubbly script, *I hate them all*.

The smell of sugar catches in my throat.

I smooth over the words with an icing spatula. I blend them with the blue frosting underneath, hoping it will look like a deliberate gradient of color.

I mix a darker aqua and I try again, shoving away the memory of Victoria and Brigid prodding and laughing at Lock while their boyfriends grabbed me like I had a body that wouldn't bruise.

My gloved hands grip the metal counter. "Why am I still so angry?"

"Did you really think you wouldn't be?" Jess asks.

I thought that if I got back my bisabuela's gift, the rage wouldn't keep blazing through my body. I thought if I found the thread of magic I lost, I could pretend it was the only thing that got ripped out of me that night.

"You know what we're going to do?" Jess leans against the counter. "We're going to make some cakes, and we're going to frost them with everything we wish we could say."

"What do you mean?" I ask.

"Anything," Jess says. "Everything."

"And then what do we do with them?"

"We bring them to the retirement home near the church," Jess says. "Your tía wanted us to do that anyway." She picks up an order form, half-filled out, one of my aunt's vague requests. *Just bring them a few rounds and a sheet cake for the birthday party.* She gives us a similar one every month, to take to the place where my abuela had so many friends.

"You want to bring cupcakes with our angry rants to a senior citizen community?" I ask.

"Yeah, why not?"

"Because I don't want them to see that?"

"Sprinkles, querida," Jess says. "Sprinkles cover a multitude of sins."

So we do it.

We bake, cool, and frost the simple rounds and sheet cakes, and we write it all.

We start with names of every abstinence-only pamphlet Lock and I had to fold. *You Can Never Get It Back. Our Greatest Treasure. The Gift You Can Only Give Once.*

"I'm still skeptical," I say.

"Watch and learn." Jess pats sprinkles onto the tops and sides.

They stick to the frosting. All our secrets disappear.

"Voilà," she says.

So we write everything else.

The fact that Jess's mother thinks being queer must be a phase because Jess is *such a pretty girl.*

How brown girls always get more skirt-length checks at school.

And everything I've wanted to say about that night.

I call them what they are. Violadores. Predators.

Four names, and what they did.

You can make me quiet but you can't make me forget.

Jess frosts a cake with the words *F**k Everything*, the asterisks neat as little flowers. Then she packs it into a box.

"You forgot to sprinkle that one," I say.

"No, I didn't."

"You're serious?"

"Oh, come on, I know at least ten little old ladies who will think it's hilarious."

She's not wrong.

I fill another frosting bag, and my hands get ahead of me.

Across the top of the sheet cake, in deep pink frosting, I write *It happened.* Over and over, in uneven writing.

Jess watches, not stopping me, not saying anything, just giving the words the space I haven't given them until right now.

It happened.

It happened.

It happened.

Violadores

My locker slams shut so hard it almost takes off my hand.

"What is wrong with you?" Victoria is standing next to my locker door.

I look around. Everyone else has already scattered.

The scarf looped around my neck and the smell of rage frosting in my hair is a barrier between me and my fear. I am nothing but bored with Victoria. She can burn herself out hating me for all I care. She can gloat about the fact that I'm not going to tell anyone anything.

I sigh pointedly. "What do you want?"

"I want to know what the hell you thought you were doing with PJ's cake."

"What are you talking about?"

"What you wrote," she says.

What I wrote.

I track back over the piñata cakes. The bachelorette cake. The silver-dusted sheet cake for Flora Merriman's husband retiring.

My stomach drops.

The cakes for the senior community.

Somewhere in all that frosting and all those sprinkles, in

raging with Jess, I boxed up the wrong cake. I hid the wrong words with sprinkles and left one of my secrets uncovered. Eight to twelve residents at the retirement home must have gotten pieces of cake that said *Congratulations, PJ*, and the Delahookes got one that said . . . what?

"His whole family almost saw it," Victoria says.

But I don't hear her.

I'm too deep into wondering what they found when they opened the bakery box.

Maybe it was *Tu hijo y sus amigos son todos violadores*
Your son and his friends are all predators

Or the worst one, the one that sounds most like a threat. *You can make me quiet but you can't make me forget.*

"You know what, I don't even care." Victoria waves a hand between us. "I hope your boyfriend likes the pictures."

My stomach buckles. "What?" The word barely wisps out of me.

Victoria says over her shoulder, "Tell him he can keep them."

Take the Heart, Leave the Rest

By the time I find Lock, he's already behind the school. He sits in his truck, head down. For a second I wonder if he's crying. But he isn't trembling or putting his hands to his face.

He's looking down.

I know, even without seeing them, that his car is probably littered with Polaroids.

I see the asphalt passing under my steps. I see my hand reaching for the door of his truck, finding it unlocked. But I climb into the passenger side before I've really made the decision to.

"Lock," I say.

His eyes stay on the squares patchworking his lap. He is staring at them, breathing hard.

"Tell me it's not true." Lock's voice is as low as an engine idling.

The pictures show my hands on his thighs, my hair brushing his jeans, getting caught in the teeth of his unzipped fly.

It's mostly hair, but you can tell it's me.

They don't show PJ and Chris's hands, or Brigid's laugh, or the orders Victoria is giving.

"Lock," I say.

"Tell me"—his voice rises before he pulls it back down—"tell me I have this wrong."

In the one he's looking at right now, my brown hands stand out against Lock's jeans. It looks like I'm holding him down.

That's not how it happened.

But the Polaroid's borders don't tell that. The shot is too close up. It shows my hands on his thighs, but doesn't show that they landed there when PJ and Chris threw me onto him. It shows my hair splayed, but doesn't show how much I'm trying to hide under it.

This picture tells as small a piece of this story as it shows of Lock's body.

"It wasn't my choice," I say, the words rasping out of me.

"You think I don't know that?" he asks. "I know you. I know this wasn't your choice. I know you would never do this."

I stare at him. I've gotten so used to the idea that the truth would be unbelievable, that it's startling to be believed.

"But you know what *was* your choice?" he asks. "Not to tell me. You didn't tell me you were in that room. You didn't tell me what happened to you at the same time. And you sure as hell didn't tell me that they made me part of it, and that they made you part of what happened to me. You didn't think I deserved to know any of that?"

He's yelling, and it's only when I open my mouth that I realize I'm ready to yell back.

"You told me you didn't want to know," I say.

"Don't," he says, fast and hard. "Just don't."

I breathe so I won't yell again. Whatever rage he has for me, I deserve. It's mine to take and absorb.

Yes, he told me not to tell him. But he didn't know what he

was saying no to. I heard what I wanted to hear. I heard a way for us both to pretend it never happened. That's what's gotten us here, how hard I've been chasing the tiny sliver of light in my brain that says if I pretend it never happened, then it never did. I chose that for both of us, and he didn't even know.

"This whole time." He shakes his head at the steering wheel. "This whole time, I thought"—he breaks off, flinching, like he's rerouting himself—"but I was never going to be anything to you except the guy who was in your mouth when you didn't want me there."

The sense of my own body falls out from under me. This is my whole body dissolving at once.

Lock has said what I haven't let myself think for months, and he said it out loud.

"I've been inside you twice," he says, his voice hard. It sounds angry, but under that film of rage is hurt I wish I couldn't see. "And you didn't bother to tell me about the first time."

I want to tell him he's wrong. I want to tell him that the night we were in my bed, every time he touched me, kissed me, set a hand on my hip, my body was mine again.

But any try at saying that dies on my tongue. It feels so small compared to what he now knows.

"Why did you even want me inside you again?" he asks, and this time I can barely hear him. "Why would you even do that to yourself?"

Before I can explain that it wasn't something I *did* to myself, that it was something I wanted, he keeps going.

"And why would you let me do that without telling me the truth?" he asks. "Did you even think about how wrong that might make me feel?"

My tongue can't get a grip on a full sentence.

Lock stares out the windshield, even though there's nothing to look at but the creek bed across from the school. "You want to know why I started taking the trees?"

I think of how the secret forest would look right now, all wrong in daylight, washed out, the branches bleached to their bones.

"Because that's how I felt after that night," Lock says. "Like I got ripped out by the roots."

His voice thins out as he talks.

I know that feeling of being torn out of what you were, and what you were being torn out of you. I know that PJ's and Chris's and Victoria's and Brigid's hands tore the hearts out of us and left the rest behind.

But I also know that until Lock reminded me there were parts of my body that were still alive, I felt like the heartwood of me was too sick to grow anything.

"You can hate me for this," I say, touching the edge of a picture that's not touching him. "You should."

His laugh is hard and grim. "You really don't get it. I don't hate you. It wasn't your fault." He shakes his head, not looking at me. "I don't blame you for anything that happened that night. I blame you for letting me make decisions without information you've had this whole time. The day I met you, I needed to know who you were, and that I am a thing they used against you."

"You're not a thing."

"I am a thing." He's almost yelling again, but it's made thin and brittle by how hard he's trying not to cry. "I am a bad thing that happened to you, and you are a bad thing that happened to me. That's all we'll ever be to each other. And you didn't tell me. You let me think I was alone in that room."

The words chill me so completely they're a sheet of ice between us.

For months, I have thought of him as someone I've wronged, as someone my unwilling body wronged.

I never thought that if he knew, he might have guilt that mirrored mine.

"How did you do this?" he asks. "How did you look at me every day and every day make the decision not to tell me?"

I say his name again, knowing how useless it is even before the last of the sound leaves my tongue.

"Don't," he says. "Every time I look at you I hate myself for what they did to you with me, and I hate you for deciding I didn't need to know."

I have had months to understand being both the one acted upon and the one used to act on someone else.

He's just had the minutes since he saw the Polaroids.

Before that, he thought it must have been Brigid's or Victoria's lipstick on him, some girl who'd had a choice, who'd decided for herself, and who'd been laughing at him ever since.

He never had a reason to think that lipstick belonged to a girl who fought to keep her mouth off him.

Now that he knows, it's crushing him, the weight of being both hurt and used to hurt someone else. I recognize it with a sickening familiarity. I understand the depth of the mistake I've made.

I should have told him the day I tried to take the blame with Whitcomb.

Or when I introduced him to Jarritos Tamarindo.

Or before he kissed me over pan dulce.

Or before he fixed my bed and I pulled him onto it.

I should have told him before someone else did.

He deserved to know before his fingers brushed mine, before he set his lips against mine, before he said yes to me unzipping his jeans.

By keeping this from him, I have made so many choices for him.

"Get out," he says, still looking forward.

"Lock."

"Please." He doesn't yell it. He just stares out the windshield and says it. "Forget my name. Forget you know me. That's exactly what I'm going to do with you. That's the only way I can exist around you. The only way for both of us to survive each other is to forget we ever met."

He doesn't even sound angry anymore. That's how I know he means it. Even when he's gone over his rage so hard that it's thinned out and threadbare, he will still mean this. Even if he forgives me, he'll mean this. And for all I know, he's right. Maybe I need to forget him as much as he needs to forget me.

So I get out.

I don't look back until I'm across the street.

He's bent forward, eyes shut tight, forehead to his palms, the backs of his hands against the steering wheel. He's shaking in a way that's either him sobbing or him about to scream into his forearms, and I look away before I know for sure which one.

The Snow Queen

Every moment of our life, it goes with us. It lives forever.

My father's words won't leave me alone as I stand at the railing above the tide pools, sea spray misting my face.

Every moment of our life, it goes with us.

Those words echoed in my head when I tried to help Lock.

It's not like it was shitty advice. But good advice is only good if you can manage not to screw things up worse while taking it.

I lean on the railing, watching the tide foam over the rocks.

It's still my abuela's voice I think of when I think of La Reina de las Nieves. It's her accent gilding the words about a boy named Kai, and a girl named Gerda, and a queen in her palace of ice, her snowflakes so big they seem like wings.

But there are parts that are mine now, ones folded into my nightmares like color into sugar paste. The shadow horses, stealing the thoughts of hunters. The little robber girl, the only brown character in the whole thing unless you count the reindeer.

The red shoes Gerda throws into the river to find Kai.

A wave splashes onto the rocks, tossing spray like a handful of coins.

I would throw anything I own into the water if it would make that night not have happened, if it would give Lock back to himself. My favorite pair of shoes, strawberry-colored ballet flats that aren't quite red but might be close enough. The snow tree Lock saved for me. The pieces of me that are as heavy and slack as wooden doll parts.

When Gerda offers her red shoes to the river, the waves seem to nod, so she does it, she throws them into the water. But because the river hasn't actually taken Kai, it throws the red shoes back. It doesn't accept them because it can't hold up its side of the bargain. It can't give her what she's asking.

Sometimes, you throw everything you can at something. Gerda losing the boy she loves. A boy getting broken down in the same night I became a girl with a glass-scarred heart. And sometimes, everything you give it washes back up, like the river, the ocean, the whole world, is telling you it doesn't have what you want.

In Mrs. Vanderlinden's class, Lock neither looks at me nor makes a point of not looking at me. I try to shrink out of his peripheral vision, but I can't help looking for the glint of every mirror shard I've left in him.

Brigid's lowered voice sounds far away, but pulls me back.

"Vic says any time after eight," she says to the girl next to her. "Nobody else is coming until probably ten."

Lock flinches, and I know he heard.

To PJ and Chris and Brigid and Victoria, it's just another party.

But to Lock and to me, an Astin party will always mean one thing. One night.

Lock pulls out his crocheting and works the needle across gray yarn.

Brigid raises her hand. "Mrs. Vanderlinden?"

Mrs. Vanderlinden nods at her.

Brigid twists toward Lock. "I can't concentrate with him doing that."

Lock freezes, looking caught.

Rage rises in me.

"Don't do this," I say under my breath, to Brigid, to Mrs. Vanderlinden.

Brigid glances at me, then at Lock again. "It's very distracting."

My rage spins and grows hotter.

Of course now she finds it distracting.

Lock has been doing this since the first day. And he's almost completely behind her. How would she ever see him unless she turned back?

Mrs. Vanderlinden looks pained.

Lock is as still and stricken as I always imagined the boy in the story, Kai, unmoving on a lake so frozen that it has become a mirror. He looks as uncomprehending as Kai, staring at the puzzle the Snow Queen lays out in front of him, trying to make something of the broken pieces in his hands.

Brigid sits up straight in her chair. "It says in the student handbook that no behavior contrary to learning will be tolerated in the classroom environment."

Mrs. Vanderlinden's face goes beyond pained to bereaved. She's on Lock's side, I can tell, but the handbook isn't.

"It's okay," Lock says, folding the yarn over. "I'll put it away."

Mrs. Vanderlinden's gratitude settles over the room, as heavy as her sadness.

She starts talking about cuneiform, stone calendars, the specifics of recording history into rock.

It takes Lock about a minute and a half to start biting his fingers.

He stares at the floor, and I wonder if he even knows he's doing it, digging his teeth into his own fingerprints.

A new understanding kicks at my stomach.

The crocheting.

The paper clips in Principal Whitcomb's office.

How Lock kept stirring the cazuela even when it could have sat on the stove.

It was all to avoid this, this nervous habit of biting his own hands.

I cannot leave him like this, stranded on that frozen pond, surrounded by impossible puzzles, handling jagged pieces of broken glass so cold they might as well be ice. If hating me will pull him back, I want it.

Because I am too much of a coward to face him at school, I go to the stolen forest later, to look for him.

I don't find him.

All I find is a forest of silver glass.

The blue spears of the chaste tree. The delicate violet of the wild lilac. The lichen-velveted branches of apple and redbud branches. The snowflake stars of the crepe myrtle.

They've all turned to slices of mirror.

The branches are still wood, in their soft shades of brown. But everything on them is silver glass. The pink cups of the lily magnolias and blue sloe-thorn fruits look crafted from the gleaming gray of the ocean at dawn. Mirrored leaves hang from the branches, heavy and sharp as knives. Blossoms look as hard as clusters of salt crystals.

There, standing in front of this field of hard, glinting branches, I know.

I know that Lock will never know me as La Bruja de los Pasteles, a girl who speaks the language of sugar shells and salt, and hierbas folded into dough.

He will always see me as what I am, a girl with a heart that is nothing but scar tissue around glass.

I am not a girl who kisses the frozen boy, who warms him with her tears, who melts the mirror shard from his eye.

I am the girl who kisses him to make him forget, who makes him numb to the cold so he does not realize it is killing him.

I am not Gerda, the flush of her cheeks and the warmth of her hands thawing the boy she loves.

I am a girl with a heart made of frost, a Snow Queen dragging this boy into her palace of ice.

I am a girl who loves things, and then watches them turn hard and still as broken glass.

Carry the Heart

I expect it to slip from my grasp, fast as water. But the gift my bisabuela left me, the one I've lost and gotten back, stays. I know which customers need to be kinder to their own hearts, and will be reminded by eating the soft pastry of almohadas, and who will feel leavened by the crunch of orejas. I know who will feel brighter and more alive after tasting the pineapple and guava in rieles.

But it's as hollow as the ground left behind when roots are torn out. I got back the thing that mattered most to me, that made me who I was, that gave me a name. But I did it at the price of Lock's whole world.

When something this big shifts everything, your heart never stays where it was. It can't. It has to move with everything that's cracking open around it, or it gets lost.

Lock didn't know it, but he had it right the first time, that day outside my house. The only way to survive me is to forget I exist.

I ring up cocoles de anís, and the smell of the aniseed cuts into me.

A woman in a tailored suit comes in, bringing the smell of good perfume with her. I tense.

If my shifts at the pastelería have taught me anything, it's how often rich people want things for free. Families with six-car garages will demand special orders at no additional cost. Businessmen wanting two-hundred conchas for a Cinco de Mayo party will take offense if we ask for a credit card up front. The same women who call the subdivision of three-bedroom constructions the Beverlys live in *the little houses* will insist on a refund if they think the frosting is *daisy* yellow instead of the requested *mustard*.

"Can you recommend something?" the woman asks, taking off her sunglasses.

Her expression is hard, cheekbones emphasized by both makeup and the muscles in her face.

But the pursing of her lips and the flinty look in her eyes show me the hollow in her. Not all of it. The don my bisabuela gave me never lets me know all of someone. But it's a hollow I notice because I have a similar one in me.

I don't know what happened to her or how long she's been carrying it. But the shape is so familiar it makes my glass-scarred heart ache with recognition.

My hands reach for the pan dulce we shape like las golondrinas.

She pays without a word, before I can try to give it to her for nothing.

I want to know if it works, if a little part of her will stitch back together when she tastes the dough of the pajarito.

But she is already gone. And I am left with how little I can do.

Grenadine

An hour after closing, I am supposed to be frosting a cake that a group of bridesmaids will pick up tomorrow afternoon. *Here Comes the Bride*, for a bachelorette party. Piped flowers. Sugar pearls.

But the cake is as blank as the inside of the bakery box. I have not written *Happy Bachelorette*. I haven't written anything on the cake.

I have written—on the metal counters, on the oven door, on the side of the mixers—one word.

One word, in red frosting, a hundred times.

No.

No.

No.

The one word I can't say.

I kneel on the floor, frosting bag still in my trembling hands, my palms stained with the dye that looks as bright and red and fake as strawberry syrup.

I both hate him, Lock Thomas, and I owe him more than I can ever pay back. I hate him for something that is not his fault, because he wasn't even conscious to say yes or no. I hate him for being both the boy that I violated, and the boy whose body was used to violate me, even though he was too far under to have a choice.

I hate him for how cleanly and sharply what happened to him mirrors what happened to me.

The first time I met Lock Thomas I thought he was drunk, and I put him in an empty bedroom to sleep it off. An empty bedroom in a house so big, I thought no one would bother him in the time it took me to find my purse and my keys and come back for him.

Now I slump against the refrigerator, sobbing into the empty kitchen, the rubber mats pressing their imprints into my knees and thighs. The red icing is bright and thick in a way that makes me think of the grenadine and the ribbon of sticky white in my stomach that night.

"Ciela?"

I startle, scrambling up as I look toward the back door.

For months, I have been holding myself together with silence and sugar water. But at the sound of my own name in my best friend's voice, my name as a question, I fold. I break apart, like pan dulce between her fingers.

The Iron at the Center of the Star

An hour and a half later, Jess and I have gotten all the red frosting cleaned up. My trembling hands clear it away, Jess checking that none of the dye is left behind. Now we're at my house, and I'm washing the frosting red off my skin.

I blot my arms dry and go toward my room.

I stop cold in the doorway.

Jess is reaching for my closet door.

"What are you doing?" I ask.

"Looking for your extra blanket. It's supposed to get cold tonight." She touches the knob.

"Stop," I say. I almost yell it. I need it to be hard enough to warn her away from that world of silver glass. If she opens that door, she might let more of it out into the world, or worse, into her.

She drops her hand away from the knob and stares at me.

I crawl onto my bed, ready to burrow under as soon as Jess walks out, which I'm pretty sure she's about to do.

But she sits on the edge of the bed.

"What happened?" she asks.

"I just had a moment," I say. "I'm fine." I try to add a laugh to it. "Really."

"I don't mean today and you know it."

"I told you already," I say.

Her inhale sharpens. "What really happened?"

"Why are you still asking me that?"

"Because someone has to."

I can't say this out loud. Not now. I need the first time I say this out loud to be some time other than right now.

"Look, if you don't want to tell me, you don't have to." Jess's words are so soft, I wonder if the whole story is printed onto my skin, like how my abuelo developed old film, the images appearing in solution.

"But if you do," Jess says, "I'm listening."

Her words snap something in me, an icicle breaking off. Everything in the world is reminding me what I did.

Lock, biting his fingerprints down to nothing.

The secret forest, turning to mirrored glass.

"I hurt him, okay?" I blurt out. "I hurt him."

I can hear how angry I sound, how angry I am, and I'm sure it's scaring Jess off.

But she just asks, "How?"

"I put him in a room where something bad happened to him."

I say it, and I am back in that upstairs guest room, the one that seemed impossibly white. White bedspread, white curtains, white-varnished dresser.

I am holding up a boy I think is drunk. He's not slurring but he's talking so quietly I can't understand him. I'm telling him, *You're lucky you're cute*, as I leave him on that white bed.

"But how is that your fault?" Jess asks. "How did you hurt him?"

Now I have found my keys. I am walking back into that room to check on him, maybe take him home or wherever he's staying. I startle in the doorway, because now it isn't just the boy on the bed, it's PJ and Chris, and Victoria and Brigid, standing around him like they're deciding what to do with him.

"I put him in that room," I say.

"But how does that mean *you* hurt him?" Jess asks.

I am still there, and it is still happening.

I stop in that doorway. Confusion flashes across PJ's and Brigid's faces, but a light comes on in Chris's and Victoria's eyes.

Graciela thought he was cute. (Victoria)

Uh, she's a lesbian, remember? She only likes girls. (PJ)

She likes everyone. (Victoria)

The memory of the words echo, trapping me deeper in that night.

She likes everyone. After months of them just assuming Jess and I are both lesbians, of them being too lazy to learn any other word for me, of me not minding sharing Jess's word but then hating it because of how it sounds on their tongues, *this* is the moment they throw it aside.

She likes everyone. The crudest, most reductive acknowledgment of who I am and how I love, at the worst possible time.

What do you want to bet she'll do it? (Chris)

No, she won't. (Brigid)

I bet she will. (Victoria)

Let's be open-minded here. (PJ, still stuck on the last part of the conversation. He tips a beer bottle toward Brigid and Victoria.)

Maybe she wants to do something with one of you.

Gross. (Victoria)

I take one step back toward the door.

Then I take another look at the boy, a blur of blue jeans and plaid flannel shirt on a white bed.

His breathing comes shallow and patchy, like he's fighting for it.

That by itself wouldn't have told me. But it slots together with other things I didn't notice at first. How he didn't smell like alcohol. How I'd seen him earlier at the party, flipping a plastic cup off the stack, pouring Dr Pepper, drinking it, nothing added. How he'd looked at me in a shy but sober way across the kitchen downstairs.

How unlikely it would be that he went from Dr Pepper–sober to completely trashed in half an hour.

I couldn't leave him here, drunk and alone in a stranger's house. Drunk and alone is bad enough, dangerous enough. This is worse.

This boy isn't drunk. He's been drugged.

The second I realize is the same second I notice the break of tan-pink in the blue of his jeans.

He's not all-the-way dressed anymore.

Victoria and Brigid have unzipped his pants. I can tell they're the ones who did it by how close they are to the bed, how expectantly they stand near it. They've pulled out his erection, one he either got in his sleep or that they prodded him into.

I can't leave him here on that bed, limbs splayed, hair in his face, fly open.

I cannot leave him like this, not with PJ and Chris and Victoria and Brigid looking like they want to tear pieces out of him.

She'll do it. Chris takes me by the wrist and leads me, stumbling, into the room.

I don't want to do anything, I say.

Come on, PJ says. *It's not even really sex. You'll still be a virgin.*

For a second of remembering, I almost wish Principal Whitcomb had been there to witness it, where all those pamphlets, all the abstinence-only lectures have gotten us. *It's not even really sex*. The inflated value of us being virgins, the offhanded dismissal of anything short of what will lose us *The Gift We Can Only Give Once*.

I trip further into the memory.

She's not a virgin, stupid, Victoria says. *She was with Jess, remember?*

Brigid gives an offended scoff. *He means a dick virgin, obviously.*

The boy on the bed doesn't stir. I can't even call his name to try to wake him up. I don't know it. I can't pull him back so he'll help himself, help me, help us both. Maybe both of us together could fight off the four of them, but on my own, I am nothing against the will of their hands.

I don't want to, I say, pulling against them.

Victoria shuts the door behind me.

I shake my head, because I do not want to remember the rest of this. Them shoving me toward the bed, laughing, encouraging me, telling me he's a prude and I'll be doing him a favor, really.

How the mood in the room turns when I resist.

Chris grabs me by my hair first. PJ's nails dig into my arms. They throw me forward so I lose my balance, and I catch myself with my hands in front of me.

My palms land on the thighs of the boy's jeans.

For a second that encourages them.

See, I told you she'd do it.

Don't let go of her, Victoria says.

PJ and Chris shove my face toward the boy's crotch, but I clench my teeth shut.

Come on, PJ says. *It's not gonna hurt. Just relax.*

They push me toward him, harder, enough that my cheek brushes his thigh. The teeth of his zipper catch pieces of my hair. But I keep my lips pressed together.

"It wasn't your fault." Jess's voice floats through the memory but doesn't break me out of it. "Whatever happened, it wasn't your fault."

I want to grab on to her voice, pull myself out of the endless white of that room and back to the bright color of my own bedroom, back to the safe brown of our bodies instead of the white of four bodies that are forcing me and one I cannot save.

But it happens.

Victoria says, *Enough of this shit. I'm bored.*

She throws a cup of ice water or ice something on me.

It soaks my shirt.

"Ciela?" Jess says.

The cold hits me hard enough to knock the breath out of me.

"Why do you think it was your fault?" Jess's voice cuts in.

I am still there, trying to keep my teeth clenched.

"How could it possibly be your fault?" Jess asks.

But a gasp, the shock of that cold, pries my lips apart.

They take that moment to shove me forward, and put my

mouth over him, and once they have me there, they can keep me there.

In the memory of that night, my lips part, and right now, my lips part, and I am screaming an answer to Jess's questions:

"I opened my mouth."

The words break out of me.

They rattle against the windows and the walls of my room. They echo into the hall and across the house. They bring the sound of breaking glass.

Once they are out of me, there is nothing holding me up. I am a star that doesn't have enough heat and metal at its core to keep from collapsing in on itself.

I give in, like I did that night.

I give in for the second it takes PJ and Chris to use my gasp, my open mouth.

I give in, staying still with this hard, unwilling thing choking me.

I give in, the salt of my tears dampening this boy's jeans.

Pinched, wavering noises come from the boy's throat. PJ and Chris roar their approval. *Hear that? He likes it.*

PJ and Chris hear what they want to hear. They think he's moaning, that they've orchestrated the best wet dream in the world. They don't hear what I am close enough and sober enough to hear, that the boy isn't groaning. He's whimpering.

He doesn't like it. Even in his sleep, he wants me off him as badly, as desperately, as I want him out of my mouth.

He's trying to come up from his dreams and fight, but whatever they've given him is holding his body down.

It's as heavy as their hands.

He whimpers again, and I gag when I realize he might be

whimpering because I'm gritting my teeth, digging them into him without meaning to. I try to leave my mouth slack so I won't hurt him.

I try to stay still until it's over.

But PJ and Chris move my head, pulling my hair back and forward, with Victoria and Brigid giving instruction.

She can't just lie there.

Help her.

She doesn't know what to do with a dick. Help her out.

I give in.

The boy's body gives in.

It trembles out that ribbon of white.

I clench my throat.

Aw, come on. This from PJ.

Yeah, you can't go that far and not finish the job. Chris.

Swallow it. Victoria.

Swallow it. Brigid.

Swallow. All of them.

I am counting the threads in Lock's jeans so I can forget, for one second, that part of him is in my mouth.

Swallow. All of them, a low cheer, like a chant at a night game that never quite gets synchronized.

PJ and Chris keep me there until my throat cramps and gives.

I give in.

I give in.

I swallow.

I swallow this ribbon of white I never wanted in my throat, and that this boy never wanted to give up.

I swallow this part of him that will always be inside me,

unwilling and unwanted, even after Chris and PJ take me off him.

I swallow.

I swallow.

I swallow.

That part of him is in me still. It clings to my stomach. It laces my blood. If I think about it, I can taste it in my own saliva, like salt and lemon pith.

I could have made the choice, an actual choice, to take him between my legs a thousand times. I could have held him, my arms across his back, my lips brushing his neck, as that part of him finished inside me. But it would never have changed this moment in that white room, of me giving up, giving in, swallowing.

I have something of Lock in me that I never wanted.

He has some of himself in me that he never wanted to give up.

I come back, to this room, my room, where there is no Chris or Victoria or PJ or Brigid, but only my best friend I have been lying to until this moment.

There is no heat in me, no iron core.

For months, I have wondered why Chris thought he could grab me by the wrist, why Victoria thought she could shut the door behind me.

But as I sob into my brown hands, my hands that remind me there are other colors in the world than white, my brain rakes over the possibility that PJ and Chris and Victoria and Brigid always saw my body—its color, its curves—as permission.

I was a brown girl who lived fearlessly in the softness of my own body, and who, at the worst moment, opened my mouth.

I opened my mouth, and I violated a boy who was too drugged to fight back.

Then I betrayed him months later, when I pretended my body was not a landscape he had visited before, against his will and against mine.

I never forgot any of this. But I lived in the lie, because it let me live.

To survive after that night, I had to put us in different rooms. And I had to decide that it wasn't him in my mouth, that it wasn't my mouth on him. That it wasn't our classmates forcing together an unconscious boy and an unwilling girl.

That it wasn't my lipstick, the color a faint stain on my mouth as I left him in the hospital.

That I didn't know exactly the shade left on his skin and the fly of his jeans.

This is why I couldn't say it. To Jess. To my tía or my mother. Not even to myself. Because what Chris and Victoria and PJ and Brigid did turned me not just into a girl who survived something, but a girl that a boy had to survive.

Jess sighs, so quietly it sounds like the trees brushing the windows. Tears tremble the air at the back of her throat.

She does not touch me.

She does not try to tell me again that wasn't my fault.

She simply does what she would have done for me if I had let her, months ago.

She sits with me, quiet, so that for as long as she's on the edge of my bed, I don't live with this alone.

As Heavy as the Sky

When I close my eyes, I see all the white in that room, or the silver of broken mirrors, or a secret forest stripped of its color and life.

But when I think of one thing, my brain goes quiet: Jess saying I found the magic I lost because I fought back.

For months, I have hated PJ and Chris. I have hated their hands gripping my hair and my arms. But how much I hate Victoria and Brigid has come on slower, so slowly I didn't even realize until the weight of it became something I couldn't hold up.

PJ and Chris were the ones with their hands on me. But Victoria and Brigid were the ones with the ice and the camera. The cold that made me gasp for breath, and the little squares that tell the story exactly the way they want.

I can't do anything now about the cold I could not stand, about the breath I had to take. But I can do something about those little film squares, hanging over us as heavy as the sky.

"Jess?" I say, my voice hoarse from not talking for the last hour.

"Yeah?" she asks, looking at me for the first time since I screamed those words, *I opened my mouth.*

This time, I say the words I haven't been able to say since that night:

"I need help."

Lock the Door

Jess parks on the street and gets out. "If you don't meet me back here in ten minutes, I'm organizing a rescue team."

I shut the passenger side door. "I'll do the same for you if you get stuck answering questions about the Laurel honors program."

Jess goes into the party first. Her unexpected appearance draws enough excited shrieks that it sounds like she's been across an ocean instead of at a liberal arts college up the freeway. I almost wish I were in the room to roll my eyes. Sure, everyone liked Jess when she was at Astin, but in the muted, noncommittal way people like the smart girl who shares her class notes or keeps the spreadsheets for any club she joins. Now that she's gone to college early, they act like they were her best friends the whole time.

I slip in behind Jess a minute later. My ponytail and jeans are a lot less conspicuous than her glitter headband, silver eyeliner, and faux leather jacket.

The smell and sound of almost all Astin parties hits me the minute I'm through the door. Soda. Vodka and any other kind of alcohol everyone swears has no smell. The flat smell of chips that get spilled everywhere more than eaten. The rise and fall of voices and music that's being argued over.

The details of the house catch me, like they're snagging on my jeans. The marble steps in the front hall. The vases Victoria moves so no one breaks them. A chandelier that throws shards of light on the high-pile carpeted stairs. Each familiar thing leaves me shivering under my sweatshirt.

But I get to the top of the stairs. I pass the room with all the white. I don't look, half-afraid that I'll see my silhouette and Lock's on the bed, surrounded by four laughing shadows.

I find Victoria's room.

It's a mess, but a mess that looks more like a disarrayed catalog than a bedroom—clothes with tags still on, new makeup in its boxes. I try not to step on the sweaters and skirts left on the floor.

Branches scratch the windows and the side of the house. That, even more than the room I had to walk past, makes my heart buckle. That oak has boughs and roots so sprawling that Lock and I could never dig it out ourselves. He'd love this tree, how it mirrors itself above and below ground. I doubt he ever saw it that night.

I check every drawer—desk, dresser, nightstand.

I find the stack of Polaroids at the back of a vanity drawer, under a mess of eyeshadow palettes, blush compacts, brushes rattling around.

The shots are close up, most of them, and as bad as the ones in Lock's truck. They show my hands on the thighs of his jeans. They show my mouth on him without showing the hands holding me there.

But there are few that hint at the edges, suggesting the rest of the story, how Victoria and Brigid passed the camera back and forth. One shows a splash of Victoria's hair, bright from being touched up every two weeks. Another, Brigid's ash-blond ponytail. The corners of their smiles. The baby blue of Brigid's nail polish and the sugar-cookie pale of her fingers. PJ's hands on my brown arms. Chris's varsity ring caught in the dark tangle of my hair.

These are the pictures they didn't give Lock, because they're the ones that are the most damning to them. And they're my last chance to fight back. They are the one thing that can stop the four of them from leaving condoms on Lock's car or throwing ice on me in the hall.

I hold my body tight as I leave Victoria's room and pass that room that will always be sweat and salt, cold and the dye of my lipstick. Even out of the corner of my vision, I know we're there, the parts of us that got left there and that we'll never quite get back.

I can't change what happened. But I can make sure it doesn't happen again tonight.

I take as deep a breath as if I were going underwater. I slip into that room, without turning on a light, and shut the door behind me.

The click of the latch throws me back into that night. It shoves me into the moment they all left, once they were done with Lock and me.

So much of this room is the same. The overly staged stacks of photography books, the new-smelling sheets, all the things that made it obvious it was a guest room. It's so much like that night that I can hear their voices.

On their way out, they laughed, Chris saying, *You could take him the rest of the way if you're feeling generous.*

Then the door shut.

At first, I didn't move. I held my breath, my cheek where they'd left it, on Lock's thigh. My throat was burning, my tears leaving damp trails on his jeans.

My breath trembles in my throat.

My fingers on the doorknob bring me back to now. Hearing my best friend downstairs brings me back to now.

My thumb clicks the round button in the center, locking the room from the inside. What happened then won't happen in this room tonight.

I slide open the window, push out the screen, and swing myself into the nearest branch of that great oak. The contours of its boughs lead me down, and I could swear the wind is letting out a breath.

The Heart Spills Out

I take two round cake halves from the bakery oven.

All of me has poured out, like the middle of a piñata cake. It happened a little at a time, to my tía, to Jess, to Lock. I want to bake something that does the same thing, spilling out its heart, but all at once.

Sometimes, the only way I can understand something is to turn it into sugar.

The kitchen smells like citrus and pine, like the blue mejorana my aunt kneads into my tío's favorite bread. Once the cake halves cool, I hollow them out, and the air turns sweet with anís and cinnamon.

I fill the piñata cake with every color candy we have. I frost the halves back together and coat it all in the sprinkles his sister loves and that Jess and I used to cover all our rage. When the knife slides in, it will come with the rattle of bright candy at the center.

This is how it was for me, says the vanilla lacing the batter.

This is what living with it was like, murmurs the cinnamon, warm and deep as the bark in his secret forest.

This is how fast I came apart, the colors in the center whisper.

Ever since my bisabuela's magic came flickering back, I thought it was because I was paying a debt I owed. I thought

I had to make things right with a boy whose body was violated with my body, who took the sting of mirrored glass that was my fault.

The thing I've missed this whole time is that I didn't lose that magic because of what I did to Lock, or even because my mouth was used against him. I lost it because, months ago, one night broke me open and my heart spilled out, like candy from the center of a piñata de estrella.

It's taken me months to understand this, but now it burns like live ash at the center of my heart.

I don't want Lock to go months without knowing this. I don't want him to wonder why his heart has broken open and is spilling out of him.

I close the cake into a pink bakery box.

I set it outside Lock's apartment door. I knock, but leave fast enough that by the time the door opens, I'm already gone.

The Girls in the Pretty Dresses

aving a beautiful time.
I would say wish you were here, but we really don't.
Love you, mija.

On the back of the postcard is a picture of green and pink and yellow balloons against a deep blue sky. I tuck it into the corner of my mirror, between the glass and the frame.

I find my yellow apron, the one I wear every year for La Noche de las Golondrinas. I've been selling trenza danesa alongside my tía every year since before she hired me to work the counter at the pastelería.

La Fiesta de las Golondrinas is the big showy celebration of the swallows every spring, but tonight holds all the lore of being quiet and a little bit secret. It's the night we search for mud nests in the hollows of cliffs, or under eaves and crossbeams. We watch the undersides of rusted-out railroad bridges, looking for the stirring of wings.

PJ and Chris and Victoria and Brigid and all the Polaroids in the world couldn't stop me. Especially now that all the Polaroids in the world that matter to me are in my closet, guarded by mirrored edges.

As I reach for my sweatshirt, my arm brushes tulle and age-softened lace.

The dress, the one that looks like antique moonlight, the one my mother bought me at the thrift shop. It hangs over the back of a chair, glittering at me.

When it catches the glow from the lamp, it looks like starlight waking up.

My mother wants me to believe I can be any kind of girl. Even the kind with a laugh so buoyant it sounds carbonated. Even the kind who wears pretty dresses to look for swallows at night. Even the kind my tía convinces to put pan dulce under their pillows, swearing it will make them dream of future loves.

I may not have my abuela's little dolls anymore, her brown-felted proof that I could be one of those girls.

But I have my own body.

I put the dress on, just to see how it looks.

I fluff the skirt around my legs.

My thighs are soft under the tulle, some of the filmy layers shredded with wear. But that only makes them softer, like I'm wearing a gown of spider silk.

My hands are slow at it, out of practice, but I find my way to coating my eyelids in gold, the tint of my skin turning it copper. I add pewter eyeliner that picks up the silver threads in the dress.

I twist my hair into a loose bun that will keep it off my shoulders and out of my face.

I slip on my pair of strawberry-red low-tops. Even if I had Gerda's perfect red shoes, they wouldn't hold up through a night of serving pan fino.

On the way out, I reach for the lamp, and catch myself in the mirror.

I am a girl with skin the same color as my mother's and my tía's, and eyes as dark as my father's. And with the rose-hip pink on my cheeks, I could almost be one of those girls who shows up tonight in a new dress. I could be one of the girls who believes if they eat half a novia or beso and put the other half under their pillows, they'll dream of their true loves.

Almost.

Before I click off the lamp, I grab the first red lipstick I find in my makeup drawer.

My hands shake as I take the cap off the gold tube. I haven't worn red lipstick since seeing mine on Lock. I will never forget how the color, my shade, looked on his raw skin.

But even with my fingers trembling, I can decide that red lipstick won't be another thing PJ and Chris and Victoria and Brigid take from me.

I put on a coat of it, blot, then another coat. And because I'll have my hands full, I slip the tube of lipstick between the cups of my bra, the short stretch of band and underwire holding it in place.

Seriously? Jess says every time she sees me do this. *You're gonna just draw it out of your bra, como una espada?*

What? I ask. *Then it's always in reach. Plus this way it's warmed up and it goes on easier.*

That's kind of brilliant. Disgusting, but brilliant.

I click off the lamp.

PJ and Chris may have had their hands on me that night, holding me where they wanted me. Victoria and Brigid may have sent that shock through me that made me gasp for breath.

But the brown of my body and the red of my lips, these things are still mine.

The Night Swallows

y the time I get to the old bridges, tourists and locals are crowding the western edge of the wilderness park. They watch for signs of the swallows fluttering out of their mud nests.

"Tan linda." My aunt takes my hands when she sees me. "For a minute, I thought you were one of them." She shrugs toward the tourists' daughters in mint-green tulle, sky-blue frills, honey-yellow lace. Dresses that look borrowed from attics or bought from the fancier vintage shops around here.

And two familiar figures. Jess, in a mauve tea-length that belonged to her tía abuela. She's laughing with Liz, who wears peach organza that makes her eyes so blue it's a little startling.

Right now, they're two girls caught up in each other enough to believe legends about night swallows and lucky hearts.

"Take your caffeine, ladies." Pilar hands us each paper cups of coffee. "We've got a crowd."

Jess gives Liz a temporary farewell, so close their eyelashes must touch.

I hand her an apron and eye her outfit. "I always knew you were a romantic."

"I admit nothing," Jess says.

My tía turns back to the bakery boxes in the trunk of her car.

The silver in her hair seems to glow when she lays out sweets for families and for girls in their hopeful dresses. She makes change for the tourists while I pick up the sugared dough with loose sheets of wax paper.

Our most popular pan dulce, no surprise, is the pajaritos we shape to look like swallows. On nights like tonight, we fold a little more sugar and lavender into the dough.

Whenever a customer hesitates, I whisper to my tía, and I am as much La Bruja de los Pasteles as I've ever been. Polvorones tricolor for a group of little kids. Peinetas for two sisters whose hearts have been broken within a month of each other. Pan nevado for a reluctant spirit. Batch-baked double pajaritos for a couple who's feeling timid in love, since the wings are touching.

It has always belonged more to my family than me, this pinch of sugared magic I lost. It's how I know to bring elotes, bread shaped like ears of corn, to a family welcoming a new baby. Las magdalenas de maíz to a woman finishing chemotherapy, because she needs something mild enough to keep down but with enough flavor to remind her she can still taste. Cuernitos de crema to a couple who found each other again forty years after meeting in high school.

Dr. Emmott and his husband come by.

"What do you recommend?" Dr. Emmott asks.

I hand them the pastry fans of abanicos, the tips coated in spiced chocolate.

"Eat these," I say, brazen and sure, "and you'll be in love forever."

"That's the best deal in town," Dr. Emmott says, making change with my tía.

His husband smiles as shyly, as if they were on a first date.

Pilar senses the shadows of our next customers first.

The three faces resolve in front of me.

Violet waves in the exaggerated way four-year-olds wave when they think you're worth acknowledging.

"Lock's not here," she says, as though I'd asked.

"She can see that, Vi," Nate says, giving me an apologetic look.

My aunt makes small talk about las golondrinas. "Have you heard about the night swallows?" she says, sweeping Violet into the story.

I study Lock's mother and stepfather like I would any other customers, considering whether they need polvorones or palmeras.

No. Roles de canela. The same, for both of them. I can tell from how they breathe in the cinnamon that I'm right.

I reach for a galleta de gragea, so covered in sprinkles you can barely see the sugar dough, and hand Violet the wax-paper-wrapped cookie.

"Your usual, ma'am," I say, trying to make my voice bright.

Pilar leans toward me. "¿Estás bien?" she asks, quiet enough that Lock's family won't hear.

"Yeah," I say, my voice tight. "Of course."

But the moon above me looks as hard and silver as a mirror. The stars are nothing but flecks of broken glass thrown across the dark velvet of the sky.

"Why don't you go get some air, mija?" Pilar asks.

"We're outside."

Pilar gives me a look.

She's giving me an out, and I know I need to take it. I need the minute. "I'm just gonna fix my lipstick."

"Please do," Jess says in between making change. "It's simply dreadful." She copies the fancy accent my tía uses for all things Astin.

"Horrid," Pilar says, chiming in with her rendition.

"Ghastly," my tía says, raising hers to new heights. "Who could even look at you?"

"You all are the worst." I take off my plastic gloves.

But they're still laughing as I leave, and so am I.

The wilderness park's closest bathrooms are enough of a walk that by the time I get there and back, the panicked fluttering in my chest will settle. It has to.

A hand catches my elbow.

I look down.

Not Jess's. Not my aunt's. Not Pilar's.

The hand is white, not brown.

It belongs to Lock's mother.

"Give him time," she says, her face soft, and sad. "Give you time too."

I want the absolution this woman is offering. I want to fall into it like sleep.

But then I remember she probably only knows that her son lived through something, and maybe that I lived through something, not that we lived through the same thing. Not that the same moment floods over us every night like a tide coming in, taking us under.

Like trying to remember the words in a forgotten language, my brain tries to land on what pan dulce I could give Lock to tell him all the things I never said.

With a puerquito, I would tell him I loved his mother's

stories about the stuffed pig he always carried with him as a little kid, the ears soft from the wear of his hands.

With a concha sugared as teal as the scarf he crocheted me, I would tell him that kissing him felt like proof that there was still some of my heart left, that one night didn't rip it all out of me.

With pan de muerto sprinkled in marigold petals, I would tell him that I believe the dead places in us can come back to life.

But sometimes the truth cannot be folded into dough, or laced into vanilla sugar, or sprinkled in like the color of nonpareils. Sometimes the truth is as heavy as glass.

Everything You
Think Is Yours

In the dark behind the bathrooms, I press my hands into my skirt, feeling the worn lace and tulle. They remind me I am not a hollowed-out version of La Bruja de los Pasteles. I am not a girl with broken glass for a heart. I am just another girl in a fluffy dress, ready to slip pan dulce under my pillow.

"What the hell did you do?" Brigid's voice scrapes past my ear.

I stare out toward the dark hills of the wilderness park, deep green and blue and almost purple in the night. I do not look at Brigid Marchand.

By giving Lock those Polaroids, PJ and Chris and Victoria and Brigid have already played their best hand. They can't hold it over me anymore.

"You were in her house?" Brigid asks. She sounds offended, but underneath the indignation, something rattles, like she didn't think girls like me would ever bite back.

"I have no idea what you're talking about," I say.

Her next words seem to die on her tongue.

Brigid Marchand wears jeans that cost more than I make at the bakery in a month. Girls like Brigid aren't breathlessly hopeful enough to do what the girls in pretty dresses do, asking my tía for the pan dulce that will make them dream of future amantes. Girls like Brigid consider those girls too starry-eyed, too pathetic, to even consider.

I look at this girl who has done anything Victoria tells her to. I want to ask her if it's worth it for what will pass to her once Victoria graduates.

Instead, I say, "I want you to listen to me very carefully." My voice is flat as the scrub fields. "I'm not saying I stole those pictures. But if I did, I would tell you that if you ever come near Lock or me again, I will make sure everyone sees the ones that show the most of you. Your mother. Your father. Your coach. Your college counselor. Father Byrne—he's supposed to write you a character recommendation, right?"

Her face tightens.

There may be enough of me in those pictures to break down everything I love. But there is enough of Brigid and her friends in those pictures to deny them so many things they think they're entitled to. And to anyone like PJ and Chris and Brigid and Victoria, that is the deepest insult you can give them, threatening what they think is owed them.

A new understanding twists her expression.

They hated me for resisting because it offended them. It never occurred to them I would, or could, bring their world down.

When a hand grabs my arm, my first thought is that it's Brigid's. She wants to dig her nails into my skin, pull my hair, whatever tantrum she thinks is going to make me crumple like the paper we wrap galletas in.

She can slap me. She can leave the pattern of her rose-gold bracelet on my cheek. I will lift my chin through whatever bruise or split lip she gives me, and she will know I mean everything I said.

But it's not her hand. She's still standing in front of me. Then comes another hand. And another one. They come out of the dark like the night is growing them.

It's only when the smell of aftershave hits me that I realize PJ and Chris are here, that I should have known they were here the whole time.

Little White Rooms

I throw an elbow into a rib cage. I'm not sure if it's Chris or PJ's.

Whoever it is swears, and then holds me harder.

I kick at the other one. It doesn't move him.

A hand grabs my side so hard the wind goes out of me, taking my scream.

I fight.

They win.

Just like months ago, they win.

For the minute of me resisting their hold, trying to twist out of their arms, I think they're going to drag me so far into the wilderness park that no one can hear me.

I try to scream again.

A hand clamps over my mouth.

I bite it.

Swearing again, but the hand stays.

Someone must have spotted a night swallow, because a wave of wondering cheers rises from the far crowd. It muffles whatever noise I can make.

They drag me forward.

I fight, wrenching my limbs and my hips to get them off me.

They win, still.

Again.

We are deep into the dark when I see where they're taking me.

It looks like a tiny white room, all pale upholstery and artificial light. It's as washed out and pristine as that room in Victoria's house.

It can't be here, that white room.

I squeeze my eyes shut to blur it away.

But when I open again, it stays.

I press my eyes shut again.

It doesn't clear. It glows like a single bulb in a dark room.

How did they get it out here?

They throw me into the pale light.

My body hits the back seat, and I understand.

Victoria is already in the driver's seat. She twists around, a polished hand on the back of the headrest.

Chris jumps into the front passenger seat.

PJ crams into the back with Brigid.

With me.

The doors close.

They click, locking.

I scramble against the windows, but it only tires me out, drying my throat and tongue.

"What did you do?" Victoria asks, sounding more irritated than panicked.

"Where did you put them?" Brigid asks.

They are all talking at me.

What did you do?

Where are they?

Where did you put them?

Where are they?

Where are they?

Not talking at me.

Yelling at me.

My throat cramps.

Brigid is holding my arms, nails digging in.

I am back there, in that room.

Victoria reaches and grabs hold of my hair.

It may have been Chris and PJ who pulled me deep into Victoria's waiting car. But now they just watch, their bodies nothing but force and threat. They look useless with incomprehension, like they are only now understanding the mess I have become for the four of them to clean up.

Victoria's fingers tangle into my hair. "Where are they?"

My body goes slack.

I am no more solid than pink sugar and flour. My flesh is the crumbling dough of pan dulce. My skin dissolves like a sugar shell. I am something to be prodded, and broken apart, and consumed.

Victoria yanks my head back. "What did you do with them?"

Something digs into the place between my bra cups.

I wonder for a second if PJ is jabbing me there. But he's still watching, eyes flashing to the windows.

Victoria lets go.

My head falls forward. The throbbing makes it feel too heavy to lift again, so I'm staring down my own dress.

A coin of gold and paper winks between my breasts.

The glint of a lipstick tube, the red label.

I have to blink a few times, especially with Brigid yelling

in my ear. But the white lettering on the red label comes into focus.

The same shade I wore that night.

The same shade that ended up on Lock's body, from my unwilling mouth. A color shared between those two violated parts of our bodies.

That color, the deep scarlet, blurs together with the red frosting that my hands left all over the bakery kitchen.

My hands said in sugar what I couldn't say out loud.

I still can't say it out loud. My tongue is too dry, and my mouth is still cramping.

But I have said it in this color before. I can do it again.

My mother's voice—*Whatever the question, red lipstick is the answer*—keeps my fingers steady enough to reach into my bra. It's a small enough gesture that, at first, the four of them don't catch it. They're expecting me to throw myself at the door or grab at the back-seat lock.

As fast as cutting the waved sugar top for conchas, I pull out the lipstick, leaving the cap between my bra cups. Como una espada, like a sword, just like Jess said.

I twist it up.

On the perfect white of Victoria's car interior, I write *NO*.

I write it hard, crushing down the bullet top of the lipstick. It smears into the upholstery.

Victoria screams, more indignation than horror.

I write it again, on another patch of pristine white.

NO, in Forest Rose #72.

Brigid pulls back.

"What is that?" Victoria shrieks. "What is she doing?"

I write it again, this time on the back of the passenger seat.

Chris swears over and over. PJ shrinks away like he thinks the red might be blood from my period.

Brigid grabs me, but the lipstick is so deep in my hand, she hasn't yet figured out what I'm painting with.

NO, I write on the seat, the color all over my hands.

NO, I scrawl across the seat belt.

They are still grabbing at me. The way they shove me covers my dress in lipstick stains.

I don't stop. My brain is humming with the word, with the color, with the feeling that I am painting both Victoria's precious car and that white room all at once, that if I went to Victoria's house I would find every *NO* mirrored on the white bedspread and curtains.

For once, the sliver of mirror in my heart is not cutting into me but making me flinty and fearless.

NO. I am writing it for me, with my throat too tight and dry to say the word out loud. I am writing it for the boy who is on that bed, dragged too far under to say it at all.

"What are you, stupid?" Victoria yells. "Get her out of here."

Brigid throws the door open.

PJ shoves me out, lipstick used up but still in my hand.

I crash onto the brush-softened ground.

I hear the shift of their weight.

They are not just letting me go.

In a second, they are coming after me.

I glance back into the distance, back toward where the crowd is, then into the thicker dark of the wilderness preserve.

Back toward the light is Jess, my tía, Pilar, Dr. Emmott, Lock's family, people I know.

But to make it there, I'd have to outrun PJ and Chris and Victoria and Brigid. They will have enough light to see my path. They will get to me before I get to everyone else.

So instead I spring to my feet, and I run into the dark, toward the corner of the wilderness park I know better than any of them.

The Mirror Season

By the time I get to the stolen forest, my lungs are dry ice. The fever heat of running crashes up against the cold air.

The trees still glisten with their coating of glass. The branches bend with it.

That glass is what's been turning over in my brain as I ran here. I try to snap a blade of it off the lily magnolia.

It won't move. The silver leaf won't give from the branch.

I try another one. I move it back and forth, to ease it free.

It stays in place. All I've done is stain it with the lipstick that ended up on my hands, Forest Rose #72 tinting the glass.

I hit it.

A tip no bigger than a sugar cube snaps off.

I drive the side of my fist into another leaf. It barely moves.

Now I am crying, but holding it tight in the back of my throat, because any noise will help them find me faster.

I try again. I slam the side of my fist into the mirrored leaf again, then again. The edge cuts the side of my hand but I keep going. I hit it again, and again, until it gives, and I'm holding a knife of jagged glass. If they find me here, if I have to use it, I can.

I turn around and find a silhouette in the dark.

"Ciela?"

The noise that breaks out of me is almost a startled scream, my hand holding the slash of silver out in front of me. But the sound from my throat breaks off when I recognize him. Then I'm crying, half from relief at it not being PJ or Chris and half because Lock can't be here, not now.

Lock shows me his palms, hands and clothes covered in dirt like he's been planting a new tree. "What happened?" He eyes the piece of glass I'm still holding between us.

His voice spreads that chilled and hot feeling from my lungs through my back.

I lower the piece of mirror. I have to fight for each breath, but I get just enough to speak.

"I couldn't say it," I rasp out.

"What happened?" he asks again, impatient, panicked.

"I couldn't tell you"—crying harder breaks up the sounds—"because I couldn't say it out loud."

I trace the horror in his expression to the red stains on my dress.

But I already have too many words on my tongue.

"It was never you hurting me," I say. "Every nightmare I ever had, it was never you hurting me. It was you getting hurt, and me getting hurt, and waking up and knowing that it happened, and it would never not have happened. That's why I couldn't say it. And I'm sorry. I should have told you. I thought it was better if I didn't, but I called it wrong."

Just like I called it wrong that night when I thought he was drunk, when I put him in that room, when I came back upstairs.

No.

I cut off the thought, fast as tearing parchment paper off the roll at the pastelería.

No.

I stop myself. I turn back from the path I've taken every time I've thought of that night, the one that looks for every mistake I made, every small thing that might have provoked them, or given them permission, or left us open to them. But none of that is really mine. They assumed permission because they wanted to. We were not open to them. They broke us open.

If I don't pull apart things I actually did wrong from things that weren't my fault, I'll never really be able to apologize for anything. Deciding everything is your fault is as meaningless as deciding nothing is. If I don't want to be the other side of the coin that is people like PJ and Chris and Victoria and Brigid, I need to stop. I need to apologize for what is my fault, for what I did wrong, but not for the wrong that was done to me.

"I'm sorry," I say, giving Lock the simple, unadorned words I've owed him this whole time. "You deserved to know who I was before you did anything with me. And I'm sorry I didn't tell you."

"Why didn't you?" he asks.

My throat clenches. "Because I needed to be a person to you."

He blinks. "What?"

"I thought about you every day after that night," I choke out between breaths. "But you weren't a person. I didn't know you. You were something that happened to me."

I am making no sense right now, and I know it. I keep trying.

"But when I met you, when I got to know you, you became someone to me," I say. "And I knew if I ever told you, I wouldn't be a person, I'd be a thing that happened to you. I wanted us to be more than things that happened to each other. I needed to be more than something that happened to you."

It still doesn't make any sense. I am handing him the truth in pieces because there's not enough to keep it together. I am offering him the truth the only way I can, unassembled, because I haven't even let myself touch it enough to put it together. And I'm ready for him to hold the pieces in his palms and say *what is this, what am I looking at?*

But his eyes fall shut. When he opens them, the faint light of the far-off highway, together with the moon, shows the mix of grief and understanding.

"You didn't rip me out of the ground," I say.

Before he was ever someone I fell in love with, he was a friend who understood, who got it, who showed me there was earth I could come back to life in.

I wipe my hands on my skirt, smearing it with more lipstick. "You're not that night, and neither am I."

Lock stares at my hands and my dress.

"It's not blood," I say. It comes out more frayed than I mean it to. "It's lipstick."

He looks at me like he doesn't believe me. Then it clicks for him. It takes him a second, but he gets it, that this is a color he knows.

As he opens his mouth to say something back, the sound of footsteps crushes over the ground.

Their shapes appear. First Chris and Victoria. Then Brigid and PJ trailing behind.

Their heavy steps are something I feel on my skin.

They have already done what they wanted with parts of our bodies.

Invading Lock's secret forest is a new kind of violation.

And I've led them here.

I feel the crunch of breaking glass in my hand, hear the crackling sound of pieces grinding together.

That feeling, that small sound, is a weight in my chest worse than trying to get my breath back.

Flecks of silver spill from my fingers. The one thing I could fight back with, and it's splintering apart.

But Lock doesn't realize. He's watching those four shapes come close enough that we can see their faces.

With my free hand, the one that does not hold a crumbling shard of mirror, I try to take Lock's hand, to keep him from biting his fingers.

But Lock doesn't slouch or curl into himself.

He straightens up.

He stands a little in front of me, like he's trying to shield me.

"No," he tells them.

The word is so level and final they actually draw back.

The blunt sound of that word turns something in me.

Yes, I gave in.

Yes, I opened my mouth.

But just because I gave in doesn't mean I have to give in forever. Just because I opened my mouth that night doesn't mean I never can again.

Just because they never would have listened to that one word then doesn't mean I never get to say it.

My *no* comes out of me so hard it turns into a scream. It echoes off the sky.

That night may have left a shard of mirror in me. But now it's becoming the bright star of my rage.

PJ and Chris and Victoria and Brigid go still.

Months ago, I didn't cry, and I didn't scream, because I thought if I started crying or screaming I'd never stop. But now I don't care if I scream forever. If I scream forever, they will have to hear me forever.

The echo off the hills keeps the sound going.

The moon trembles.

The stars flinch.

That's when I feel it, something in the air like a familiar voice, one I haven't heard in a long time.

The sky lets out a breath. Air spills from the clouds.

The Santa Anas stream across the wilderness preserve, fast and thick as a river. They lift my hair off my shoulders and pull the last pieces of mirror from my hand.

The trees rattle, glass knocking together.

I open my eyes, breathing hard.

I have used all the air in my body on that one word, this one scream, and now I have to let the Santa Anas breathe into me.

The most delicate pieces of glass on the trees crack. One branch splinters, then the next, from the flashing leaves on the smoke bush trees, to the silver blossoms on the wild lilac, to the globes of fruit on the shoe-thorn branches.

So much of my world has turned to mirrored glass. But right now, my rage is enough to break it apart.

The Santa Anas blow harder, singing through the dark. The branches shrug away their crystals of mirrored glass. The blossoms toss aside glass petals. The boughs throw off silver blades. The Santa Anas spin them into a storm. They lace the air, catching the wink of every star.

But this is not as quiet or distant as the stars. This is a storm as loud as the screaming I've let off my tongue. It's as hard and close as waves smashing over the tide pool rocks. The wind blows my hair hard enough that I feel its cold fingers on the back of my neck. It seals my skirt to my legs and Lock's shirt to his chest.

The wind roars its current through the hollow of the wilderness park. It shrieks through the branches of the secret forest, stripping away one layer of silver dust at a time. It's so loud it takes my scream, folding it into its noise as easily and smoothly as mixing sugar into batter.

This is a storm made of the kind of snow I've heard about but never seen, the white glitter of diamond dust that only happens when the world is truly freezing. This is a storm like the stories my abuela told me, legends of screaming winds carrying blades of obsidian. Except instead of the glittering white of the coldest snow, or the gleaming black of obsidian glass, this is the searing silver of broken mirrors.

For months, I've thought a white room had taken all the color in me, bleaching everything as silver and gray as a mirror. But now, as more of the glass breaks off the branches, it catches the light from the sky, and splinters it. It fractures the white, like prisms cutting light into rainbows. It brightens the air, reflecting back every color.

The pieces break into finer dust, like salt crystals. Then again, into a snow so fine that it's the lightest touch on my skin. Lock feels it too, shutting his eyes and letting it blow over him. This storm may be loud, and hard enough that we have to brace ourselves to stand against its current. But we do, because this is ours.

Chris and PJ and Victoria and Brigid recoil, like the fine dust of the mirrored glass is far sharper to them. They draw into themselves like they're caught in a storm of rough, silver sand. They hold their hands to their eyes like shards have gotten in.

And when they do lift their heads to look at us, there's fear in them, like their own slivers of mirrored glass are making them see the hard glint of our will.

They stare in shock. And then they run.

They run from us because our rage and these mirrors make them see what they are.

They run from us because they have just now noticed we are as sharp as broken glass.

Nothing Gets Lost

We find our way out of the dark. Lock makes sure I get to Jess and my tía and Pilar. I make sure he finds his mother and Nate and Violet.

When I don't hear from him, I don't come after him. I don't call him. I let him go.

All that's left to me, all I have to do, is to give Lock the same space I've had. Enough time to understand my own body as something violated and something used to violate. Enough to know that his body is more than those two things. He is more than that night tried to make him.

We both are.

La Reina de las Nieves and I, we may have lived in the cold for so long we think we are made of it. But our bodies, our hearts, are as alive as the ground under the snow.

When I go back to the pastelería, I find a little more of La Bruja de los Pasteles' magic, like spotting one Easter egg at a time in overgrown grass. I recommend the perfect mantecadas to a church council that cannot agree on altar decorations, knowing the gentle vanilla in the dough will help them compromise. I slide a cocada to a city college student who's chewing on the end of her pen over her next exam, and she lights up as though she understands it will make her brave. When we get our next order for a piñata cake, I fill it with bright candy as though I am filling my own heart with color.

I bring Dr. Emmott and his husband a box of polvorones. I can almost see the sheen of their love as they touch the sleeves of each other's sweaters, a gesture so small and casual I wonder if they realize they're doing it.

The orange and coconut smell of los ojos de buey soaks into my clothes. The air in the kitchen warms as I pull out trays of pajaritos, the swallow bread whispering its hope that all our golondrinas will come back one day.

I am, a little at a time, a girl who speaks in sugar and chili powder. I find the great storm on Jupiter in the rust and gold sugar of mango chamoyada. I smell the season turning, the cold coming, like the smell of lavender and pine.

My careful hands mix color into the sugar tops for conchas. But this time they're not solid pink or white, or even the bright swirl of las conchas de sirena. For these ones, I fold in dye the blue of the bakery walls, the pink of a lawn flamingo Jess once put in my locker for my birthday, the yellow of a sweater I wore the night I met a boy from Lancaster or the moon.

As the pan dulce bakes, the sugar tops settle and bloom. Each color blurs softly into the next, like the rare spring rainbows over the wilderness park.

Together, the pink, yellow, and blue look like a flag Jess showed me once during Pride. She said it stood for what I am, how my heart works, how I love.

I want to stand for what I am, how I love, how my broken heart still works. Even if there are cracks in me. Even if my heart is scar tissue around a sliver of glass.

So I mix these same colors again, this time into the recipe

for polvorones tricolor. The sugar cookies each look like their own little flags.

I'm folding dough for the two-color polvorones we call sol y sombra—sun and shadow—when the bell on the front door rings.

I strip off my gloves, tacky from handling dough. When I see the silhouette against the orange light, I'm about to ask *What can I get you?*

Then my eyes adjust. I recognize the shape of his hair, his shoulders, his jeans.

The light behind him is too bright to let me see his face.

He's not afraid. His back isn't rounded. He doesn't slump.

"Ciela," he says, his voice steady but low.

There's an intensity to how he says my name. He sounds almost surprised to have found me, like he checked the school and the secret forest and everywhere in the whole world before thinking of the pastelería.

I don't take off my flour-dusted apron.

I don't take a full breath before we cross the linoleum squares under us.

"Is it okay if I touch you?" he asks, with the wounded consideration of someone who will never forget being touched when he didn't want it.

I may be afraid of cold water and the sudden movements of anyone in the halls at school. I may be afraid of grenadine and the whirring sound of automatic sliding doors. But I am not afraid of Lock Thomas.

Lock and I put our arms around each other so fast that my forearm almost hits his back.

His hand doesn't slip down to my hip bone. My mouth doesn't find his.

For right now, we don't stand in the same space where I fell in love with him. We don't stand where he fell in love with a girl, not realizing she was broken in a way that mirrored so closely the way he was.

For this minute, we are friends, with matching broken hearts. He is telling me how sorry he is that he turned on me in the space of a few white-bordered photos. I am telling him how sorry I am that I could never say out loud the worst thing that happened to me, that I still don't know how to say it, that I have to hand it to him in pieces.

I hold on to him tight enough that he's crying into my hair. He sobs so hard it's like something crashing through him, a storm breaking against a sea wall. I can't tell if I'm screaming into his shoulder. There's no sound, and I don't know if that's because I'm not making any or because his body is taking it.

I hold him. He holds me.

I am held. He is held.

We let ourselves break apart. But somehow, with my hands gripping his shoulders and his hands across my back, there's enough surface tension to keep us inside our own skin.

The next time this boy is on my bed, we are not laughing. My hands are not going for his belt. He is not stripping off my sweater. I am setting pan de yema onto his tongue, and he accepts it as solemnly as a blessing. When he takes it, swallows it, I find the shimmer of light in him, like glass catching the sun. It is something beautiful and sad, not the wonder and surprise of our customers when they realize, yes, what they wanted was the woven dough of una reja or the soft give of una almohada.

This is different.

I was right, about him, about this being the kind of pan dulce he needed. I am not happy about being right. Because now I realize why it was this, and not pan nevado or una corbata. The yellow and spice of el pan de yema are pouring light into the darkest, coldest corners of this boy's heart.

This is not the kind of pan dulce he might have needed if last spring had never happened. I will never get to know that, what kind of sugar and dough would have lit up his heart a year ago. I will never know that Lock.

But I know this one, the boy who needs light flooding into parts of him that have gone dark. And I am, in some way smaller than my hands, bringing him back to life.

We cannot keep each other together. Neither of us can do that for the other. It's our own work. But we help each other keep track of the pieces.

We make sure nothing gets lost.

Sticky Notes

This is really what you need right now?" Jess sounds skeptical but like she's trying not to sound skeptical. She knows everything now, from that night at the party to what happened in the secret forest. And when she asked me how she could help, I don't think this is remotely what she was thinking of.

"This is exactly what I need right now," I say.

We are standing in what Jess calls her mothership, the office supply store just up the freeway. Specifically, in the section with all the sticky notes.

"Will you pick for me?" I ask, staring at the display in front of us.

Jess lights up like I've asked her to pick my winter formal dress. I may speak the language of flour and sugar, but Jess speaks the language of gel pens and color-coded files.

She looks between me and the racks of different sizes and colors, assessing. "What are you using them for?" she asks.

"Everything I should have said months ago."

Telenovela

A couple of days after my parents get back from seeing the hot air balloons, I tell them.

Not to their faces. I couldn't watch the shifts in their expressions if I spoke the words.

I tell my parents by writing it on a series of sticky notes and leaving them on the fridge.

I write all of it.

What happened in that room.

At the hospital.

With Lock.

It takes two pads of sticky notes, two different colors, so many squares of paper that by the time I'm done I have covered all the takeout menus, the miniature calendar, the magnets from the dentist's and the dry cleaner's.

I hide in my dark bedroom when I hear them come home, when I know they're reading them.

I brace for their footsteps on the stairs, and for every question they'll have.

My mother comes upstairs with eyes reddened in a way that tells me she's been crying.

I sit up, tensing for everything she's about to ask.

But all she asks is if I'm hungry.

I blink into the hallway light, casting her in silhouette.

"Sure," I say, cautious.

She nods, goes downstairs.

They don't ask me questions, not tonight.

They don't try to hug me, or comfort me in a way that would do more for them than me, something I am so grateful for that I will light candles at my abuela's church over it.

We order takeout. We eat it in front of the TV, watching my mother's favorite telenovela.

We cry, each of us, about these things I have just said in squares of magenta and turquoise paper.

When my mother cries, she pretends it's about Severino declaring his love to Ana Brenda.

When my father does, he pretends it's about Lupita's death-bed confession to her son, Carlitos.

When I do, I pretend it's about Clara and Evelina finding out they're sisters.

We sit there, watching the actors in their sunset-bright lives, and for right now, everything I live with, I don't live with alone.

Everything We Have

The detectives tell us that Lock and I will be interviewed separately. They say we cannot talk any further about the specifics of that night, not yet. We are already witnesses to each other's assaults, and I can't blame them for not wanting to fray what I'm guessing is a pretty tenuous case. A brown girl and a boy from a dust-road town, against families who have their names on plaques all over the county.

They give us this instruction, not to talk to each other about that night, almost apologetically. As though Lock and I really want to rehash the details. But the truth is it gives us an excuse not to, not to compare notes, not to match up the edges of when the night goes dark for him, and when it becomes searing white for me.

Lock breaks this instruction only once.

"I want to give them the pictures we have," he says as soon as I pick up the phone. "But we won't do it if you don't want to."

I glance toward my closet. When I threw the photos in there, I was half wishing the mirror pieces would slash them into confetti.

"It's your only shot," he says. "And you know that. But we're not doing it if you say no."

The breath goes out of me, spooled away by how right he is.

The pictures I have are the matching set to the ones Lock has. His show more of me, and him. Mine show more of PJ, Chris, Victoria, and Brigid.

There will be little doubt about the assault on Lock, about the fact that he was drugged. Blood work records attest to the state of the boy I left in the emergency room, and an admitting nurse will testify to the lipstick found on him when they checked him for injuries.

But the question of who did it, not so much who left that lipstick but who is responsible for it being left, will remain. Lock's word that I didn't do it voluntarily, that I never would, will be the word of a boy who was unconscious while it happened. The first detective my parents and I talked to told me the good news is I won't be charged, since neither Lock nor his parents are about to blame me. But the other side of that good news—and I knew there was another side, I could hear it in the detective's voice—is that it'll be the turn of a coin whether any of my story will hold up.

It will come down to my word against the four of theirs. Those pictures could be a steadier voice than mine, one that says, with every frame, that I'm not a liar.

"Lock," I say. "If we do this, it's not just going to be words anymore. Anyone who sees our files will actually *see* it."

"That's exactly why I want to do it," he says. "I want to give them everything we have. I want to fight back with everything we have."

He tells me to think about it.

After we hang up, I stand for a while at the closet door. I knew I'd have to open it eventually.

I turn the knob, bracing for all those pieces disintegrating into shards or silver dust. I crack the door, and the first thing the vein of light getting in shows me is the photos. They're still where they landed when I threw them in.

When more light gets in, it doesn't splinter over thousands of glass edges. It shines over a solid, gleaming surface.

The papel picado, the rock candy, the leaves, the ribbon, the dolls, they haven't turned back like the creek bed. But they haven't broken into shards either.

All that glass is now a smooth plain, a mirror covering the floor of my closet.

I kneel down, my hands meeting my reflected hands, like a girl looking into a frozen pond.

After

In the gray light of the morning, Lock Thomas could almost be a boy I'm meeting for the first time. His hair blows into his face like he forgot to get it cut. His jeans, white t-shirt under his Carhartt jacket, are the opposite of our school uniforms.

But everything hovers between us, tinting the air.

How I didn't know that Lock laughing when I told him about the sticky notes was exactly the response I needed until he did it.

The way we want to kiss each other again but don't exactly know how, like it's a thing our bodies can't do if our brains think too hard.

What we're doing today.

"Lock?" I ask.

"Yeah?"

I set my hand against the bark of the crepe myrtle, the one I still call the snow tree.

"My dad told me once that every moment lives forever," I say. "Do you believe that?"

"Yes," Lock says, no hesitation.

My heart feels as fragile as the new blossoms on these trees.

"That means what happened is happening every minute," I say. "It's happening now. It's happening forever."

"Yes," Lock says, the overcast light cooling the brown of his eyes. "But so is this."

He looks up at the boughs. First leaves and scatterings of blue and purple blossoms dot the bare branches.

"So is this." He barely touches a belt loop on my jeans, above where my second tattoo is healing. Jess read me a draft of her term paper while the artist put the color in.

It's a second rose hip, this one on the other side, a reminder that my whole body, not just one piece of it, is mine.

I take his hand and put it on my waist, to show him he can still touch me.

He brushes pieces of hair out of my face, only for the wind to put them back.

Even when I say yes, and he says yes, even when I tell him I want it and he tells me he wants it, he's awkward about setting his lips against mine. It's so hesitant it feels like a first kiss.

I kiss him back, a little harder, but not as hard as I will the next time, or the time after that. I let this be a first kiss, because it's his first time kissing me, and knowing. It's his first time kissing me, Graciela Cristales, the girl who brought him into that room, the girl who fought and then stopped fighting, the girl who took him inside her first without wanting it, and then, months later, again, when she did.

There are a hundred thousand moments I want to be forever more than I want that night to be forever. I want to teach Lock the alchemy of turning flour and water and yeast into something living. I want him to show me how he figures out the exact vitamins to give each stolen tree, some mix of chemistry and botany and brujería. I want us to watch the colors these trees put on and take off from season to season, the living painting of his secret forest.

But in a few minutes, our families will be waiting for us. My mother and father. Lock's mother. (My father gave Lock's stepdad directions to the tide pools, so he can take Violet.) They're sharing the weight of this day, when we will answer all the detectives' questions, tell them everything we know, give them everything we have.

"Hey." Lock grasps my hand and tilts his head toward the lily magnolia. "Look."

Wings flash through the branches.

A few swallows dip and soar above the boughs. I catch the soft brown of their backs, their wings shot through with violet and sage that only shows in flashes.

They whirl through the first blue of the chaste tree, and then ride the wind toward the hills.

This is probably the last we will see of them before next spring. Maybe by then, spring won't make us shudder with the thought of white rooms, and salt torn from our bodies. Maybe, instead, we'll wait for the brilliant first bloom of these trees, the settling of a hundred thousand wings.

That night left each of us holding pieces of broken glass. And ever since, we have been gripping them. We have been clenching our fingers around them, the edges cutting into our palms, our blood on the silver.

We may never be able to set them down for good. They may be in our hands forever, something we're always holding. But we don't have to grip them. We don't have to hold them so tightly that they're forever cutting our fingers.

Instead, we hold them as lightly as we can. We let them rest on our palms. We don't help them do the work of drawing our blood.

We live with them.

We learn the ways that broken things can catch the light.

Author's Note

This book is a work of fiction.

I wish I could tell you none of it was true.

This book began with "The Snow Queen," one of the most beautiful and disturbing fairy tales I encountered growing up. As a child, I knew I was meant to identify with Gerda, the purehearted girl who sets out to rescue her childhood friend Kai. But instead I was drawn to the broken mirror, enthralled and frightened by how a tiny piece of glass could change how the whole world looks. And the Little Robber Girl, the only character in the story who, with her brown skin and dark hair, looked a little like me and my primas. And the Snow Queen herself, who made me wonder what happened to leave her so cold she feels most at home in ice.

La Reina de las Nieves is portrayed as the queen with the frozen heart. But no one asks how she came to be stripped of all her warmth. No one asks if she was once a girl watching snowflakes and imagining them to be stars against the blue night. No one asks her if her palace of ice is a world she rules or a room she's been locked into.

This book draws on my experiences as a survivor of multiple sexual assaults. Perhaps most of all, it draws on the experience of a boy and I finding out we had been assaulted by the same person, and that the same people seemed to stand by and let it happen.

The specific circumstances have been changed for this book, both to protect this boy's privacy and to maintain the integrity of a case that, as I write these words, is still pending. Like Lock and Ciela, this boy and I decided, together, to report.

I've been writing a book about being sexually assaulted before I know if I—Jane Doe, according to the legal system—or the boy—John Doe—will ever get justice. And there have been times when I wondered if this was a wise decision for my own mental health. But after reporting, the Snow Queen kept calling me back. She whispered that my reimagining of her had to come from my heart as a queer Latinx survivor. It had to be about how one thing can be so sharp it changes your world forever.

It had to be about the boy who got dragged into the cold along with me.

I think I had to write this book before finding out if John Doe and I will get justice. It's the same place this book leaves Ciela and Lock, not knowing, but knowing they have to tell their story.

Moving from a place of feeling broken by sexual assault to feeling ready to speak up for myself has been one of the most difficult processes of my life. Reporting is one of the biggest steps I've made toward finding my voice, and starting to talk about how our society's conversations about sexual assault are failing women of color, boys, and queer and trans survivors.

I wrote this book while figuring out I'm nonbinary. This

meant I had to face down not only my own trauma but how it had terrified me into hiding my gender identity. Telling Ciela and Lock's story became not only about telling the emotional truth about what happened to John Doe and me. It became about contending with how a more girl-identifying side of me dealt with sexual assault (by pretending it didn't happen), and how a more boy-identifying side of me dealt with it (by pretending it shouldn't hurt me). Probably unsurprisingly, there's a lot of me in Ciela. And there's a lot of John Doe in Lock. But there's a lot of me in Lock too.

John Doe and I sometimes wonder when the legal system's names for us will leave room for the fact that gender isn't binary. We've wondered what I could be called instead of Jane Doe (Jess Doe?). It's what we talk about when we don't want to talk about the fact that to tell the truth, we had to give up our own names.

Some of you reading this may know who John Doe is. Some may try to guess. You may or may not be right; survivors often don't fit the description the world expects. John Doe gave me permission to disclose his identity in talking about our story. But I'm not going to, at least not in these pages.

Respect for John Doe's privacy may be my first reason for not telling you his name here, but it's not the only one. I'm not telling you John Doe's name, because if you're ever lucky enough to meet him, I want you to meet him not just as a survivor but as the brilliant, funny, caring spirit he is. I want you to know him as more than John Doe. You deserve to know him that way. He deserves to be known that way. Yes, I know that there may be little chance that you and he will ever encounter each other. But I have to leave him, and you, that possibility. I have to believe in it, in our survivors' hearts being seen not just for the cracks that run through them but for the light spilling out from inside us.

Some days I believe in that light. Some days I can't. Some days I'm okay, and some days I'm really not. If you're not okay, please be kind to yourself about that. And if you're not okay, please get help. I wish I had earlier. While my biggest recommendation is to start with someone you trust, whether that's a family member, a friend, a medical/mental health professional, if you're not sure where to start, start with RAINN (rainn.org). I know how heavy the phone can feel. But the one blessing I can find in how long it took me to get help is that I can tell you, right now, it's not too late. It's not too late to feel better, to take deeper breaths, to startle a little less every time the world brushes too close.

It's not too late for any of us.

We survived.

Now we can live.

Acknowledgments

I often start my acknowledgments by saying how many people it takes to turn a story into a book. I'm overwhelmed by the work of everyone who makes this process, which is nothing short of magic, happen.

And right now, I'm overwhelmed not just by how many people it takes to make a book but by how many people it takes to make an author ready to write a book like this.

I'm deeply grateful for all of them. Here, I'll name a few:

Kat Brzozowski, for challenging me to find the voice I needed for Ciela's story and for being someone I felt safe telling it to.

Emily Settle, for welcoming my idea emails and for making me know this book is in good hands.

Taylor Martindale Kean, Stefanie Sanchez Von Borstel, and everyone at Full Circle Literary, for making a wonderful home for authors.

Jean Feiwel, for making me and my stories part of the Feiwel & Friends family.

Brittany Pearlman, for helping my books make their way in the world.

Rich Deas, for his amazing art direction at MacKids; Liz Dresner, for your beautiful vision for this book's cover; Marly Gallardo, for your breathtaking art.

Everyone at Feiwel & Friends and Macmillan Children's Publishing Group: Kim Waymer, Celeste Cass, Jon Yaged, Allison Verost, Liz Szabla, Erin Siu, Molly Ellis, Teresa Ferraiolo, Allegra Green, Jo Kirby, Kathryn Little, Julia Gardiner, Lauren Scobell, Dawn Ryan, Alexei Esikoff, Mariel Dawson, Avia Perez, Ilana Worrell, Romanie Rout, Ebony Lane, Kristin Dulaney, Jordan Winch, Kaitlin Loss, Rachel Diebel, Amanda Barillas, Morgan Dubin, Morgan Rath, Madison Furr, Mary Van Akin, and Kelsey Marrujo; Katie Halata, Lucy Del Priore, Melissa Croce, Kristen Luby, and Cierra Bland of Macmillan School & Library; and the many more who turn stories into books and get them to readers.

Taryn Fagerness and the Taryn Fagerness Agency, for helping my stories travel the world.

The writers who helped me revise and refine this book: Dahlia Adler, who first told me I was so queer even my dulce is pan; Lindsay Eagar, who helped me understand why we have to laugh about the things that break our hearts; Alex Villasante, mi hermana in Narnia, lipstick, and that particular shade of yellow.

Megan Manzano, for helping Ciela—and me—find our way in a corner of queer identity that resonates with how we love.

The writers who helped me keep moving forward in the months that led up to me deciding I needed to tell this story, and the months of writing it. Here, I name a few:

Aisha Saeed, who reached out when I was too brokenhearted to.

Tess Sharpe, who told me it wasn't just me, exactly when I needed to hear it.

Saundra Mitchell, who was there when I was still in shock and who helped me figure out what I was going to do next.

Laurie Halse Anderson, who told me it's okay that I'm not okay.

Nova Ren Suma, for sparkling snow magic when I was still trying to piece together the puzzle of this book.

A.S. King, for those late-night talks and for not minding when I got glitter all over your room.

Even in my most contemporary book to date, I still needed some research help, especially when it came to las golondrinas. So thank you to Dr. Charles Brown, who through his written scholarship and by phone generously answered my questions about the swallows of San Juan Capistrano; and to Jim McCoy, for the early-morning birding adventures and encyclopedic knowledge about all the wings we saw.

Also thank you to my father, for taking me to see the water so early in the morning it was still silver. My mother, for teaching me that whatever the question, red lipstick is the answer.

John Doe, for letting me share some of our emotional truth in these pages and for not letting me do the hard thing alone.

My fellow survivors: We carry our broken hearts together.

Readers, for making stories matter. Thank you.